sourcebooks
fire

Title:	Four Days of You and Me
Author:	Miranda Kenneally
Agent:	Jim McCarthy
	Dystel, Goderich & Bourret
Publication date:	May 5, 2020
Category:	Young Adult Fiction
Format:	Hardcover
ISBN:	978-1-4926-8413-8
Price:	$17.99 U.S.
Pages:	352 pages
Ages:	14 and up

This book represents the final manuscript being distributed for prepublication review. Typographical and layout errors are not intended to be present in the final book at release. It is not intended for sale and should not be purchased from any site or vendor. If this book did reach you through a vendor or through a purchase, please notify the publisher.

Please send all reviews or mentions of this book to the Sourcebooks marketing and publicity departments:
marketing@sourcebooks.com

For sales inquires, please contact **sales@sourcebooks.com**

For librarian and educator resources, visit:
sourcebooks.com/library

ALSO BY MIRANDA KENNEALLY

FOUR DAYS OF YOU AND ME

MIRANDA KENNEALLY

sourcebooks
fire

Copyright © 2020 by Miranda Kenneally
Cover and internal design © 2020 by Sourcebooks
Cover design by Jenna Stempel-Lobell
Cover images © ampcool/Shutterstock; G-Stock Studio/Shutterstock
Internal design by Danielle McNaughton
Internal [images or illustrations] ©

Published by Sourcebooks Fire, an imprint of Sourcebooks
P.O. Box 4410, Naperville, Illinois 60567-4410
(630) 961-3900
sourcebooks.com

[Library of Congress Cataloging-in-Publication Data]

Printed and bound in [XXXX].
XX 10 9 8 7 6 5 4 3 2 1

In memory of Bob Beggan,
a man who went everywhere and talked to everybody

MAY 7
SENIOR YEAR

Our first kiss was exactly four years ago today, and since then, nothing—*and everything*—has changed.

PART I

MAY 7, FRESHMAN YEAR

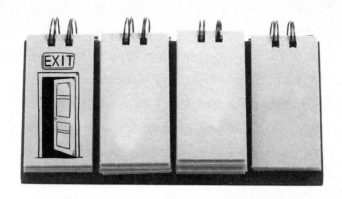

TODAY
FRESHMAN CLASS TRIP

It's six in the morning and the sun is barely up, but I'm wide awake. Normally I hit snooze four or five times before climbing out of bed. This morning? I didn't push it once. Today is the annual class field trip, and I am determined to have a real conversation with Jonah.

One day in the cafeteria a few weeks ago, he peeked over my shoulder when I was sketching the main character of the graphic novel I'm writing. He told me he likes comics too, especially *Saga*. I was too mesmerized by his curly dark hair to respond. But next time? I am totally going to open my mouth and use my words like a real person.

Mom pulls into the school parking lot. I drape my purse strap around my shoulder. "Good luck with your showing today," I say. She is a real estate agent and just put a historic farmhouse on the market.

Mom lightly kisses my cheek. "Thanks, sweet girl."

I shiver when I step out of the car. The sun is out, but the air is still brisk and smells of morning dew. I scan the crowd of kids already here and spot my best friend, Max. I jog over to give him a side hug.

"Hey, friend," he says, bending down to air-kiss my cheeks. He repositions his camera bag over his shoulder, looking my outfit up and down. I paired gray combat boots with a little white flowing tunic dress I hope will grab Jonah's attention.

"You were right. That dress is hot."

"Not as hot as this new patch," I say, checking out his camera bag. In addition to Captain America's shield, a Corgi, and an astronaut planting a gay pride flag on the moon, he's added a bright yellow pineapple patch.

"Thanks," Max replies. "Dad picked it up for me in Miami." As a pilot, Mr. Davis flies the daily route between Nashville and Miami for American Airlines, and frequently brings us delicious coconut patties from this one store at the airport.

After handing our permission slips to Coach Rice, we climb aboard the bus that's taking us to Nashville. Max chooses a seat in the fourth row.

"Too close to the teachers," I say, continuing down the aisle.

He follows me. "Lulu, I don't want to sit in the back."

"But that's where the guys sit."

Max scrunches his nose. "It always smells like gas."

We agree to sit in the middle as other kids climb aboard and stake out seats. Max carefully secures his camera bag between his feet on the floor and pulls out his phone. I lean across him to peek out the window. Jonah's still not here. I sigh dramatically.

Max moves me off his lap. "C'mon now. Don't act desperate."

I point out the window at my cousin, who's already making out with her boyfriend. "I was looking for Grace," I lie.

"No, you're desperate," Max replies, and we laugh together. We've been calling each other out on our bullshit since we became best friends in sixth grade.

I watch student after student climb aboard, waiting for Jonah. When Grace spots me, she smiles briefly. With her dark skin and wavy, chestnut-brown hair that she inherited from her mom's Hawaiian genes, my cousin is one of the most gorgeous people I've ever seen.

I straighten up in my seat, hoping she'll sit beside us, but she chooses a seat a few rows back instead. I sink lower, crossing my arms over my stomach. Her boyfriend passes by like I don't exist.

Even though I grew up with Grace, this is the first year we've gone to the same school. But as the only freshman on the varsity dance team, her circle of friends is in another stratosphere than mine, which basically consists of Max and myself.

I look hopefully toward the front of the bus when I hear someone else climb on, but it's just Alex Rouvelis, my mortal enemy. He's wearing a white T-shirt that glows against his olive skin and low-slung jeans full of rips and holes. Chunky black boots complete the hot bad-boy look. His dark hair is cut neatly and sweeps to the side. I wet my lips.

I hate him. I hate him so much.

Alex greets the bus driver, patting him on the shoulder. "Hey, Animal!"

5

"Animal!" all the other boys yell. I have no idea why they call him that, but he doesn't seem to mind. He yells, "Animal!" right along with them.

Alex's baseball teammates choose seats at the very back of the bus.

As Alex passes my row, he glances down at me.

Max gets up on his knees to pull our window down for some fresh air. "It's so hot in here," he says through a mouthful of gum. "And it already smells like farts. How is that possible? We've only been here for two minutes."

Coach Rice comes aboard last. He lifts the silver whistle hanging around his neck and toots it. "Sit down, everybody. We can't leave until you're all seated." The bus is in a state of chaos: everybody is talking and horsing around. His whistle screeches for a second time. "If y'all don't sit right now, you can stay here and spend the day writing me an essay."

Kids actually listen to that warning and put their butts in seats.

But Jonah's not here. What if he decided to stay home and play Xbox or something?

God, this is going to be the worst field trip ever. We're going to a science museum, and I don't even have my crush to lust after.

With everyone ready to go, Coach Rice gives Animal the signal to start the engine. It roars to life and the bus begins to vibrate.

"Field trip!" Alex calls out, and the boys start whooping.

Animal slowly begins to pull out of the parking lot. "Wait," Coach Rice says. The bus screeches to a halt and the door squeaks open.

Jonah rushes up the steps, his eyes darting around looking for an open seat.

"What a douchebag," the baseball players mutter.

I hold my breath as Jonah walks down the aisle toward the empty spot in front of me, but he goes right past. My body slumps in disappointment.

He sits a couple of rows back and to my right. Now how am I supposed to stare at him? It will be totally obvious if I turn around.

Maybe it's okay to be obvious. Show him I'm interested. It's not every day a guy talks to me in the cafeteria.

Coach Rice studies his clipboard as the bus begins to move again. He teaches biology, coaches the baseball team, and is one of the youngest teachers at our school. I don't think he's much older than my sister in college. "As you know," he starts, "we're headed to Nashville to the Cumberland Science Museum, which was named for—"

Laughter bursts out from the back. I whip around to see a stark, white butt hanging over a seat.

"Ugh," Max says, and I giggle.

"Ryan McDowell," Coach Rice warns, "I swear to God, if you moon me again, you're not starting in tomorrow's game."

The butt disappears, and Ryan's headful of red hair pops back up. As I laugh along with everybody else who isn't grossed out, I discreetly peek at Jonah. He's staring at another girl.

Max elbows me. "Stalker."

"But he's totally checking out Dana."

Max waves a hand dismissively. "I heard she gave some junior a hand job. That's why all the guys are looking at her."

"Because they think she'll give them one?"

Max shrugs.

I peek over my shoulder to find Jonah putting a pair of headphones on. Lightly bobbing his head to the music, his eyes continue sweeping over the girls. I hope he'll look my way. A couple of weeks ago at the movies, he was definitely checking me out. That is, until Alex Rouvelis made a rude comment about me, effectively chasing Jonah off that night.

Look at me, look at me, I chant in my mind.

But he doesn't. His eyes stop on Dana again. The other day, I saw her bending over beside her locker, putting her books in her bag. Her jeans slipped down to where I couldn't avoid seeing her pink thong. Those things look super uncomfortable.

"Should I get a thong?" I ask Max in a rush.

"If your dad found out, he'd make you join a convent." Max pulls the gum from his mouth and tosses it out the window.

Two seconds later, I hear a boy say, "Shit, there's gum in my hair."

"Crap." Max ducks his head. "It must've flown back in a window."

I crack up, clutching my best friend's elbow.

A few seconds later, my mortal enemy is standing above me.

"Hey, Alex," I say. "You've got gum in your hair."

"Wells," he replies, addressing me by my last name like he always does. "Is this your gum?"

"No," I reply, laughing again.

And that's when Alex pulls the gum from his hair and sticks it in mine.

Asshole.

SEPTEMBER
FRESHMAN YEAR

Half the time I want to kiss him. The other half? I want to kill him.

That's what I'm thinking on Election Day as I'm waiting backstage to give my speech for class president.

While I've been carefully reading through my notes one last time, my competition—Alex Rouvelis—is nosing around the ancient musical instruments that have been abandoned backstage.

I flip to my next notecard, sneaking peeks at Alex out of the corner of my eye.

He picks up a rusty trombone, pushes the slide up and down between his legs and says, "Hey, Wells, check it out. I have a *tromboner*."

I burst out laughing, which makes him grin.

Then I wipe the smile off my face. I can't show weakness by laughing at his boner joke. I need to stay focused so I can win my campaign.

I've been working on my speech all week. Like in middle school, Max helped me make posters. We went for an animal-themed campaign with signs like, "Vote for Lulu! She's got the right Koalafications." When I was hanging my posters everywhere, I kept an eye out for Alex's. I needed to see what I was up against.

Alex hung exactly one poster: PLEASE VOTE FOR ME. I ALREADY TOLD MY MOM I WON.

I smile to myself. His sign was pretty hilarious, but also? This will be easy. How can he win if he didn't campaign?

Out onstage, the principal thanks the kids who gave speeches for vice president. Then he announces my name. "Lulu Wells! Lulu is our first candidate for freshman class president."

Alex blows into the trombone. "Good luck, Wells!"

I shake my head at him and march confidently from behind the curtains onstage to a friendly smattering of applause, especially from kids who came from Coffee County Middle School. I'd been class president there for the past three years.

I'm still getting to know the people from Westwood Middle School, and as I stand in front of them, I wish I knew each and every one of their names. I should've tried to introduce myself to more of them. My sweaty palms leave damp splotches on my notecards.

I smile at the crowd and speak strongly and clearly into the microphone. "Hi, everybody, I'm Lulu Wells, and I want to talk to you about trash."

The crowd is dead silent.

I cough into my fist. "That's right. Trash. I'm running on a platform of creating a more sustainable, green school. My first act of business will be to create a trash committee so we can get in control of our recycling." The crowd groans and a boy in the front row rolls his eyes, but I press on, outlining my other ideas—planting a school garden, installing air purifiers in classrooms, and approaching the school board about installing solar panels on the roof.

I spot one girl nodding off. A couple in the back row appears to be fooling around. This is a complete disaster.

I end my speech on a high note: "And finally, I think study hall should be turned into a meditation hour so we can hone our creativity."

I grin when kids cheer for that one. "Thank you, everybody! Don't forget to vote for me, Lulu Wells, for class president."

Some people in the crowd clap politely, but most kids are checking their phones as I walk backstage. My face burns red at how bad my speech went. The audience didn't care at all. The student council plans the homecoming week festivities, runs the Thanksgiving food drive, and picks out the themes for dances. It's a big deal. But it could be so much more.

When it's time for Alex's speech, he walks out *not* carrying notecards, but that stupid trombone! Alex blows into it. *Honnnnkkkkk.*

I peek out from behind the curtain to see the crowd laughing.

"I'm Alex Rouvelis, and I'm running for freshman class president. If you elect me, you're gonna see a lot of changes around here. First up, we've gotta get rid of these hard, wooden desks. I don't know about y'all, but my butt falls asleep. All. The. Time. That's why I think we need couches in class. And forget school busses. We're gonna start traveling to school in style. In limos!" Kids in the audience start heckling him.

"Just kidding, just kidding." Alex sets the trombone on the floor, grabs the microphone, and proceeds to give an off-the-cuff speech. "For real, though, I am running for class president because I care a lot about school spirit. At Westwood, I loved putting on my baseball uniform and representing you guys on the field. I haven't had a chance to meet all of you from Coffee County Middle yet, but I know we're going to be a great freshman class. No matter if you're in the drama club, or the math team, or play football, you represent our school. And I want to represent you on the student council to make it even better. Go Raiders!"

When he walks offstage to wild cheers from our classmates, I glare at him. *He winged it.* I worked so hard to prepare, and he simply winged a great speech. It's like he intuitively knows how to bring people together. I wish I had that skill.

If I weren't running against Alex, I would vote for him.

"You forgot to mention our spring field trip," I say with a hand on my hip. "You should've promised them a trip to Mars."

He nudges my arm. "Good idea, Wells. Too bad you didn't think of it before your speech. You could win on a platform like that."

"A platform of lies?"

"Embellishments." He blows into the trombone again. *Honnnnkkkkk.*

I push the instrument away from his face. "Don't you take anything seriously?"

"Sure." A lopsided grin appears on his face. "I'm serious about pizza, my dog, and the Atlanta Braves."

He's so charming, I can't help but laugh. "I'm serious about pizza too. I love the veggie pizza you make at Niko's." Everybody knows his family owns the Greek place in town.

He cocks his head to the side. "Why haven't I seen you there before?"

I shrug. "Probably because it's always so busy." I nervously swipe a lock of hair behind my ear.

The truth is, I've seen him there tons of times.

Niko's kitchen has a glass wall, so you can watch the cooks assembling pizzas before popping them in a wood fire oven. The first time I ever saw Alex in person, he was kneading and flipping dough, laughing along with a girl who looked a lot like him. Maybe an older sister?

But gods, his smile.

I'd seen his picture online before. My cousin Grace had gone to Westwood with Alex, so he popped up on her Instagram from time to time. I couldn't wait to meet him in high school.

I admit I daydreamed about making out with him at the back-to-school dance. In reality, he didn't even look my way, much less make out with me.

Then I learned that Alex is popular. Really popular. He's the kind of guy who never has to worry about walking down the hallway alone. He walks in a pack of other inordinately attractive kids, tossing a baseball to himself, being attractive.

"Next time you're at Niko's, say hi to me, okay?" he says. "I'll add some extra mushrooms to your veggie pizza."

"I'd like that."

His eyes flick up and down my body. "I like your overalls. You look like a farmer."

I give him a look. "Thanks a lot, tromboner boy."

"Not like, an old man farmer. A cute farmer."

He starts laughing, and I join in. His joy and silliness is sort of contagious.

When our laughter fades away, he stares down at me and I gaze up at him. Quickly I glance around the dimly lit backstage.

Nobody else is here.

And it's dark. And he's so cute. And my heart is going to burst out of my chest.

He clears his throat. "I really do like some of your ideas, Lu."

"You do?" I say softly, loving how he said my first name.

He slowly takes a step closer. "Yeah. Especially the recycling."

My feet move nearer to his. "I liked your ideas too. I mean, I wouldn't mind driving to school in a limo," I flirt. It annoys me that I'm still attracted to him, even after he winged his speech. Stupid hormones.

He cracks another smile that makes my body hum in places I've never noticed before. When his eyes glance at my mouth, goose bumps explode on my skin.

Alex kneels to set the trombone down on the floor, and when he stands back up, his body is barely an inch from mine.

I lick my lips as his neck curls my way—*oh my God, is he going to kiss me?*—when the principal pops through the curtains.

Alex and I jump apart from each other.

"Alex, Lulu, it's time to vote," Dr. Walters announces,

seemingly unaware that he totally ruined the biggest moment of my whole entire life!

The principal holds the curtain open, ushering us out onto the gym floor. Kids are lining up to cast their votes, filling out ballots, and dropping them into cardboard boxes.

Alex and I stand next to each other, not moving, and not looking at each other. I touch my fingers to my throat, hardly believing what just happened. We totally got caught up in the moment. I'm too nervous to look at him.

After what feels like an eon, Alex sticks out his hand to shake mine. "Good luck, Wells."

I squeeze his fingers. "You too."

We grin at each other one last time before we separately start lobbying kids in line to vote for us.

At the end of the day, Dr. Walters's voice comes over the loudspeaker. "We've finished tallying the student council votes." He announces the names of freshman class treasurer, secretary, and vice president first. Depending on who they wanted to win, people squeal in response. I hold my breath, waiting for the finale. "And last but not least, the winner of freshman class president is—

"Alex Rouvelis!"

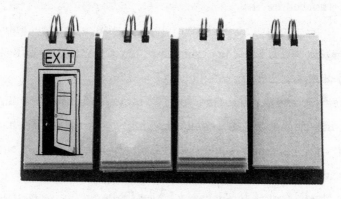

TODAY
FRESHMAN CLASS TRIP

Coffee County High's class trips are generally amazing because a super wealthy graduate of our school started an endowment before he died. Jim Worthington, who had made a fortune on medical inventions, loved traveling and wanted kids from our town to learn about the world.

Of course we have to hold car washes and bake sales through-out the year to make extra money for our travel, but the endowment allows for some nice field trips. The senior year trip is always the best because the school pays most of the cost. My older sister Lila's class flew to Rome before graduation. That year, the juniors went to Washington, D.C. It was a stretch, but I hoped our freshman class trip would be to Miami.

Nope.

We are at the Cumberland Science Museum, which is the last place I would've chosen for a field trip.

I am not completely opposed to science—without it, we wouldn't have electricity or the internet, and I'm a big fan of gravity, but I suck at balancing formulas, and dissecting animals pretty much goes against my entire belief system.

The line to get inside the museum is full of screaming elementary schoolers. One boy is digging out a wedgie. This is definitely not Miami Beach.

Max is standing beside me in line, gently combing his fingers through my hair to find any stray gum.

"I heard there's an indoor beehive in this museum," I say. "I hate that. Bees were meant to be free outside. Maybe we can find a way to set them loose."

"Lu, you're out of your mind. What if somebody got stung? You'd get, like, a year's worth of detention." Max lets go of my hair. "Okay, I think I got most of the gum."

I cross my arms. "Alex is such an asshole sometimes."

"Well, you did laugh when my gum landed on him. He probably thought you were guilty."

"Whose side are you on?"

He reaches into the back pocket of his tight gray jeans. "Want some gum?"

I gently shove his chest, making him grin as he slides a fresh piece in his mouth.

It's a good thing Max was able to fish the gum out of my long hair without having to cut it, because my hair is perfect right now. Last weekend when my stylist gave me a trim, I had her dye a deep purple streak underneath. This infuriated Dad, of course, but I don't care. It looks great contrasted against my blond waves and gives me something extra.

I run a hand through my hair. "How bad does it look?"

Max pats my shoulder. "It's no big deal. Look around. Guys are still checking you out."

I glance to see if one of them is Jonah, but he's up toward the front of the line near Dana Jenkins. That's disappointing. The good news is I still have a full day to spend time with him. I want to know his favorite comics. If he likes *Saga*, we probably have a lot in common. Maybe he likes *Lumberjanes* too?

Coach Rice passes tickets out to us and says we can go anywhere as long as we stay inside the museum, but reminds us to be back at the bus by one o'clock.

After handing our tickets to a museum employee, Max and I walk into the main atrium where Grace and her boyfriend, Ben, have already found a bench to make out on.

They've been dating for most of the school year, so they're pretty serious. She told me they're planning to sleep together when school lets out for summer and their parents are at work. Mom says that sex is something you do with a boy once you're in college and not a second before, but that's probably just Mom trying to keep my pants on.

I tear my eyes away from the Grace kissing show to focus on the real exhibits at the museum. A T. rex skeleton hangs from the ceiling, looming over me like a blimp. I read the little placard providing details about this particular skeleton, which was discovered in South Dakota.

Max gently pulls his Nikon digital camera out of its bag and hangs its strap around his neck. He points his lens at the T. rex. *Click, click, click.*

Alex, Ryan, and the other baseball players appear next to me and stare up at the dinosaur.

"Can you believe this thing? I bet its dick was huge," Ryan exclaims, making his friends crack up. "But not as big as mine. I don't know if you all know this," he says, puffing out his chest, "but they're thinking of naming this T. rex after me."

Max pointedly looks at the front of Ryan's pants and whispers to me, "More like they're planning to name an itty-bitty lizard after him."

Giggling and leaning against each other, Max and I wander into the diamond exhibit. I never knew there were so many colors of diamonds. White, pink, yellow, blue. There's even a red one.

"Look, Lu," Max says, peering into a glass box at a massive blue diamond. "Let me get your picture in front of this one. It'll look great next to your hair."

As a photographer for the school yearbook, Max is constantly snapping photos of me. At this rate, next year's yearbook will consist of only me and him. He loves taking selfies.

I prop a hand on my hip and pose like a model, showing off the blue diamond. "This diamond has 650 carats. Just like my future engagement ring."

Right as Max snaps my picture, Alex jumps into the shot. "Damn, Wells. You expect a guy to buy you a diamond like that? I already felt sorry for whoever you date, but now I wonder if I should warn guys off." He waves his arms back and forth like an airport worker directing planes with orange batons. "Attention, everybody, attention. Don't propose to Lulu Wells. She'll demand a big-ass diamond and you'll go broke."

"The only way I'd ever consider marrying you is if you gave me a big-ass diamond like that," I reply.

Max snaps pictures of us as Alex continues to wave his pretend batons. "Move along, people. Nothing to see here but a gold digger."

Kids from school walk by, laughing at Alex.

"Oh my God, I'd die if that happened to me," Marcie Wallace says to Dana Jenkins, giving me a look that's equal parts smugness and pity.

That's when I notice Jonah enter the room.

I move away from Alex, pretending to look at "the Pumpkin Diamond," one of the largest orange diamonds in the world. After a few seconds, I discreetly peek through the glass display at Jonah on the other side of the room. He's leaning against the wall, scrolling on his phone.

With both hands, I smooth my white tunic.

Jonah hasn't looked up from his screen. Since he's not checking out the exhibit, maybe now is the right time to try to talk to him. With a deep breath, I adjust my purse strap and walk his way.

Then Alex steps into my path, looking from me to Jonah. "Seriously?" He studies my eyes, then peeks over his shoulder at Jonah again. "You got a thing for him?"

Am I that transparent? I bite my lower lip, hoping Alex doesn't use this as an opportunity to humiliate me.

"Get out of my way, Alex."

"He'd never buy you a giant diamond, you know. He'd have to get his head out of his ass first, and I don't see that happening."

"Why do you think his head's in his ass?"

"He's in a room full of diamonds—some bigger than baseballs—and he's looking at his phone. That's weak."

I move to step around Alex, and he blocks my way again. "God, you're like a toddler," I snap.

I glance over at Jonah to find he's still mesmerized by his phone.

Alex pretends like he's guarding me on the basketball court, arms spread wide, shuffling sideways back and forth.

I skip to the right to avoid him, snag my boot on a divot in the carpet, and fall into one of the display cases. My elbow slams against the reinforced glass.

"Ow!"

Alex is laughing as he continues to try to block me.

"Stop it," I snap.

His eyes change when he notices me cradling my arm. A blue security light begins to flash as he rushes to help me. "Whoa, I'm sorry. You okay, Wells?"

I push him away, then rub my elbow. Right then an alarm goes off.

"Excuse me!" a voice screeches. A young woman wearing a museum employee badge is charging past students, heading our way. "You can't behave that way in here! Where are your teachers?"

"Shit," I say. "You better not have gotten me detention again, Alex."

After a quick look around the room, he grabs my forearm. "C'mon! Let's go." Alex rushes us out of the exhibit, away from the screeching alarm, pulling me behind him.

I nearly trip again trying to keep up. "Where are you taking me?" I blurt.

"I'm rescuing you from the museum lady."

Alex charges ahead down the hall. He reaches toward a door handle. Above the entrance is a sign that says Cumberland Science Museum Escape Room.

"Alex, wait, no!" I say, but he's already yanked the door open and is pulling me through.

I glance over my shoulder to locate Max, to see if he's following me, when suddenly the door slams shut behind us. Alex and I are in a dark room with no windows. All I can see is a glowing red exit sign.

"Uh, where are we?" Alex says, flicking on an overhead light, revealing that we're in a cavernous room full of science equipment. "It looks like Frankenstein's laboratory."

It's true. The room is straight out of the 1950s.

I yank on the door, to pull it open, but it's locked. Then a robotic voice comes over a loudspeaker. *"The famous scientist Rose Darwin has been kidnapped. Her robot, Isaac Newton, has been stolen and reprogrammed to attack hospitals and schools."*

Alex and I give each other a look.

The booming voice goes on, *"If you do not solve the riddles placed throughout this laboratory within an hour, the robot Newton will begin attacking hospitals and schools. To stop the robot, locate the twelve keys to unlock the safe containing its remote control panel."*

"I'm stuck in here for an hour with you?" I say. I open my purse, pull out my phone, and send Max a text: Helllllllp!!!!!!!!!!!!!!!

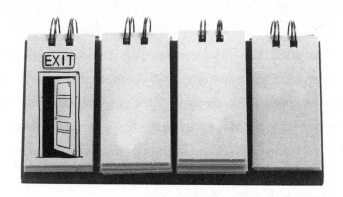

TODAY
FRESHMAN CLASS TRIP

Earlier this year, I would've killed to be alone with Alex.

Now? I'd rather be taking an algebra test.

"I don't get it," Alex says, peering around the laboratory. "What is this place?"

"I saw one of these on TV," I reply. "It's an escape room."

"A what?"

I put it in plain English: "We're stuck in here until we figure out how to escape. Don't you read signs on doors before you open them?"

"No." Alex shuts his eyes. "Let's get to work, then. I don't want to be in here for a second longer than I have to."

I sit on a lab table. "You're the one who's good at science. You get us out of here."

"You're lazy."

"I'm not lazy. This is your fault for knocking me into the diamond display."

"It's not like you have anything else to do in here."

"Actually, I do." I pull my electronic Wacom sketchpad out of my purse. It took a couple of years to save enough, but I was finally able to buy one after receiving my fifteenth birthday money. I push the power button, and the new comic panel I've been working on appears. My character Nera is lying on her bed doing homework in her family's cave.

"What's that?" Alex asks.

I ignore him. He'll make fun of it.

"What is it?" he repeats, looking over my arm. "A comic book? It's pretty good."

"Just a story I'm working on. A graphic novel, not a comic book."

"What's it about? An evil lady who throws gum at nice, unsuspecting boys?"

"No, but maybe you're on to something." I point my tablet pen at him. "That would be an instant bestseller."

Alex studies my screen. "Is that girl living in a cave?"

Pleasure fills me. I love it when people can tell what I'm drawing. "Yeah. Nera grew up in a cave after an asteroid hit the Earth and destroyed most of civilization."

Alex furrows his eyebrows. "She had time to move a bed into a cave before the asteroid hit?"

"In my story, people know for a year that the asteroid is coming and have time to prepare. Her family builds a shelter in the caves near their house in Niagara Falls."

"And the asteroid destroys most of the world?"

"So far as Nera knows. When she finally leaves the caves, she discovers some clans living outside, and the clan leaders are descendants of the former president and vice president of the United States. Now they're enemies."

"I don't think that's plausible. I mean, the chances of an asteroid that's big enough to destroy the planet actually hitting us must be in the millions."

"It happens in my book."

"I don't buy it."

"It's just a story!"

"I'm only trying to help. I know a lot about science."

Show-off. As irritating as he is, deep down I'm pleased Alex gave me feedback on my work. When I tell my parents about my drawings over dinner, they nod and then interrogate me about whether my homework is finished. Max always looks at what I draw, but he never gives critical feedback.

But Alex...Alex is telling me his true opinion. That's hard to find.

He's still annoying, though. "By the way, this is the worst field trip ever."

Alex grins evilly. "I knew you'd hate it."

"What are you talking about?"

"Remember when you protested biology class because we had to dissect frogs, and I told you that it's important to study frogs for the sake of science, and you were all like, 'I hate science almost as much as I hate you, Alex.'" He mimics my voice.

"Yeah..."

"That's why, as class president, I recommended the Cumberland Science Museum for our field trip."

I shake my head. "You seriously suggested we come here to piss me off?"

"Worked, didn't it?" he says with a laugh.

"If I didn't know any better, I'd say you're obsessed with me."

"Just getting even." He crosses his arms over his white T-shirt. His face grows still and serious, and it dawns on me why he's trying to get back at me. There's only one thing that puts him in that kind of mood: baseball.

JANUARY–FEBRUARY
FRESHMAN YEAR

Losing class president to Alex sucked.

Like pit of my stomach, pride punching, sucked. I was super pissed and couldn't even look at him for a while.

Now? We pass in the hallway between second and third period every day, and sometimes he even deigns to give me a knowing smile during algebra class, but he never tries to continue what we started backstage.

When I told Grace about the almost-kiss, how we got caught up in the moment, and how there hadn't been a repeat, she said, "Lu-babe, I don't know how to tell you this gently, but I've known Alex a long time. If he wants a girl, she'd know it, because he'd be obvious about it. He's confident about stuff like that."

So he probably didn't truly want to kiss me? I wasn't sure if I wanted to kiss him either.

Or did I?

Finding world peace would be easier than sorting that out. Maybe I should just ignore him for all eternity.

But since he's president of our class, and I have things I want to get done, I decide to approach him after the final bell one day.

"We have soccer, football, and baseball fields, and a tennis court behind the school. There's even a putting green for the golf team to get in some practice before hitting the course at the country club."

Alex puts his hands in the back pockets of his jeans. "What are you getting at?"

"There's a tiny plot of land beside the baseball field. What can I do to convince the school we need a garden?"

"Why do you think we need one?"

"Have you eaten in the cafeteria?" I raise an eyebrow at him. "The food sucks ass. They don't even have a salad bar for people like me."

"People like you?" He cocks his head. "Is something wrong? Are you sick?"

"No, I'm vegan. I don't believe in eating animals. It's bad for the poor animals and bad for the environment. The meat industry is one of the leading causes of climate change."

Alex stares at me like I'm from another planet. "What do you mean you don't eat meat? Are you sure you're not sick? Maybe you just haven't had really good meat. You should try my grandfather's lamb shish kebabs."

"Alex, please work with me here. I didn't win the election, but I'd still like to help make this school better."

He gives me a quizzical smile, like he can't figure me out. "You should start a petition for your garden. I need to know this is more than only you talking before I can take it to the student council, and on to the principal."

As Alex suggests, I draft a petition and over the course of a month, I get 250 kids to sign it. More than half the kids in our school! Some of them are definitely into the idea of a sustainable garden because they hate the crappy processed cafeteria food, but Max says he heard some of my classmates only signed my petition because they want to plant a few marijuana plants next to the carrots.

Regardless, I have the signatures I need. I only need to find Alex and show him.

After the final bell of the day rings, I hustle out of class and jog down the hallway toward the gym, where I see Alex heading toward the locker room.

"Alex," I call, bolting after him.

His teammates see me, and start jostling Alex around, teasing him.

"The garden girl's coming!" one of the seniors says, and Alex's face turns red. He rushes to the locker room door, but I skid to a halt to block him.

I hand him the petition. "Here you go. Two-hundred and fifty signatures supporting a school garden. Will you present it to the student council and principal?"

Alex takes a hard look at it, flipping through all the signatures. His eyebrows furrow. "I'll pass it along," he says finally.

I bounce on my toes. "Thanks, Alex."

He sucks his bottom lip into his mouth and nods, not looking at me. Amazing to think that just a few months ago he nearly kissed me, and now he can't even look my way? My stomach falls. Whatever. I'll focus on convincing the school to get a garden, not on some boy.

But a few weeks later when I ask about my petition, a strange expression comes over his face. His forehead crinkles up, as if he's worried. "Oh. I'm sorry, I haven't had a chance to give it to Dr. Walters yet. I've been busy with batting practice and working."

I put a hand on my hip. "Maybe you shouldn't have run for class president if you didn't have time for it."

He takes a step closer. "I do my job. I helped plan the homecoming parade and the talent show."

"You could be doing more."

"I swear to God, Lulu. I'm sorry I'm not as perfect as you, but I've done what I'm supposed to do. I didn't sign up to build your garden."

He turns his back on me, sitting at his lunch table with the other baseball players.

Fine. If he won't help me, I'll do it myself. I'll go to the next meeting of the school board and make a case.

But then it happens. A bulldozer appears by the baseball field and begins to dig. Construction workers quickly erect a new structure that looks nothing like a garden.

It's a batting cage.

I'm so angry, I could hit a hundred baseballs right now. I went to all the trouble to collect 250 signatures on a petition. I feel like a fool.

The next day, I approach Alex in the library during study hall. He's sitting at a table with Ryan McDowell and their teammates, goofing off and laughing, even though we're supposed to be silent during study hall. But when the teachers love you as much as they love him, you get away with anything.

Hell, just the other day in algebra class, Mrs. Monroe asked, "If there are five times as many oranges as apples, eight more bananas than apples, and three times as many pears as bananas, and the sum of the apples and oranges is equal to the sum of the bananas and pears, then how much fruit is there? Alex?"

"Easy," he replied, folding his hands behind his head, leaning back in his chair, "it's a fruit salad."

Mrs. Monroe just laughed and laughed, and he didn't even have to answer the question.

In the library, Alex sees me coming and starts rapping his pencil nervously on the side of the table.

"Alex."

"Wells," he replies. *Tap, tap, tap* goes the pencil.

"Did you know about the batting cage all along?" I ask with a weak voice.

He shrugs, not meeting my eyes.

His friends look back and forth between us. Ryan rubs his hands together. "This is gonna be good."

All Ryan needs is popcorn to watch our show.

"I spent all that time collecting signatures on my petition and talking to you about it," I start, "and you couldn't even tell me to my face that the land was never available?"

Alex shifts in his chair. "Look, I'm sorry," he says softly. "I didn't figure you'd be able to get all those signatures..."

"I didn't figure you'd get all those votes for class president either."

"*Damn*," Ryan says, as their teammates go, "Ooooooh!"

"I can't believe you," I say.

"Lulu, c'mon," Alex replies.

"C'mon, *what*?" I throw my hands in the air.

"Shhhhhh!" The librarian glares at me.

"Don't you ever care about anybody but yourself?" Alex asks.

"I do care about others. That was the whole point of a garden. Healthy food for everybody."

"Hear, hear," Ryan interjects. "Meatloaf Monday was the worst day of my life."

I grin at Ryan's joke, which makes Alex scowl.

"But what about me?" Alex says.

"What about you?" I reply. "You could eat the vegetables too if you want. Or do you not eat vegetables? Do you only drink other people's blood?"

A tiny smile quirks on his lips, but it goes away more quickly than it appeared. He stands up from the table and begins to speak more quietly. "The batting cage is important for me."

"Why? You can practice on that big baseball field, you know."

"I need all the batting practice I can get, okay? I'm great at first base, but my hitting could always be better. I need to be able to hit eighty-mile-an-hour fastballs." He pauses. "So I can get a scholarship."

"A scholarship?"

"Yeah, my family expects me to work at their restaurant the rest of my life. I need a scholarship to go to college."

My eyebrows furrow. Not going to college seems impossible. My parents have been talking about college since I could crawl. As the town dentist, my father fully expects me to find a good job, and my mother is all about girl power and thinks women should bring home just as much money as men. My sister, Lila, graduates college next year and plans to apply to law school. She'll be a district attorney before you know it.

For me, college is the expectation.

Alex is probably overreacting. "I'm sure you'll get to go to college," I say. "Now back to the garden—"

He holds up a hand to stop me from talking. "You don't know anything about me."

"Whose fault is that? You wanted to be class president so bad, but you're always busy. You never have time to talk to me about my ideas—"

"You're so selfish, Lulu. You only care about you and your *big* ideas," he snaps, making air quotes. "I'm sorry, but the only land left is the school's front lawn, and like that's gonna happen," he says sarcastically.

"There's gotta be something we can do."

"I can't suddenly create more land. I'm not God."

"You could get rid of your batting cage."

"Gah! You never know when to shut up."

All his boys go, "Oooooooh" again.

Alex shoulders his backpack, grabs his books from the library table, and storms off.

What an ass.

I'm so angry with Alex, and hurt that he misled me and made me look like an idiot getting all those signatures, that I skip class, ride my bike to the hardware store, and buy a heavy-duty padlock.

Last period I sneak outside, lock the batting cage, and throw the key in some thick bushes. I sit up in the back of the stands.

Then the baseball team arrives for batting practice before their game against Winchester.

Alex pulls at the gate. It doesn't open. He rattles the fence as the other players try to find a way in.

Coach Rice examines the padlock. "What the hell? Where'd this come from?"

"I guess we'll have to warm up on the field," says Jeremy, one of the senior captains.

Coach Rice shakes his head. "I promised Winchester they could take batting practice on the field since we have the new cage."

"What are we supposed to do?" the captain snaps. "We have to warm up."

"Y'all can go play catch next to the parking lot," Coach Rice says. "Just don't hit any cars. And unless I can find a bolt cutter, no batting practice today."

Alex's shoulders droop as the coach heads off toward the school, presumably to try to find bolt cutters. Alex puts on his baseball mitt and pounds his fist into it as if frustrated, and throws his head back to look at the sky. When he lowers his chin, he sees me sitting at the top of the stands. I duck my head down, but it's too late. He saw me.

He glances at the batting cage, then back in my direction, and I can see him working out the math in his mind. "Wells?" he calls out. "Did you lock the batting cage?"

The players begin to turn my way and start shouting.

"Where's the key?" one guy yells at me, but I can only shrug.

There's no way I could find it in those thick bushes. I wish I could, though. I'm starting to regret this...

"What a fucked-up thing to do," one player says.

"What a weirdo," another guy adds.

The captain comes to stand by Alex. He drops a hand on his shoulder, and speaks loudly enough for everyone to hear him, "Keep your girl problems off the field, Rouvelis."

Alex's face turns redder than his Red Raiders uniform.

The only player who doesn't care is Ryan. He thinks it's hilarious.

"Damn," he says with a laugh. "Lulu knows how to hold a grudge."

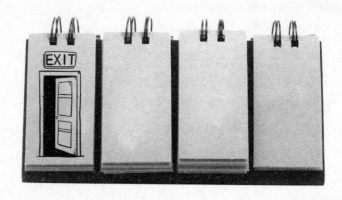

TODAY
FRESHMAN CLASS TRIP

"So you planned this entire field trip to get back at me for locking the batting cage?"

Alex cracks up.

"You're such a pain in the ass." I rotate my arm in slow circles. It's sore from where I banged it against the glass.

Alex glances at my arm. "Is your elbow okay?"

"I think so. I might have a bruise."

He moves closer to examine it. His brown eyes meet mine as his warm fingers brush across my skin. I'd never noticed he wears leather bands around his wrist.

"I'm sorry," he says.

His gentle touch makes my heart race. I quickly pull my arm

from his grip. "You know what you should be sorry for? Putting gum in my hair. That was so gross."

"But it was your gum."

"No, it was Max's."

Realization dawns on Alex's face. He cringes. "Oops."

He touches my elbow again, as if to check on it.

I can't believe he convinced the school to come to a science museum to get back at me. It's not like I haven't already paid the price for that prank.

After the baseball team turned me in for my crime, the principal gave me two days of detention. This mortified my father. People who came to his office for a teeth cleaning would not stop talking about it because in Manchester, baseball is a religion. Me locking the batting cage was an affront to the patriarchy or something.

Worst of all, it embarrassed Grace.

She texted me: Why'd you have to do something so weird? Everyone's talking about you—not in a good way

Me: I'm sorry. I didn't mean to hurt you

Grace: Please start acting mature or high school's gonna suck for both of us

She started avoiding me at school after that, even though we still had our occasional weekend sleepovers. It killed me when I realized that if Grace and I weren't cousins, she wouldn't even talk to me.

"I really am sorry about the batting cage," I tell Alex. "It was a stupid thing to do. I was just so angry at you."

His brown eyes meet mine. "I get that. I would've been mad too, if I'd gotten all those signatures for nothing."

"Okay, so we're even now," I say.

"Agreed."

I need to get out of here. I peer around the escape room. I once wrote a dystopian story about a girl who gets trapped inside a military compound and figures her way out. Unfortunately my characters' qualities do not translate to me. I am shitty at solving any kind of puzzle.

My phone buzzes with a response from Max.

Max: Where are you?

Me: Stuck in an escape room with Alex!

Max: 😂 😂 😂

Me: Help me already!

My phone doesn't buzz with his reply until a minute later: Talked to a museum lady. She said nothing bad will happen to you in there. You are supposed to solve the quizzes to escape.

Me: No shit, Sherlock. Tell them to let me out!

Max: They'll let you out if you want.

Me: Great!

Max: It's not like you could solve your way out of there anyway.

Me: EXCUSE YOU, OF COURSE I COULD 😳

Max: Prove it then. And while you're at it, you can spend some QT with that hottie sexpot Alex.

Me: You are the worst best friend ever!

Max: You love me.

"Wells!" I glance up from my phone screen to find Alex glaring at me. "We only have fifty-five minutes left to find the keys so we can unlock the safe with the remote control."

"C'mon, Alex, that's not real. A robot isn't going to destroy hospitals and schools."

"Look, the sooner we find the keys, the sooner we get out of here. I need to pee."

"Then you better hold it." I raise my eyebrows. "I bet I can find more keys than you."

He stares me down. "You're on."

My eyes scan the room. The place is full of lockboxes, beakers, old TV sets and computers, dials and buttons, Bunsen burners, and a framed photo of Albert Einstein. A bright red clock counts down our remaining time.

I start opening drawers in a desk, looking for keys, while Alex is crawling on the floor, his stupid perfect butt sticking up in the air.

"I found something," he calls. "There's words written under this table. It says, 'This clue is not really a clue and will not help you in your escape.'"

I discover a chalkboard with an equation written on it. Algebra is the worst, but this problem is simple enough that I can solve it. *Open lockbox *** 8x—3 = 3x + 17. Code = 7777*

Using the chalk, I work through the problem and come up with an answer of 4. The second I'm finished, Alex runs for a little lockbox with the number 4 on it. He punches in 7777, opens the lid, and pulls out a sheet of paper.

"Hey!" I say. "That was my clue."

"I found it first."

"I did the work." I march over, grab the paper from him, and hip check him to the side. He hip checks me back and looks over my shoulder at the paper.

It says *5_8_7_* with blank spaces in between the numbers. I set it aside to look for other clues. I open a tall storage container.

Inside I search the shelves. Aha! A black light. I flip it on and shine the purple beam on the floor and walls, not sure if I'm looking for something or if it will be another non-clue like the writing under the table.

Meanwhile, Alex is now wearing protective goggles.

"What are those for?" I ask.

He strikes a pose. "I look hot, right?"

Rolling my eyes, I continue scanning the laboratory with the black light until random letters appear across the ceiling. *A-Y-O-E-F. Lockbox 2.*

"A code?" I ask.

"Look here," Alex replies, leading me to a stack of crates in the corner. Each one has a letter on it and a number. I find the crates with *A-Y-O-E-F* and match up the numbers.

"5-6-4-1-2," I say, and Alex walks over to a lockbox labeled 2. He punches in the numbers. The lid pops open.

"Eee," I squeal, shuffling over to look inside. My arm brushes his as we pull out a key together.

Alex gives me a high five. "Good job, Wells."

Eleven keys to go. We continue working together to find more keys all over the room. Behind loose bricks, panels in the walls, a grate in the floor. We have to solve math problems and riddles. I find a ring of ten keys that don't work on any locks in the room. Another worthless clue that wastes time.

"It's funny that the robot's name is Isaac Newton," Alex says as he's searching the shelves again.

"Why is that funny?" I ask. "Didn't he discover gravity?"

"Yeah, he did. I saw this documentary about him on the History

Channel. It said Isaac Newton didn't think his greatest accomplishment was discovering gravity. He was most proud of being a virgin."

"What?" I pause to look at Alex. "Maybe that's why the robot's so angry and wants to destroy schools," I joke. "He's horny."

After about fifty minutes, we're down to one missing key. Time is running out. We need to find a code to open the remaining lockbox.

Alex and I are running around the room, yanking open drawers, moving beakers, and checking behind bookcases, searching for anything that might be a clue. With two minutes to spare, I pick up the photo of Albert Einstein. I turn the frame over to remove the back, finding a folded sheet of paper with three more random numbers. Would it match up with the other sheet of paper that said *5_8_7_*?

I dart across the room to the original numbers, press the papers together, and hold them up to the light. Alex appears above my shoulder to stare up at it. *5-6-8-3-7–7.*

Alex punches that number into the final lockbox. It opens. I yank the key out, stick it in the safe with the other eleven keys. It swings open.

"We did it," I shout.

His arms come around me in a hug. My body stiffens at first, but he feels so good, I slowly begin to relax against his chest. Our hug feels warm, and soft, and safe, with a strong electric buzz.

"We saved all of the hospitals and schools from that asshole robot," Alex says.

I chuckle into his shoulder as he pats my back. "Yeah, we're a pretty good team."

The door slides open. Natural light floods in. We peer out to see Max in front of a group of kids from school staring at us, our arms still looped around each other.

"You did it!" Max says. "You got out."

"Dude, were you hooking up with Lulu Wells?" Ryan asks.

"You hooked up with Alex in the escape room?!" Max whisper-yells at me.

"I can't believe Alex made out with that hippie," Marcie Wallace says, giving Alex a wistful look.

I shake my head. "Guys, we didn't hook up in there. We were too busy escaping."

My classmates mutter, "Yeah, right" and "I call BS."

Then something happens that I never expected: Jonah approaches Alex, going in for a fist bump. "Nice one, man."

I narrow my eyes. Is Jonah kidding me? Any interest I had in him suddenly disappears.

Alex looks him up and down, refusing to answer the fist bump. "Get out of my way, Jonah."

Jonah's face reddens as he shuffles backward, melting into the crowd.

"This is not how I expected today to turn out," Max murmurs to me. "It's like your life became a reality show."

"Can we go check out the gift shop?" I say, feeling uncomfortable about what just happened. Not only about Jonah's comment, but about the hug. I can't believe how good it felt to be in Alex's arms. But he's a jerk, right?

I look back at him. He's busy telling Ryan about how Isaac Newton was proudest of being a virgin.

"You and Isaac have a lot common," Ryan tells Alex, deadpan, and I snort with laughter.

Alex gives me a grin, his brown eyes twinkling, seeing right through me, as if he knows how conflicted I am about him. How can one person be so annoying and yet so charming?

APRIL
FRESHMAN YEAR

Mom pulls her car up in front of the movie theater in Murfreesboro, the next town over from Manchester.

"What time should I pick you up?"

"Ben's parents are giving me a ride to a party at Tina Hardaway's house," Grace says. "Mom and Dad are okay with it."

Max unclips his seat belt in the back seat. "Lu and I might get food afterwards, Mrs. Wells."

Mom looks at him through her rearview mirror. "Is that code for going to the party?"

"Nah, I'm serious," Max says. "I need some Rocky Road."

"We're just gonna go across the street to the mall, Mom."

"Okay, okay," Mom replies. "But if you want to go to a party, I don't mind as long as we can pick you up before your curfew at eleven. Your father and I just need to know where you are and how to reach you."

I shift in my seat. Max and I don't get invited to parties. Especially not at the house of Tina Hardaway, a senior on Grace's dance team.

After giving Mom a kiss goodbye, I follow Max and Grace into the theater. There are so many kids from school here, the lobby might as well be the cafeteria.

We pick up our movie tickets and head to the concession stand.

"What can I get for you?" the concession stand worker says in an overly chipper voice.

"Twizzlers, please," I reply.

"A large popcorn and Milk Duds," Max says.

"Water, please," Grace replies. "Oh! There's Ben." In a flash, she abandons us, throwing her arms around his neck as he meets her with a kiss.

I sigh, watching them.

"What's wrong?" Max asks.

"I'm jealous."

"Don't be," Max says under his breath as he passes his dad's credit card over to the concession worker. "She could do so much better."

Max has his reasons for disliking Ben. He told me all about how Ben's friends bully him in the locker room. And while Ben never joins in, sometimes he laughs.

I can't help agreeing with Max—Ben is not good enough for my cousin. She's kind, gets far better grades than me, and is a great dancer. Ben, on the other hand, has basically refused to acknowledge Max's and my existence since he started dating Grace.

"Yeah, Ben's a dick," I say to Max as I pass a ten-dollar bill to the worker. "But I just, like, want to make out with somebody."

"Me too," Max says wistfully.

I give him a look. Max has at least kissed a guy—someone he met last summer in Kentucky at church camp—but my experience with boys adds up to zilch.

I take Grace's water from the counter along with my Twizzlers, turning around. Grace is tugging Ben my way, even though it looks like he'd rather have an invasive medical procedure than be seen with me.

"Hi, Ben," I say. He nods and scrubs a hand through his hair, focusing on a display for some upcoming Pixar movie.

"Doesn't Lulu look great tonight?" Grace asks. "We gave each other makeovers."

He glances at me again, but doesn't respond. "I'm gonna talk to the guys for a minute, babe," Ben says, kissing the top of her head and vanishing into the arcade.

Max watches Ben walk away with narrowed eyes. "What, does he think we have a disease or something?"

Grace fidgets, adjusting her purse strap. "I'm sorry, you guys," she mutters.

I touch her elbow. "I know."

We might not think Ben is good enough for Grace, but the feeling is mutual. He doesn't think we're good enough for her.

She bumps her hip against mine. "And was I right about that lip color or what? Guys are checking you out already."

Grace had convinced me to wear some of her siren-red lipstick. Some guys from school were definitely peering our way, but they could easily be focusing on Grace. She looks glamorous as usual, wearing the new fuchsia lipstick I suggested along with her regular lush eye makeup.

Dana Jenkins and Marcie Wallace appear out of nowhere. "Grace, can we talk to you about dance camp for a sec?" Marcie asks.

"Sure," Grace says, then turns to Max and me. "Some of the junior varsity girls are thinking of applying to this sleepaway dance camp in Florida this summer, and I might go with them."

She walks off with Dana and Marcie, drifting even farther away from me.

Max and I sit on a bench together. I cross my legs beneath me and open my Twizzlers. Max pours Milk Duds into his large carton of popcorn. He nods at the Pixar poster of a girl fawning over a merman. "Why can't it be about a merman who's in love with a human boy?"

"That sounds sooo much better," I say. "But how would that work anatomically?"

Max thinks as he chews on his popcorn. "I bet the merman's fin disappears when he comes on dry land, and then he's hung like any other dude."

I burst out laughing, leaning against my friend, and he leans back into me.

The lobby door swings open and Ryan McDowell enters. With his freckles and perfectly gelled red hair, Ryan looks like a super cute Weasley brother. Lots of girls would use a love potion on him.

Alex Rouvelis follows behind Ryan, wearing a short-sleeved hooded sweatshirt over a long-sleeved black shirt, distressed jeans that fit just right, and a backwards Braves cap.

I suck in a breath and sit up straighter.

Two sophomore girls approach Alex and Ryan to say hello.

As Alex smiles and flirts with the girls, Max and I pretend not to drool.

Max nudges my side. "Looks like we're not the only jealous ones."

Even though Ryan has a sophomore girl hanging on his arm, he's staring at Grace, who has resumed kissing Ben over in the arcade.

"That's ridiculous," I reply. Alex and Ryan are the most popular guys in our class. And I heard Ryan's family has more money than God, Jesus, and the Holy Spirit combined. "Ryan's not jealous. He can get anybody he wants."

"Not me," Max says. "Ryan's too pasty. He looks like Elmer's Glue."

I giggle. "That's not nice."

"Just telling the truth. I'm not attracted to guys who look like mashed potatoes. But Alex? Yeah, I'd hit that."

I look over at Alex. *Were those jeans made specifically for him?* "You have bad taste, friend."

Max snorts. "You know, for someone who hates him so much, you sure spend an awful lot of time looking at him."

I tear my eyes away from Alex and rip into my Twizzler with my teeth, to avoid having to respond. Of course Alex is cute, but never in a million years would I have a chance with him after everything that's happened between us. Besides, why would I want to make out with someone like him? I'm still not over how he convinced me to collect all those signatures. I basically had people signing a petition that did nothing but prove I'm a total loser.

Three of Ben's friends walk by on the way to the concession stand. "Hot date with Garden Girl tonight, Max?" asks Paul Clark, a boy in my homeroom.

Another boy mutters something I can't hear, but I'm pretty sure Max can because his face blushes.

"Do you smell something?" I ask Max.

He sticks his nose in the air. "Yeah, smells like a dumpster fire."

Ignoring us, Ben's friends laugh as they walk away.

Max looks like he wants to cry and scream at the same time. I know it's hard for him, being the only out gay kid in our small town.

"Do you want to leave?" I ask.

He shakes his head. "No way in hell am I missing out on Thor and Loki."

Right then Alex walks up to us. "Hey, Max."

After a moment of shock, Max sets his popcorn on the bench and jumps to his feet.

"My papu—my grandfather, loved the pictures you took of our baseball team for the yearbook."

"Oh cool, thanks," Max says.

"I wanted to ask, do you ever take pictures on the side? Because Papu's seventieth birthday is coming up, and I want to get him something special, so I was wondering—" He stops to take a breath, adjusting his ball cap. "I was wondering if you'd be willing to take pictures of his restaurant? Niko's? I was thinking I could frame a couple for him."

Max's eyes light up. "Yeah, no problem. Let me give you my number, and we'll work something out."

"Thanks, man."

"But you know what?" Max says with a sly grin, as I lift a Twizzler to my mouth. "You should ask Lulu to draw Niko's. Her drawing would be much better than any picture I would take."

I bite the Twizzler in two, choking a piece down. "What?"

That's when Alex notices me sitting on the bench. His eyes linger on my face longer than usual. He glances at my red lipstick. "After she locked my batting cage, I can't imagine what she'd draw. Niko's completely empty with no customers? Niko's on fire?"

My face burns. "I'd never do that. I love Niko's."

I glare at Alex and he glares at me. His eyes return to my lips. His expression softens for a second before his eyebrows furrow.

"Look, man, I'd be happy to take some pictures for you," Max says, and Alex gives him a fist bump.

Max and I take our seats in the theater, which are right in the middle for "optimum Thor viewing" according to him.

During the previews, my eyes scan the theater. Grace and Ben sit a few aisles in front of us. Max shovels popcorn into his mouth while surreptitiously sneaking glances at the guys' basketball team. Ryan makes out with the sophomore I saw him with earlier.

My eyes land on Alex, who's laughing at a preview. His stupid grin hypnotizes me.

Alex looks my way and catches me staring. *Shit.* I jerk my head to face the screen.

After about twenty-five minutes of previews, I lean over to Max. "It feels like we've been here for hours. I'm ready to go home."

"Shh," he whispers.

I reach into my Twizzlers bag to get another, only to find I'm on my last one. "Do you want anything from the concession stand? I need more candy."

Max shakes his head, stuffing more popcorn in his mouth.

I hunch over so I don't block people's view of the screen, edge out of my row of seats, and head to the lobby. It's nearly empty now that the movies are starting. I decide to stop in the restroom first. On my way out, I notice my sneaker is untied.

I kneel to tie my shoe, and a pair of white sneakers appear before me. As I rise back to my full height, I discover the shoes belong to Alex.

"Please tell me the previews are over," I say. "I'm literally about to die of old age."

"Sorry, they're still going strong."

"I've got time to go get more Twizzlers, then."

"That's where I was headed. I'm craving Junior Mints." He gestures down the hallway toward the lobby.

"Junior Mints?" I say, rolling my eyes. "That's so cliché."

"I wish I'd snuck in a bag of Jolly Ranchers."

"Jolly Ranchers are my favorite."

His eyes light up. "Mine too. Especially the lemon."

"Ugh. You're wrong about everything, aren't you?"

He chuckles. "Let me guess...you like the green apple?"

"No, cherry. Anyway, you couldn't have brought them to the movies. You'd be that guy making noise with the crinkly wrappers, and everyone would be going 'Shhhhhh!' at you."

He smirks at me.

"Did you do something different with your makeup?" Alex asks.

I touch my fingers to my mouth. "I borrowed Grace's lipstick."

"Oh." He stuffs his hand in his jeans pocket.

After going to the concession stand, we walk back to the theater, and on the way we pass Jonah Zotter from school and two older guys I don't recognize.

"Hi," one of them says, checking me out.

Jonah looks back and forth between Alex and me, raising his eyebrows. "Hi, Lulu," he says, and I return his smile as I walk by. He's cute.

Alex sees this happen and stops to stare over his shoulder at the guys for a long moment. When he turns back to me, his eyes travel up my body to my face.

Out of the corner of my eye, I see him looking at me again.

"Watch out for this one, guys," Alex calls out to the boys, and the smile falls from Jonah's face. "She's a handful."

"Ugh, you're such a dick," I say, and turn back toward the theater as Alex chuckles behind me.

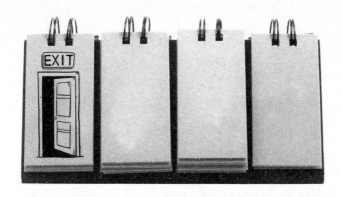

TODAY
FRESHMAN CLASS TRIP

After escaping from the escape room, I walk around the museum gift shop with Max, gossiping and browsing.

"You need this," I say, showing him a keychain made of fake brains.

"Nah, I don't have a car." He strides across the shop. "Now this? This I could use." He stands next to a full-size skeleton.

I snap a picture of Max and Skeletor for my Instagram, then I wrap my arm around the skeleton's waist, as Max takes pictures of me with his fancy yearbook camera.

"Come here often?" I say to the skeleton, cracking Max up. I love making him laugh.

That's when Grace and Ben come into the gift shop and dart over to me. "I heard about you and Alex Rouvelis," she says, grabbing my arm, and then whispers, "I remember when you had a thing for him before."

"Yeah, what happened?" Ben asks, leaning over her shoulder to hear my response.

He is a classic follower, and since Alex deigned to hug me, here Ben is—*following*. If Grace's douchey boyfriend wasn't here, I'd tell her about hugging Alex, and how it felt like waking up in a pool of sunlight on the beach.

I search frantically for a way to distract her and put off this conversation until Ben isn't around. "Look," I say, pointing over her shoulder. "Flamingos."

"Huh?" she replies.

I give her a pointed look, to try to get her to play along. "You *love* flamingos, right?"

She mouths, "Ohhh," to me, and presses her hands to Ben's chest, staring at him like a kitten who wants a treat. "I want a flamingo."

Ben leans down to kiss her. "Let's pick one out, babe."

"Gross," I say under my breath. They wander over to the display, where Grace stands on one foot pretending to be a flamingo, and Ben kisses her again.

"Get a room," a voice calls out. It's Ryan, back again, sauntering into the gift shop with Alex and their teammates.

"Guys," Max calls out to them excitedly, "let me get your picture with the skeleton for the yearbook."

"Yesssss," Ryan says.

Alex drapes his arm around the skeleton. "Let's do this!"

I smooth my hair back nervously, then pretend to look at postcards. I peek at him through the rack as Max takes his picture.

Ryan moves the skeleton's jaw up and down. "Alex, show me on the skeleton where the bad man touched you."

Alex groans, "Shut up, dude."

After finishing his photo shoot, Max rests his camera against his chest and joins me behind the postcards, leaning toward me conspiratorially. "So, what really happened in the escape room?"

"We solved some riddles together. And we hugged."

"You guys were all over each other. That's all you did?"

"Of course," I whisper, but I can barely believe how much I enjoyed that hug. Alex bothered me a lot this year, but he's had his good moments too, especially today. And can we talk about how his skin made mine sizzle? "I guess...I guess I wouldn't be opposed to more, though."

Max claps his hands. "This is brilliant. You're a real-life, enemies-to-lovers story." He rubs his chin as if coming up with an evil manifesto. "This will make a great spread in next year's yearbook," he muses.

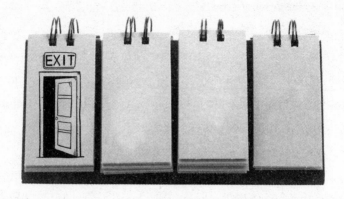

TODAY
FRESHMAN CLASS TRIP

Before we leave the museum, Max has one last thing he wants to do: visit the planetarium.

We stand in line to get tickets, playing with our phones and chatting.

"Why are you so into the planetarium all of a sudden?" I ask.

Max looks up from his screen with glittering eyes. "While you were in the escape room, I met a boy."

"Shut up!" I bounce up and down on my tiptoes. "Why didn't you tell me sooner?"

Max's freckled cheeks turn a rosy pink. "We exchanged numbers, but I wasn't sure if he was for real or not. I mean, I wanted to see if he actually texted me first before I said anything."

"Who is it?"

"He goes to Riverdale."

"But they're our rivals," I say with mock-seriousness.

Max, tall and lean with stylish brown hair, spreads his arms out wide. "Does it look like I play sports? And I've never heard of rival yearbook photographers."

"If there were, you'd kick everybody's ass."

"I know, right?"

"It sucks he goes to another school, though."

"I'm kinda glad he does, to be honest."

Max came out to his parents two years ago when he was thirteen, and while they weren't surprised and fully supported him, they acknowledged that our town isn't the most open-minded place in the world. Riverdale is in Murfreesboro, a more progressive town about half an hour away from us. Max's parents had even talked about moving there to make things easier, where people and churches would be more welcoming, but they'd lived their whole lives in Manchester. It was important to their family to stand by who they are, even when other people are prejudiced jerks.

"What does the planetarium have to do with Riverdale boy?" I ask. "Does he have a name?"

Max leans closer to whisper. "Blake. He sent a text that he's going to the planetarium and asked me to meet him there."

"The planetarium is so romantic. I swear, you are so much better at flirting than I am."

Max buys us tickets for the planetarium. As we are heading inside, Alex walks by with the baseball players. He gives me a little wave and I nod back.

Max watches this and declares, "Huh. He's into you."

"Do you really think so? I mean, we've been fighting this whole year."

"Just calling it like I see it."

Max and I go into the large, oval auditorium of the planetarium. A guy sitting near the back motions at us. Is that Blake? He's cute. Only one seat is open beside him, so I let Max take it and choose a spot in the next row. Bored, I begin to braid a chunk of my hair.

Right then, Alex enters the planetarium and scans the space. I abandon my braid, slowly slipping down in my seat to hide, but he spots me anyhow. He jogs up the steps to take the seat next to me. I grip the armrests. Is this really happening?

The dim lights fade to black. Bright stars dot the curved ceiling and blink in mesmerizing swirls. I know this is meant to be educational, but I marvel at how much it feels like we're camping under the stars. Light violin music plays over the speakers.

I should include a scene in my novel where my characters lie on the ground, staring at the billions of stars in the sky. Nera would curl up against Ander's side and she'd inhale his scent...

I take a deep breath. Next to me, Alex smells fantastic, like soap and shampoo. My heart leaps into my stomach.

Then a booming godlike voice begins to speak. "In the beginning, there was the sky...both beautiful and mysterious."

Someone mutters, "This is worse than church."

Alex, however, leans his head back and gazes up at the twinkling stars. He rests his arm on our shared armrest. His hand brushes mine. Then his pinky.

The ceiling explodes into a swirl of bright oranges, pinks, and purples. The violin music crescendos. My heart goes supernova.

When he looks over at me, I don't turn away.

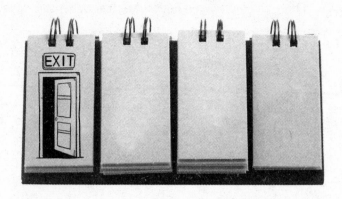

TODAY
FRESHMAN CLASS TRIP

My stomach is still fluttering as we head back to the bus for lunch. In the darkness of the planetarium, it was easy to get caught up in the idea of romance with Alex under the twinkling stars. We kept catching each other's eye during the show, but in the bright light of the museum hallway, reality is quick to set in.

As we exit the planetarium, Alex clears his throat. "I'd better go find Ryan."

"Me too. I mean, I should find Max."

"I'll see you later?" he asks softly, and smiles when I nod.

He rejoins his friends, and I latch on to Max's elbow to stay standing upright. Did Alex really touch my hand? What does it mean? I need to check my horoscope ASAP.

Max and I climb onto the bus, taking our same seats from earlier. He secures the camera bag between his legs.

"So, how'd it go with that guy?" I ask. "Blake?"

"He was cute..."

"But?"

"I asked if he wanted to go to dinner or on a date or whatever, and he said he's looking for something more casual." His voice cracks. "He wants to hook up and that's it."

"Ugh." I squeeze my friend's hand. "You're better than that."

A small smile forms on Max's face. "We're both better than that."

"Hells yeah, we are. We're like, royal family material."

"Prince Max sounds great," Max jokes. "But seriously? It sucks. Why is finding a boyfriend so hard?"

"You're telling me." It's not every day that Max meets a guy he might be able to date. I feel for him.

Coach Rice blows his whistle. "Everybody sit down so we can go eat. It's time for lunch."

"Foooooooood. Foooooood," the guys chant, making the girls laugh at how much they're acting like cavemen.

"We have something special planned for you," Coach Rice adds.

"Please tell me it's Taco Bell," Max says.

"We're going to the mall food court?" Ryan calls out, and kids start whooping.

"Better," Coach says. "We're going on the Tennessee Riverboat for lunch."

Everyone cheers even louder, because for some reason, boats make people lose their minds.

61

The bus drives through downtown Nashville to the riverfront beside 2nd Avenue. This area, the heart of Nashville, is filled with honky-tonk bars, a museum in honor of Johnny Cash, and the Country Music Hall of Fame. Across the river is where the Titans play football.

We walk up the plank onto the riverboat. Burgers, hot dogs, fries, and coleslaw are spread out on banquet tables. The coleslaw probably has mayo in it and the fries possibly could've been fried in animal fat, so I can't risk eating them. I do not see any vegan options. Not a surprise.

Max scans the food. "This sucks. What are you gonna do?"

I pat my purse. "I have snacks."

He passes me his camera bag for safekeeping. "Meet you outside? We can grab a table on the deck."

I walk out to the stern, pulling my sunglasses down to cover my eyes. The sun blazes on my skin. The greenish water of the Cumberland River rushes behind the boat. Now this is what I call a field trip. All I need is a bikini and a towel to lay out on the boat deck, and I'd be in paradise.

My classmates are still inside, lined up for food. I sit alone at a table, open my bag, and pull out an apple, pretzels, and a baggie of mixed nuts. I dig in to my pretzels, wishing I had brought one of my almond bars to eat. My stomach rumbles. Being held captive in an escape room is a real calorie burner.

"Wells."

I look up to find Alex holding a paper carton.

"I brought you lunch."

"Thanks, but I don't eat burgers and hot dogs." I toss a pretzel in my mouth.

He passes me the carton. "I know. When we made the plans for today, I made sure they had vegan stuff for you."

I open it. Inside is a pasta salad with avocado and chickpeas. It smells delicious. This is the sweetest thing anyone's ever done for me.

I glance at Alex again. He's staring at me. His smile reminds me of the first time I saw his picture. How I fell for his deep brown eyes.

Without thinking, I set the carton down and stand up, throw my arms around his neck, and kiss him. He pulls back, his mouth falling open.

I look away from his soft lips. Stare at the waves churning behind the boat propellers. I feel dizzy.

What did I just do?

I kissed Alex Rouvelis.

I should throw myself overboard.

"Shit," I mutter, bowing my head.

"Hey," he says quietly, putting his fingers under my chin, lifting it so I am looking straight at him. He murmurs, "Wow."

"Wow," I agree.

He wraps his strong hands around my waist and I rest mine on his shoulders, and his body melts against mine as our lips meet again. And again.

Again and again and again.

PART II

MAY 7, SOPHOMORE YEAR

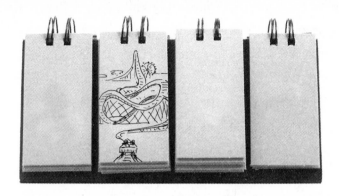

TODAY
SOPHOMORE CLASS TRIP

I'm beginning to think the field trip gods are out to get me.

Roller coasters and heights have always given me motion sickness and vertigo.

So, of course, the sophomore class trip would be to Six Flags Over Georgia, home of ten state-of-the-art roller coasters guaranteed to make you lose your shit.

Using his bullhorn, Coach Rice yells for our class of one hundred to gather round the entrance to the park.

"Here are the rules," Coach Rice booms into his bullhorn. "Make sure you stay with someone at all times."

Max, Grace, and I nod at one another, silently agreeing to stick together.

I feel like I haven't seen Max much lately because he spent the spring semester crashing on yearbook production. I'm excited we'll be together today. And ever since Grace broke up with Ben, we've been hanging out more, especially since she apologized for blowing me off a lot freshman year. Family is family. Besides, she understands what I'm going through. It's been a rough couple of months for both of us.

Horrible roller coasters aside, it will be fun to spend the day with my friends. The best thing about Six Flags is that it has a water park, and I fully plan to spend a lot of the day sunbathing in the lazy river.

"Everyone should have a partner," Coach Rice continues. "If you don't have one, stick with a teacher or chaperone."

"Coach," Ryan calls out. "I want to be your buddy."

Coach Rice ignores Ryan and goes on, "We're leaving at exactly eight o'clock tonight. Make sure you're back here in the parking lot by then."

Mrs. Schmidt, the health teacher, tugs on his arm and murmurs something to him. Coach says, "And don't forget to wear sunscreen." She mutters again in his ear. "And make good life choices!"

Once the lecture is over and we each have a wristband that will let us onto park rides, everyone scatters like a confetti bomb.

With a quick, blank glance at me over his shoulder, Alex gets in line with Ryan for the turnstiles to enter the park.

Alex looks as good as ever, wearing navy-blue shorts, a gray V-neck tee, scuffed white sneakers, and his Braves cap turned backward.

It's hard to believe he won't be my buddy today, that we won't be riding the teacups together, making out and feeding each other cotton candy.

I don't want Alex to think I'm lurking around him, so I stop to study a map of the park that's as big as one of my bedroom walls.

Grace points at the Hurricane Harbor water park. "I can't wait for the lazy river."

"Me too," I say. It's supposed to hit ninety degrees in Atlanta this afternoon and my pasty vampire skin could use some sun.

Max's eyes dart around the map. "My God, look at all these roller coasters. I'm going to ride them all."

Grace bounces on her toes. "I'm in."

The ten gigantic roller coasters take up much of the map's real estate. God, I hate them. I note the silly baby rides (that I secretly want to ride).

Ultimately I have one goal at Six Flags today: eat a bunch of funnel cakes.

I know I'm vegan, but when it comes to funnel cakes, I cheat. My dad bought me my first one at the county fair in kindergarten, and I've loved them ever since.

I point to Boomtown Funnel Cakes on the map. "There it is."

"Isn't it a little early for dessert?" Grace asks.

"If I'm going to have at least three funnel cakes today, I need to get started early. Do you think they'd let me take a funnel cake in the pool? Like on a float?"

She eyes my body. "Is that why you wore that baggy T-shirt? So you could eat loads of funnel cakes?"

"It's a billion degrees out and I want to be comfortable." I return the favor, eyeing my cousin's slip dress that doesn't seem sturdy enough to survive a single roller coaster ride. "Why would you wear *that*?"

"In case we meet guys from other schools. Or maybe even college."

"I imagine all the college guys are in class today. It's a weekday."

"Maybe they decided to skip," Max says, nudging me. "It would be good for you to meet somebody."

I'm not ready for that. I don't want to date anybody but Alex. He begged me to get back together, but it's not that simple. Ever since I ended our relationship after spring break, my heart has been falling, falling, falling like I'm on a never-ending roller coaster. I regret getting on the ride, but at the same time, I don't. We had ten months of great memories together.

"I don't want to meet any guys," I say. "I want my funnel cake. Hey, can funnel cake be my new boyfriend?"

Max tilts his head to the side. "Isn't dating a food against the law?"

"C'mon," Grace says, hooking her arm in mine. "It's been forever since you and Alex broke up." *Less than two months is not forever.* "I think Caleb Hernandez is into you," she adds. "He kept looking your way on the bus."

Max furrows his eyebrows, twiddling his fingers in front of him as if he's searching for something to do with his hands. Normally his camera is attached to him like skin, but he couldn't risk breaking it at Six Flags. He looks almost naked without it.

"Caleb reminds me of a young Enrique Iglesias," Grace adds. "I follow him on Instagram for his dancing." She whips out her phone and pulls up a picture of Enrique wearing a trucker hat, standing in front of a crowd of thousands.

Max leans over Grace's shoulder to see her phone screen. "Oh my God, he's so hot."

Grace groans. "Right? Just looking at him might get me pregnant."

"Me too," Max replies.

Grace holds the phone up for me. "Don't you think Caleb looks like *my boyfriend* Enrique?"

I scrunch my face, not wanting to talk about boys. "Can we go now?"

Max gives me a sympathetic look. "Sure."

"Let's ride the Scream Machine first," Grace says.

"Yesss," Max replies, giving her a fist bump. "But then I want to try the bungee-jumping platform."

"What about my funnel cake?" I say.

"Great idea," Grace says, glancing around. She opens her backpack and gestures for us to peek inside at her silver flask, likely containing vodka she stole from Uncle James. "We should definitely coat our stomachs before having one of my cocktails." One of Grace's favorite things to do is spike a Diet Coke with vodka and call it a Skinny Bitch.

"You want to drink and then get on a roller coaster? We'll get sick as hell."

"Fine," Grace says, zipping up her bag. "We'll save it for the bus ride home."

"Party!" Max and I reply together as if we're twins.

As we're walking in the direction of Boomtown, I glance over my shoulder to find Alex standing with Ryan and other players from the baseball team. Two girls from the dance team are with them: Dana Jenkins and Marcie Wallace.

When Alex and I were going out, Marcie stared at him all the time.

I can't blame her. He's grown nearly a foot in the past year, his body stretching to over six feet tall. I had to stand on my tippy toes to kiss him. A stool would've helped. And thanks to all his work in the weight room during the off-season, his body is strong and toned. He looks like he could be playing for the Atlanta Braves already.

As Alex's group is talking, coming up with their own plan for how to tackle this massive park that's bigger than a small country, he reaches into his pocket and pulls out a Jolly Rancher. He pops it in his mouth. Marcie holds out a hand, and he fishes out another Jolly Rancher for her. Then she reaches out to grab his hand.

He stares down at their fingers clasped together and doesn't let go.

Oh my God, he's holding her hand. Oh God...are they together? I still think of him every waking minute—how can he move on this easily? *This quickly?*

When we were still together, he'd meet me by my locker before first period with a kiss and some other treat. Grape tomatoes he nicked from his grandfather's restaurant for me. A pencil decorated in hearts. Cherry Jolly Ranchers.

In return, I'd give him a lemon Jolly Rancher and a handwritten note featuring pictures I doodled of him. Of us. He hung my notes on his bedroom wall beside his bed.

Every morning after we'd swap gifts, he'd slip his hand in mine and walk me to class super slowly, so we could spend as much time together as possible.

I miss him so much.

And now he's holding *Marcie's* hand?

"I can't believe him," I growl.

Max steers me away from Alex. "Funnel cake time."

"Can I get two?" I ask.

Grace glares at Alex and Marcie. "You can have as many as you want, Lu."

"Great. I'll throw both of them at Alex."

"Now we're talking," Max says, putting an arm around me.

I can't believe he gave her a Jolly Rancher. That was our thing. Asshole.

MAY
FRESHMAN YEAR

A Year Ago

"We're going out to eat at Niko's," Dad says.

"Nooooo," I cry overdramatically in a Darth Vader voice. What if Alex thinks I'm stalking him after I kissed him on the riverboat a few days ago? "Anywhere but Niko's."

"Louise," my father scolds. "It's the only place in town that has food you'll eat. I'd be happy to go eat a steak at Crockett's Roadhouse."

"You know we can't go there, Dad. They fry everything in animal fat. Gods, even like, the salad is covered in those fried onion straws."

Dad groans, touching his stomach. "I know. They're so good."

Since Dad is dead set on going to Niko's, I spend half an

hour primping. I carefully apply my makeup and ensure my hair is perfectly disheveled, my purple streak hanging over my shoulder seductively. It's a warm May night, so I put on a cute, white cotton dress that bares my shoulders.

After Alex and I kissed several times on the boat, he sat with his friends during lunch, and I—totally dazed—returned to Max, who nearly had a coronary when the gossip got around that I had been making out with Alex.

But after that? Nothing happened. We didn't sit together on the bus ride home from Nashville. Everyone knows that's what couples do. They sit together toward the back and make out and sometimes do naughtier things, provided it's dark and no one can see.

Alex grinned whenever he saw me in the hallway at school, and I smiled back, but it was almost like our brief make-out session on the boat never occurred. *Was I that bad a kisser?*

"Just go talk to him," Max whined yesterday.

I shook my head, glancing at Alex from across the cafeteria where I sat with my poster protesting the lack of a school garden. "It was a fluke."

"It doesn't sound like it was a fluke. I didn't see it myself, but Marcie told everybody you tried to suck his face off. Listen, I'm not a scientist, but you don't suck somebody's face off unless you've got chemistry."

Honestly, I like Alex a lot. I like him so much, I'd probably eat a chicken pot pie if he begged.

When I finally emerge from my room, Dad gapes at me. "I said we were going to Niko's, not prom."

Going to Niko's might as well be prom. Alex will likely be there.

Mom puts her magazine down and beams at me. "You look cute, sweet girl. I hope you don't get pizza on that dress, though."

I spend the entire car ride to Niko's fidgeting, smoothing my dress. Alex is totally going to think I'm stalking him.

We arrive to a packed parking lot. Saturday nights are always bustling at Niko's. The hostess seats us at a table with a white-and-red checkered tablecloth by the window overlooking sleepy highway 41, where only the occasional car trickles by, headlights bright under the purple twilight.

As I pretend to read my menu, I peek toward the kitchen through the glass wall. Alex is helping to quickly prepare the dishes I can smell from our table. Workers call out instructions and rapidly pass plates back and forth.

That's when Alex looks up at me through the glass.

Behind him, a burst of fire shoots up from the grill.

He stares at me, his eyes moving down to my dress, then back up to my eyes.

I turn my focus to my parents and *only* my parents, so I won't seem totally desperate.

I rip up my paper napkin into bits as Mom talks about staging the lake house she's working to sell, while Dad tells us some kid tried to bite him while he was filling a cavity. In other words, a typical week.

Then Alex approaches our table with a plate and a bowl. "I thought you might like to try our bruschetta, Mr. and Mrs. Wells. On the house," he says with a polite nod as my parents gush over him, saying thank you. He's dressed in a plain white T-shirt and worn jeans. Looking at him makes me hot all over. I gulp down some water.

"And some tomatoes from my yia yia's garden for Lulu," Alex says, and I smile at the small bowl of tomatoes he places in front of me.

"Alex," Dad says, shaking his hand. My father knows everybody because he's the only dentist in town. "Heard the team won your final game the other night."

"Yes, sir, we've had a great season. We went twenty-three and five, and we're headed to the playoffs."

"Thank God," Dad replies. "I worried that Lulu messing with your batting cage would throw off the team's mojo." Dad turns to me with a stern look on his face. "Did you tell Alex you were sorry for locking the batting cage?"

"You know I did. And Alex said he had a great season," I reply, popping a tomato in my mouth. "See, no harm done."

"You mean," Alex starts, "except for that all the seniors on the team threatened to murder me."

I peer down at my lap. In retrospect, locking the batting cage was dumb. I didn't think about what it would do to his standing on the team. I didn't think of the other players. I didn't think about how it would embarrass Grace.

What if that silly stunt cost me a chance with Alex?

But when I glance up, he's laughing along with my mom. "I couldn't believe she locked the cage," he says.

"I don't know where Lulu gets her wild ideas from," Mom says. "Not from me or her father, that's for sure."

"Her imagination is why she's such a good writer," Alex replies.

And I melt right there on the spot.

A waitress whispers in Alex's ear, pointing her thumb toward the kitchen.

"I gotta get back," he says. "Just wanted to say hi. I hope you enjoy your dinner."

After he leaves, my parents can't stop talking about him. He's like the son they never had or something.

"He's president of the class and has great grades," Mom says.

"He's going places," Dad announces as he munches on his free bruschetta.

I roll my eyes. "Maybe you should adopt him, then. I have to use the restroom."

I excuse myself. Again, Alex looks up through the glass and watches me walking across the restaurant, his eyes full of heat.

In the bathroom, I dab cold water on my wrists and neck, trying to cool my jets. My dress feels tight. My skin burns. My lips pulse with want. I run a hand up and down my arm, caressing myself, seeking relief. What is he doing to me? My body has never reacted to a boy this way before.

When I'm done in the bathroom, I exit into the narrow hallway to find him standing there.

Alex. All alone.

The tiny space highlights how much taller he is than me.

He takes a deep breath. "Can we talk?"

"Here?"

Without a word, he takes me by the hand and leads me farther down the hall into a supply closet full of napkins and tablecloths. The door clicks shut behind us.

"What'd you want to talk about?" I ask.

"This," he replies, his lips crashing to mine.

I cling to him as his hands move up and down my back,

sweeping over my bare shoulders, electrifying my skin, providing the relief I desperately need but couldn't find on my own.

We reenact our kiss from the boat, and somehow, even though we aren't out on the water under the sun—it's better than the first time. We discover each other's rhythms. Biting his lower lip makes him groan, and him running fingers through my hair makes my knees wobbly.

Kissing him is a drug, making me lose my sense of balance. I lean against Alex, trying to stay upright and accidentally knock him into a shelf full of napkins that fall all over the floor.

"Oops," I say, stopping to pick them up.

"Forget it," he replies, pulling me back against him, pressing his mouth to mine like he needs me to breathe.

Again, we kiss and kiss until—

The closet door swings open.

"Alexander Rouvelis."

Alex yanks back from me, lips ruby red and swollen, his hair a disaster from my hands clutching it. He closes his eyes and lets out the deep breath he took before we started kissing. He turns to face the large imposing man in a black suit.

"Papu," Alex replies, patting down his hair. "Lu, uh, this is my grandfather. Papu, this my Lul—I mean, this is Lulu."

Papu sets his hands on his hips, his bushy mustache twitching. "Is this any way to treat a lady? Mauling her in my supply closet?" He pauses to scan the mess of white napkins I knocked on the floor. "Back in my day, we took the girl to dinner and then necked in the car."

I start giggling.

Alex's face turns the color of Niko's famous tomato sauce.

"I need you back in the kitchen," Papu says. "We got a delivery order for ten pizzas."

"Can I have a minute?"

Papu gives him an indulgent smile. "You can have two."

The supply closet door shuts. Alex's forehead drops to touch mine. Our breathing is still heavy, still out of control.

"So, do you want to go to dinner sometime?" he asks.

I smile up at him and he smiles back. "Yeah. As long as there's necking in the car after."

He gives me a look, then glances down at my lips. "I want to kiss you some more."

"I want to kiss you whenever I want."

"Sounds great to me," he says, as simple as two plus two. "Is that your way of saying you want to be mine?"

"Yeah...and you're mine." I get up on tiptoes and wrap my arms around his neck, answering with a long kiss that leaves us both breathless.

And then we use all of the two minutes we have left.

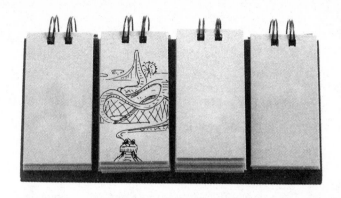

TODAY
SOPHOMORE CLASS TRIP

The hot May sun blazes down as Grace, Max, and I set off into the park.

It's only ten in the morning, but kids are everywhere. We navigate around a pack of elementary schoolers on our way to Boomtown. Skylift chairs soar above us across the park. Off to my right is an attraction where kids can drive trucks along a cabled road. The sound of screams punctuates the air. The roller coasters poke out above the trees like swirling dragons, looping and preparing to strike.

"I'm worried Mr. Worthington's field trip endowment is running out of money," I tell Grace and Max. "I mean, last year we went to a science museum and this year we're at Six Flags. What if next year we end up going to the city park, or God, back to that science museum?"

"It's not running out of money," Max says. "The seniors are going to Paris this year."

"I wish we could've gone somewhere other than a theme park," I reply. "I mean, weird stuff happens at these places."

"Like what?" Grace asks.

"Did you hear about the kid who dropped his phone when he was riding a roller coaster, so he jumped a fence to go find it and got decapitated by said roller coaster?"

Max makes a horrified face. "That's terrible. I thought you were going to say Minnie Mouse and Pluto got caught doing it at Disney."

A laugh sounds behind us.

I turn to find Caleb Hernandez standing there. Grace mentioned he was looking my way on the bus. Now he's following us? I bite the tip of my thumb. I'm sure I'll eventually date another guy, but only one guy interests me...and now he's holding hands with another girl.

Caleb walks up to us. "Can I hang out with you guys today?"

How straightforward. I don't know him well, so it's kind of surprising he'd come right out and ask.

"Sure," Grace rushes to say, without even consulting us.

"It's better to have an even number of us for riding rides purposes," Max says, and Caleb smiles brightly at him.

I will admit he does look like a young Enrique Iglesias, i.e., he is gorgeous and also looks like loads of trouble. Over six feet tall, Caleb plays for the school basketball team and has dark brown skin and these unbelievably beautiful light-blue eyes. Like me, Max has never really been into sports, but one night when he was photographing a game for the yearbook, Max claims that Caleb's blue eyes hypnotized him, and after that, he suddenly became a huge basketball fan.

"What are you guys doing first?" Caleb asks.

"Funnel cakes, then Scream Machine," Max replies.

"Yesss."

"Oh no," I say. "Not another wild-ass ride lover."

"That's me," Caleb says cheerfully.

I agree to get the snacks while Grace and Max find a locker to stow our backpacks until we're ready to hit the water park later. Caleb stands in line beside me, crossing his arms across his chest as he studies the menu.

"You didn't want to hang out with your team today?" I ask.

Caleb gives me a noncommittal shrug. "I see them all the time."

"I see my friends all the time too, but I'd rather be with them than somebody I don't know well."

"Field trips are sort of like a mini vacation, you know? They're a good chance to get to know people."

I laugh nervously, wrapping my arms around myself. He's not wrong. Field trips are like vacations. In some ways, they might even have a bit of fantasy to them.

Last year, I ended up with a boyfriend I never could've imagined.

I order two funnel cakes—one for me and one for Max, and Caleb chooses a hot dog, which grosses me out. We meet up with Max and Grace at the picnic tables. I take a huge bite of my funnel cake, feeling guilty about the milk that made it, but not guilty enough to stop eating.

"Oh my God, yum," I say.

"Double orgasm," Max replies as he digs into his.

"Triple," I reply.

Meanwhile, Grace stares longingly at my funnel cake. As a dancer, Grace is always trying to stay in great shape, and she rarely indulges.

I hold my plate under her nose. "C'mon. One bite."

She licks her lips, ogling my food. "Okay, fine."

Her one bite turns into ripping off a huge piece. I will definitely have to buy another one of these.

Max dips his finger in the sugar and wipes a big streak across my cheek. I shove him away. Then he does it again before I can stop him. This time he tries to lick the sugar off me, and I grab some sugar and shove it onto his face.

Grace checks her phone. "Would y'all grow up?"

"Want some?" Max reaches out to touch her face, and she jumps up from the table, darting away. She grabs some of the powder and throws it at Max.

Caleb grins as he watches them goof around. Maybe he's not so bad.

If Alex is moving on, maybe I should try harder to get over him. I mean, it's great that this park is huge. Maybe I won't run into him. Still, I bet I'll spend the entire day wondering if he's getting it on with Marcie in the fun house. Ew.

Maybe I should spend today having a great time with my friends and try to put him out of my mind.

It is nearly summertime, after all, and summer is all about fresh beginnings.

SUMMER
AFTER FRESHMAN YEAR

One day at the start of summer break, Alex shows up at my house with Princess Peach.

My sister, Lila—who's home on break before her senior year of college—answers the door. "Lu! Alex is here."

I painted my toenails orange and don't want to mess them up, so I hobble carefully to the foyer.

My sister raises her eyebrows at me and mouths, "Wow."

"Hi," I say to my new boyfriend, grinning so hard my face hurts.

He holds up his dog's leash. "Want to come for a walk with us?"

"Come in while my nails finish drying?"

I want to put on a cuter outfit than my cutoffs and ratty T-shirt too.

Alex walks into the house. At the sight of Princess Peach, my cat, Winston, goes scampering up the stairs, probably to hide under a bed. The dog barks up the stairs in Winston's direction. Alex tightens the leash and follows me into the kitchen, where my mother gives him a sweet tea while he waits for me to change clothes. The dog lies at his feet and stares up at him lovingly.

Lila follows me up the stairs to my room. As soon as the door is shut, she flops down on my bed and squeals like a middle schooler. "Lu, Alex is so cute."

Her opinion means a lot. My sister is much prettier than me and was popular in high school. Not only was she in the show choir, she often played big roles in school musicals. Like me, she loves to dance.

My hands shake as I pick out a cute, little, red one-piece romper and start to change. "I worry he's *too* hot for me."

Lila glances up from her phone screen. "Why do you say that?"

"He's gorgeous, and funny, and has so many friends."

"And you're friendly, pretty, and smart. He's lucky to have you. Don't ever act like you're second-best around him, okay, Lu? Always remember that you deserve a great guy. And use condoms!"

"We've only been dating two weeks."

"You should always be prepared. Besides, Grace texted me all about how you guys were going at it on the riverboat." Lila returns to playing with her phone. "I'll order a bunch for you and have them shipped to the house."

I peek over her shoulder. She's searching online for condoms.

"Oh, hell no!" I lunge for her phone but miss as she yanks it away. I face-plant onto the bed, and we dissolve into giggles.

I go back downstairs. When Alex lays eyes on my red romper, he swallows hard.

"You look beautiful, Lu," he says.

Mom squeals like Lila, and pulls out her phone. "Let's get a picture of you two for Grammy and Aunt Lilibeth and the ladies down at the office and the girls from church." At the rate she's going, the picture will be all over the world by lunchtime.

She poses us next to an arrangement of wildflowers erupting with color, like a box of crayons. "Now, Alex, put your arm around Lulu, and, Lulu, you put your hand on his chest."

Lila dies laughing.

"Oh my God," I mutter under my breath.

Mom ignores me and Lila. "Alex, stand a little straighter and lower your chin."

"Mom, would you stop trying to stage us like a house?"

"This is my first picture of you with your first boyfriend. I need to document it. Now, Lu, you lift your right foot off the floor and lean into Alex."

I lift my foot with a groan. "I think I'll go die now."

Alex raises a leg too, posing like me. Mom purses her lips at us, and we giggle together.

Lila beams, and before we leave, she gives Alex a hug. "Do you have any older brothers?"

Alex smiles. "Not that I know of."

My house isn't too far from the city park. After we escape Mom, we walk alongside the creek, where Alex throws a tennis ball out into the water and the dog splashes around.

We hold hands and often stop to kiss, but Princess Peach barks at me when I get too close to her human.

"Come on now, Peach," Alex says to his dog. "You're gonna be seeing a lot more of Lulu, so you best stop being jealous."

The black-and-white dog whines like a little puppy and rolls around in the grass, then barks at me again.

"Let's face it," I say. "I'm a cat person, not a dog person."

Out of the corner of his mouth, Alex says through his teeth, "Reach into my pocket and get a piece of"—he begins to spell—"H-O-T-D-O-G from the baggie and give it to her. You'll be her favorite person ever."

Even though I realllllly don't want to touch it, I do what he said, and suddenly the dog is all over me. I giggle as she licks my face and I pet her soft coat.

Alex's phone beeps. He checks the screen. "Ryan wants me to drop by. He wants to play video games."

"Okay," I say, disappointed our afternoon is already over. "Walk me home first?"

"Why don't you come to Ryan's house with me?"

I hesitate. "It's all right. We can hang out tomorrow if you want."

Alex sadly sticks his hands in his pockets. "You don't want to come?"

The last time I saw Ryan, he was teasing Alex for "sleeping with the enemy" in front of our whole class. But I'm not sleeping with Alex, and it's not okay that Ryan made everyone think I am.

Grace grew up going to elementary and middle school with Ryan and Alex, and prior to freshman year, I frequently saw Ryan on Grace's Insta and Snapchat. Before she had started dating that dickwad Ben, Grace spent a lot of time with Ryan and considered him one of her best guy friends.

"I don't think Ryan likes me very much," I say.

"Ryan likes everybody."

"He's so…rich."

"Lulu Wells, aren't you a snob," Alex says with a laugh.

"Okay, okay, I'll go. But in return, you have to take me to mini golf later."

"Deal."

Alex only lives about a mile from me, so we walk back to his place to drop off the dog and ask his older sister, Demi, for a ride to Ryan's.

Ryan lives out by the country club, the area around the golf course that has gorgeous houses straight out of furniture catalogs. Mom loves selling houses out here.

I gape when we pull up to a huge mansion on a hill. I knew Ryan's father was the district attorney, but Mom once told me the real money came from his mother, who had inherited earnings from an old automobile company that had been around a hundred years ago. Her family—the Thorntons—are like the kings and queens of Manchester. Her brother is the mayor of our town.

When we knock on the front door, Ryan's mom answers. She's wearing a pristine white blouse and colorful pink skirt. Her red hair looks styled for a fancy lunch in Nashville. She smiles at the sight of Alex. "C'mon in, y'all."

I scan the foyer and formal living room. The space, filled with soft beiges, whites, and grays, are meticulously put together with not a speck of dust anywhere. Did I walk into a Pottery Barn catalog?

"Mrs. McDowell, this is my girlfriend, Lulu Wells."

Ryan's mother sticks out a hand. "Nice to meet you, Lulu. Are you related to Dr. Wells?"

"Yes, ma'am. He's my dad."

"Your parents always donate to my annual St. Jude's fundraiser. They're absolutely wonderful people."

"Thanks," I reply, wringing my fingers together. Are my sneakers tracking dirt on the pristine floor?

"Can I get y'all anything?" Mrs. McDowell asks.

"Do you have any more of those gingersnaps?" Alex says, and Ryan's mom leads us into the biggest kitchen I've ever seen.

This house and Ryan's mom remind me of a happily-ever-after.

Mrs. McDowell opens a tin container full of cookies and places some on a white plate for Alex, who says, "Ohmygoshthankyouma'am," before diving in.

Ryan appears in the kitchen. He kisses his mother's cheek, then turns to Alex. "Dude, what are you doing? I thought we were gonna play *Fortnite*."

Alex can't respond—he has a mouthful of cookies.

"I was just getting to know Lulu," Mrs. McDowell says.

Ryan bites into a gingersnap. "She's Grace Wells's cousin."

"Ohhh," Mrs. McDowell replies. "I haven't seen Grace in forever."

"Not since she started dating that douchebag, Ben," Ryan says.

"Ryan Anderson McDowell, don't use language like that in my kitchen," his mom says.

"Well it's true," slips out of my mouth.

Ryan's eyes grow wide. "You don't like him either, Lu?"

I don't want to further badmouth my cousin's bad taste in guys, so I just stand there gripping the back of a barstool.

Alex holds up his cookie and continues to chew. "I wish our desserts were this good at Niko's, Mrs. McDowell."

She beams at his compliment and holds out the cookie plate to me. "Have one, sweetie, before the boys eat them all."

"Lulu's vegan," Alex explains.

"Oh! Why didn't you say so?" She whips open her refrigerator to peer inside. "Let's see...I can offer you...a carrot?"

Everybody laughs.

"It's okay," I say. "I'm good."

"Gina!" a mean voice yells.

I nearly jump out of my skin. I wasn't expecting that. Everything is so perfect here in Ryan's perfect house.

Ryan glares down the hall. Mrs. McDowell closes the refrigerator. She pushes the hair back away from her face, takes a deep breath, and walks out without another word.

Ryan grabs the cookie plate. "Let's go down to the rec room." He stalks out of the kitchen.

We follow behind him.

"Why's your dad home?" Alex mutters.

"He took the day off because the plumber's here. We're having some work done on one of our bathrooms."

"Oh." Alex drags a hand through his dark hair. "Is it okay if we're here?"

Ryan shrugs, leading us downstairs to the fanciest basement I've ever seen. The McDowells have a gigantic couch that might as well be a king-size bed. Funny throw pillows are scattered across the couch, saying things like *Normal is Boring* and *Netflix is My Girlfriend*. A TV hangs on the wall and a fully stocked bar runs the length of the rear of the room. Through a door, I spot a gym with weights and a treadmill.

The three of us splay out on the couch with our feet up. I snuggle against Alex, resting my chin on his shoulder. He squeezes my knee. No matter where we are, we can't seem to keep our hands to ourselves. Ryan glances at us.

Upstairs, I can hear his dad yelling again. "Where's my shirt, Gina?"

"I don't know," Mrs. McDowell cries.

As Ryan slides down on the couch, his expression falls too.

Alex bites into his lower lip and focuses on starting up the game on the TV.

"I need my shirt," Mr. McDowell yells. "You'd better find it right now, or I'll miss my fucking tee time."

"You have other shirts, Mark."

"I want the green one."

I give the ceiling a dirty look. My boyfriend isn't making eye contact with anyone. Ryan looks broken.

The arguing continues on for another couple of minutes. Ryan's family problems are none of my business, but I can't believe Alex is acting like nothing is happening. I can't take it anymore.

"It's his shirt," I say. "Shouldn't he keep track of it himself?"

Alex sucks in a deep breath and gives me a piercing look.

"Yeah, he should," Ryan says.

"Is it like this a lot?" I ask softly.

Ryan looks at me contemplatively for several seconds, then nods.

"That sucks," I say.

"Yeah, it does..." He runs a hand through his red hair. "You sure you don't want to try one of Mom's cookies? They're the best."

Without giving it much thought, I reach over, pluck one off the plate and take a bite.

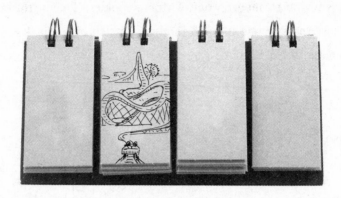

TODAY
SOPHOMORE CLASS TRIP

On the way to the first roller coaster, Caleb walks ahead of me with Max. Max says something that makes Caleb laugh, and Caleb gives him a friendly shove on the shoulder.

They get in line for Scream Machine. Which probably should be called the Vomit Comet.

The roller coaster roars overhead, rattling the tracks, rustling the trees.

"We're all gonna get decapitated," I announce with a cry.

Max throws an arm around my shoulder. "Nah. We're more likely to see Minnie and Pluto getting it on, remember?"

I playfully pinch his side. "I'm going to play a game while you guys ride, okay?"

Caleb's eyebrows pinch together. "You're not coming?"

"Trust me, you don't want to be anywhere near me if I get motion sickness."

Everybody cringes.

My friends stay in line for the roller coaster, and I decide to find a game that's in the shade.

After purchasing some tickets, I stop by the game where you toss ping-pong balls into bowls of fish. That is animal cruelty.

I take my phone out of my back pocket and make a note to email Six Flags to protest the fish game. It's too bad I can't save all the fish right now. I'd have to win them all or steal them, and that's without figuring out how to get them out of here. My classmates would be pissed if I made everyone carry a goldfish in their lap on the way home. It would definitely mess with Grace's party bus plans.

I sigh.

"Lu? You okay?"

I glance up to find Alex standing with Ryan and their other friends, including Marcie and Dana.

Ryan opens his arms wide to give me a hug. "Hey, *Lu*cifer."

"Hey, *Little Private* Ryan."

Ryan laughs, mussing my hair. "You been saving that one, huh?"

One of the hardest things about breaking up with Alex is not getting to see Ryan as often. First and foremost, he was Alex's friend, so I've tried to keep my distance. I miss being around him, though. Yeah, Ryan's super popular and seems to have a new girl every weekend, but he is kind and always asks how I'm doing.

Alex swallows hard when Ryan pulls away from me. Hurt fills my ex-boyfriend's eyes. It's the same look he's given me for the past two months. I hate that he's in pain, because I hurt just as much, if not more, but being with him is too hard. My heart can't handle it.

"What's going on?" Alex asks, looking around. "Why are you by yourself? Where's Max?"

"He's riding the Scream Machine," I say.

"That's where we were headed," Alex replies. "Afraid you'll get sick?"

I nod.

Then he notices where I'm standing. He winces when he sees the tiny fishbowls. "Are you mad about these goldfish? Thinking about how to rescue them?"

"How did you know?"

He gives me a little smile. "You're so predictable, Lu."

"Predictably weird," Dana Jenkins mutters, making Marcie snort.

I glare at the girls.

I spin around to march over to the next game. It's the one where you spray water at rubber duckies on a conveyer belt and try to knock them off. What is this game called anyway? *Murder All the Ducks?*

At least it doesn't involve real ducks. I pass over five tickets to the game operator.

Alex appears next to me. "I'm in. Can I borrow some tickets?"

I pass him some. "Get ready to meet your maker, Rouvelis."

He smirks, lifting his spray gun.

A buzzer sounds and toy ducks begin to slide by. I start spraying water at the defenseless ducks. This is a good outlet for my rage.

"You were holding Marcie's hand," I say.

He pulls a deep breath, glancing at me sideways. "Yeah."

"Are you going out with her now?" I ask through my teeth.

"No." Alex sprays water, knocking a bunch of ducks off. "Not yet."

Not yet? *Not yet?* A roller coaster roars over our heads, rattling the booth.

Ten months. We spent ten months together, and he's already thinking about dating someone else?

I whip my hose around and spray him in the face and chest, soaking his gray V-neck. The cotton sticks to his skin, highlighting his strong abs. He sputters and wipes the water from his eyes.

"What the hell?" he blurts. "Why'd you do that?"

I lift a shoulder. "You looked overheated."

"Bullshit." He shakes the water from his face.

It's immature, I know, but I couldn't help myself. He makes me feel so bad sometimes. "I can't believe you'd date Marcie," I whisper-hiss.

"You're the one who broke up with me, remember?" He gestures with his water gun.

"You never had time for me."

"I called you every night!"

"Yeah, like after midnight. I tried so many times to get you to come home from work early so we could spend time together."

"I saw you as much as I could, but with baseball and homework and Niko's, it was hard, you know?" His voice goes quiet.

"I know," I whisper-yell. "But you could find the time to hit up a party with Ryan. To go on spring break with other girls!"

"If you don't want to get back together with me, then fine," he says, snatching the Braves cap off his head to sling the water off. "But you don't get to act jealous and question who I go out with next."

"Fine."

"*Fine.*"

And that's when he aims the water hose my way and drenches me from head to foot.

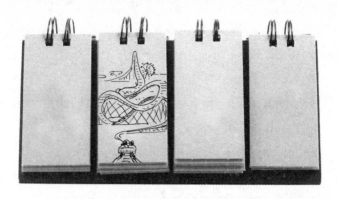

TODAY
SOPHOMORE CLASS TRIP

I storm away from the murdering ducks game, stopping in the girls' restroom to clean up.

It's like a gross, hot sewer in here. Bright florescent lights threaten to blind me. A spider has spun a web up in the dark corner.

I glance in the mirror, giving myself a sad smile. When I was with Alex, I always took great care with my appearance because I wanted to look nice for him. Now look at me. Water drips from my hair. You can see my bra through my soaked white T-shirt. Shit. This'll take forever to dry.

God, it smells like something died in here. I rush into a stall and hold my breath, working to get in and out as quickly as possible.

As I'm using the bathroom and trying not to suffocate, two familiar voices appear. Marcie and Dana.

"I don't know how I'll ever have a chance with Alex if *she's* hanging around all the time," Marcie says.

"She dumped him," Dana says.

"He's like, super into her. She's so much prettier than me," Marcie says quietly.

"You're beautiful. Alex would be lucky to have you. Plus, you're a great friend. And the best dancer I've ever seen. You could be on that TV show, *Dance Island*."

"Thank you. I just can't believe it," Marcie says in a heated tone. "We talked so much over spring break...I really thought something was there between us."

I bite down on my knuckle. Marcie was on the spring break trip? Alex spent time with her when we were still together?

He told me the senior guys had invited the girls. Did they invite Marcie? Alex knows I've never gotten along with her. How could he not tell me she was there? Did something happen between them? I choke down a sob.

She keeps speaking: "Alex was holding my hand this morning. And when I tried again just now, he brushed me off. Lulu is so hot and cold with him, and now he'll mope around the rest of the day because of her."

My heart sinks a little for her. I know what it's like to feel like you're in second place.

"Lulu was acting totally jealous," Dana says.

"That's because she's desperate for attention."

I come out of the stall and give the girls a look. They gasp.

At least Marcie has the decency to look embarrassed I caught her trashing me.

I lean closer to the mirror and swipe away the water dripping down my forehead. "I am not desperate for attention."

But all the same, I'm ashamed of my behavior. Alex upset me and I snapped, and I let my emotions take over.

Marcie takes lip gloss out of her pocket, her hand shaking nervously as she reapplies. "Why'd you break up with Alex anyway? When you were with him, you were like, in another league."

I didn't date him for popularity. I wanted him. "I'm not talking about it with you."

She gives me a hurt look, which I don't understand. It's not like we're friends.

Very calmly and as naturally as possible—which is hard considering I feel on the verge of exploding—I wash my hands, adjust my soggy T-shirt, pull my long, blond hair up into a ponytail, and strut out like I'm a model on a runway...who just went through a car wash.

I leave the smelly bathroom and step back into the blistering sun to go meet my friends as they are getting off the ride.

"Hey!" I say in a fake cheery voice. "How was it?"

"Great," Max replies. "And you were right. Grace's dress totally flew up over her head."

Grace gives him a friendly slap on the shoulder. "It did not."

Then they notice my disheveled appearance.

Grace turns her nose up at my wet, baggy T-shirt. "What in the world happened?"

"Alex happened."

"Did you take a shower together?" Max asks with hope in his eyes. Caleb raises his eyebrows.

"No, we did not take a shower. Get your mind out of the gutter, friend. Who goes to Six Flags to take a shower together?"

"You said it first," Max replies. "Weird shit happens at theme parks."

MARCH
SOPHOMORE YEAR

The Saturday morning before spring break, I need to step away from writing *Here Comes the Sun* and get out of the house. I text Alex to see if he wants to catch a movie or go to the skating rink.

Alex: *Can't. Baseball practice, then working until 11. Call you after.*

It's the same old story. After playing baseball all day, Alex works at Niko's on Friday and Saturday nights. I rarely see my boyfriend outside of school.

At least we'll have spring break together. My parents will be at work. We can spend all day watching Netflix or going for hikes or simply sitting around talking. Whatever we want! I also made an appointment with a geologist at Vanderbilt University, and Alex says he'll drive me up there so I can ask her questions about caves for my book.

While waiting for Alex to get off work, I decide to spend my night like nearly all Saturday nights: working on my book in my bedroom.

Under the glow of the twinkling lights that spell out *LOVE* over my bed, I'm busy sketching a scene where Nera meets the love of her life, Ander, as my black-and-white cat, Winston, snuggles my feet. Like Alex and me, Nera and Ander have their differences. Nera's favorite thing to do is read books her father brought into the caves, but Ander doesn't even know how to read. He never learned because when he was a little boy, his parents were too busy surviving to teach him, and then they died fighting a rival clan.

As I draw, my eyes keep flicking to check the time. By 11:05 p.m., Alex hasn't texted or called. I let out the disappointed, deep breath I've been holding for hours. I pick up my phone and dial Alex's number.

He answers after two rings. "Hey, babe. Listen, I have to stop by Goose Pond for a little while."

I shake my head. I shouldn't be surprised. This happens more often than not. Alex loves going out to Goose Pond late on weekend nights because older guys from the baseball team like to hang out there. Nearly every Saturday night, they load a keg of beer into the back of a pickup truck, light a bonfire, and party in the field by the pond.

Lots of senior girls will be there too. I wish I could go, but Alex always gets off work past my curfew. Lately I feel like the last item on his checklist after school, baseball, working, and his friends.

"Fine. Whatever," I blurt, and then cringe for snapping at him.

There's a long pause on the other end of the phone. "I'm sorry, Lu. I'd been planning to come right to your place, but Ryan needs to talk to me."

"Is everything okay?"

"I'm not sure. He didn't sound like himself. I'll call you after, okay?"

"Okay. Tell Ryan I said hi."

I decide I'm not going to be one of those girls who sits around waiting for her boyfriend. I'll use my time wisely. I hover over my electronic sketchpad, doodling a picture of Nera discovering Ander's clan living in a deserted shopping mall in upstate New York. It aggravates me that I can't draw Ander's face just like it appears in my mind.

Around midnight, my phone rings. Alex. "It's me. I'm coming over."

Tension races up my spine. I hate having to sneak him in so late. If Dad catches us, he'll flip out and put me in a chastity belt and probably ground me over spring break. Still, I need to see my boyfriend.

"See you in a minute," I tell him.

I sneak downstairs in my pajamas, avoiding the one stair that always creaks. I quietly open the back door and wave Alex inside, putting a finger to my lips. *Shhh.*

His hands weave into my hair as he pulls me in for a kiss. His lips zap me like an electrical shock. Our mouths meet again and again, his kiss demanding and confident and sexy as hell.

"I missed you today," he whispers.

Probably not as much as I missed you. "You too."

We recklessly kiss down the stairs to the rec room and lie on the couch. I use my phone to turn on some music.

He leans over me, swiping my hair away from my face. "I'm sorry about tonight."

"Is Ryan okay?"

"His dad's being a dick again. Ryan needed to vent."

I touch Alex's chest. "That guy is the worst. I'm sorry."

"I'm sorry too. I didn't mean to get here so late."

"It's okay. I understand," I say, even though it's getting harder and harder to. The same thing happened last weekend. After he got off work, he went out to a diner with his friends before coming over here. The weekend before that? His dad let him off work early to watch the playoffs with Ryan.

"I just, wish, like—"

"You wish what?"

"You'd come see me first after you get off work."

He looks confused. "Oh. I thought you knew I was saving the best for last."

"I'm the best?" I whisper with a suggestive smile.

"The bestest best. But if it makes you feel better, I'll come see you first next time."

I nod, and Alex leans in to softly kiss me. I can feel him smiling against my lips. It's moments like these when I know how much he cares. How much he wants me. And that makes me feel okay about our relationship again.

I only wish I knew what to do about all those other moments when I worry that I like him more than he likes me.

As our lips explore, our bodies draw closer and closer until he's fully resting on top of me. My heart pounds against his ribs. I caress his neck as his hand gently cups my knee, his lips teasing my collarbone. It feels like he was made just for me.

We press our foreheads together and smile. He leans back to study my clothes.

"I love these pajamas."

They're a tank top and little shorts covered with dogs. Alex's finger traces one of the puppies over my stomach. It tingles in a very good way.

"But I want them off you," he adds, and a hot flush races over my skin. My pulse drums, his hands tremble as he eases my tank and shorts off. "You're so gorgeous," he murmurs. "I love this bra."

We started going to third base a few months ago, and while at the beginning it felt scary like my first leap off the high dive at the city pool, our passion makes it better and better each time he touches me intimately.

Tonight is no different. His fingers tiptoe up my thigh, and I bury my face in his neck as he takes me sky high with his hand. I push against him, trying to get closer and closer until my body breaks apart with pleasure. "Oh my God, Alex," I groan when I crash back down to Earth. The way he makes me feel is too good. A quick glance at his face, and I see he's incredibly pleased with himself. I burst out laughing and he joins in.

When I'm finished, I curl up against him, trying to catch my breath. I eagerly reach down past his rigid abs to touch his hardness (*I can't believe how turned on he is!*), which makes him suck in a deep breath and lift his hips to remove his jeans.

"Lu," he says excitedly. "I've been thinking."

"What have you been thinking about?" I flirt.

"That I want all of you," he says, out of breath. Our eyes meet.

I pause from touching him. We've been dating ten months. It's so easy to imagine, him being my first. I haven't told him yet, but I'm definitely in love with him. But I still worry I like him more than he likes me. I need more time to think about this, to make sure he and I are on the same page before I give him everything.

I shake my head. "Not tonight," I say. "I'm not ready. And it's weird with Mom and Dad upstairs asleep."

"It's okay," he replies soothingly, but I can see the disappointment in his eyes.

Even though I'm not going to sleep with him tonight, I still help him take off his jeans—*fine, I practically rip them off*—and eagerly kiss my way down his body. He threads a hand through my hair as he stares down at me, biting his lower lip.

His cheeks flush with passion. "You're killing me, Lu."

When our clothes are safely back on—my parents could always wake up and discover us down here—we stretch our legs out on the ottoman and Alex wraps his arms around me and yawns.

His sleepy eyes close. "I don't want to leave you, but I have to get up in six hours to go to church with Yia Yia and Papu."

"I'm worried about you. You work too much." I brush the hair out of his eyes. "I'm glad we'll have some time off for spring break. Have you thought about what you want to do? I mean, besides going to Vanderbilt to meet Dr. Chadha?"

His body begins to tense beneath my hands. "About that... Me and some of the guys decided to go camping in Fall Creek Falls. Even some of the seniors are coming."

"Camping?" I say in a tiny voice.

"It's a last-minute guy thing. Ryan came up with it, and I promised him I'd go. I'm sorry."

My stomach lurches. "Okay... How long will you be gone?"

"Leaving Sunday and we'll be back Friday."

I try to put on a calm, brave front, but my voice still shakes. "I hope you have a nice time with the guys."

"You can work on your book while I'm away," Alex adds. "And study for the geometry test."

I groan. Alex is so driven to go to college that even an A–makes him nervous. In his eyes, getting a C is basically the zombie apocalypse.

"All this triangle-rhombus-ninety-degree angle mumbo jumbo makes sense to you, but I only see shapes."

He rubs the back of his neck.

"I want to write graphic novels. All that matters is that I can draw the shapes. I don't need to know what they mean, okay?"

"Keep an open mind," he says. "What if math helps you with a story one day? Who knows what might inspire you?"

"I never thought of that," I reply quietly.

He plays with one of my tiny braids. "Listen, let's make a trade. I'll help you study for geometry, and you can name a hot character after me in your book."

I tap my lip. "How about an old man? Or one of the horses? The mule!"

"Oh, now it's on." He tackles me to the floor, tickling me.

"Stooooppp!" I whisper-yell.

Alex wrestles with me, pulling me on top of him, tickling my ribs—tickling me so hard, I might lose my mind, and when I'm trying to escape...I fart.

I freaking pass gas on my boyfriend's lap. For a long moment, neither of us says a word. What if he's so grossed out he breaks up with me?

"I'm gonna go die now," I say, rolling away from Alex onto the carpet.

He clutches his sides as he laughs and laughs. "You're not going anywhere."

Then he hauls me right back onto his lap and presses his lips to mine, and by the grace of God, our laughing doesn't wake up my parents.

I text him a few times during the camping trip but don't receive any responses. Maybe he doesn't have good reception? I can't wait to tell him about Dr. Chadha and how much she'd helped me with little details about rocks that will make my book so much stronger.

Then, four days into his trip, he calls late at night. Was there reception after all?

"Lu. I miss you so much," he says in a low voice. "I can't wait to get back to you. Less than two days."

I find his call incredibly sweet...until I hear girls in the background. Laughing and partying. *"Ryan, bring me another beer!" a girl cries.*

"No, let's do mystery shots. I'll pour you a shot of something and you have to guess what it is, and if you get it wrong, you have to remove an item of clothing."

I want to punch something. "You said you were going camping with the guys."

"I am."

"But there are girls," I say through clenched teeth. *And Ryan's suggesting they take their clothes off in front of my boyfriend?!*

"Yeah, Marcos and Jeremy invited their girlfriends and some of their friends." Marcos and Jeremy are the senior captains of his baseball team. They're in charge and can therefore do whatever they want, including inviting girls on an all-guy camping trip.

"You lied to me," I say. "You told me it was a guys' trip."

"I didn't know girls would be coming."

"I can't believe this," I mutter. "You're hanging out with other girls on spring break. You're drinking with other girls, doing mystery shots. And stripping? And I'm sitting here alone."

"Don't worry, Lu. I'm not stripping, and you're all I'm thinking about. See you Saturday."

On Saturday morning, I go to his game. Even though I'm upset with him, I've missed him too much to let my anger get the best of me.

I sit in the stands with my tablet, drawing a picture of his team manning the field. I decide to print it out and give it to him tonight.

After the game, I stand beside the dugout with the other girlfriends. Coffee County lost 5–4, so I steel myself for Alex's bad mood. But when Alex emerges from the dugout, his eyes avoid mine and his jaw is set as he charges past me.

This is the first time I've seen him in a week, and he won't even look at me? I hurry after him into the parking lot, hating that I'm the girl chasing after her boyfriend.

Once we're in relative privacy next to his truck, he says, "During my game, you didn't even look up from your sketchpad once. I help you with your writing all the time, and you can't even watch me play?"

"I wasn't writing—"

He opens his truck door and tosses his glove inside. "I don't know why you even bother coming, when you'd rather be home writing."

"Alex—"

"It's kind of embarrassing, you know, when your girlfriend is off in la-la land instead of cheering you on."

"But I was cheering for you!" I flip open the lid of my tablet, which makes him scowl. "I was drawing you, you big dummy."

He looks down at the screen, and his whole face changes. He goes from angry, to chagrined, to awed. "It looks so real. It's even better than the one you did of Niko's for Papu."

"I was going to print it out for you tonight," I mumble. "As a surprise."

"I'm sorry, Lu...I'm an asshole."

He pulls me into a hug. I press my face to his chest, to inhale his scent, but it isn't comforting. How could he hurt my feelings like this? My body sags against his.

"I haven't seen you in a week, and the first thing you do is yell at me," I say with eyes full of tears. "I deserve better than that."

"Yeah, you do. I'm so sorry. How about we grab some lunch?" he murmurs into my hair, and I nod.

He continues to hold me until his phone beeps. When he checks the screen, he sighs. "Dad wants me at Niko's earlier. One of the servers called out and he needs me to cover the afternoon shift. Can I take a raincheck on lunch?"

"Same ole, same ole." I swipe a tear away.

"Lu, c'mon. You know I have to work. It's my family."

"I understand," I say. Of all the things I say to my boyfriend, that's the word I say most. *I understand, I understand, I understand.* But today, I just can't anymore. "I need to go."

I turn around and bolt toward my car, needing to get there before I start bawling in front of his entire baseball team.

"Lu," he calls out after me.

I climb in the driver's seat and slam the car door shut so I don't have to hear him. I wish I could take my own spring break trip now, to get away from these feelings. How did things change so much between us? Is having a boyfriend supposed to be this hard? Make me feel this insecure?

I thought being in love would be fun, but god damn, it makes me want to crawl under the covers and never come out. As I drive home, tears run down my cheeks.

It's after midnight Saturday night when my phone begins to flash with Alex's picture. *Alex calling.*

I pick it up. "Why do you always have to call so late? I'm beginning to think you're a vampire."

"Hi to you too, babe," he says.

I grip my quilt in my hand, trying to stay calm. "What are you doing?"

"I'm heading out to Goose Pond."

Lots of girls will be there, and they might try to flirt with Alex. They probably *did* flirt with him during the spring break camping trip. I don't believe Alex would cheat on me, but the idea still frightens me. I mean, he's not a saint. What if he was acting like a jerk this morning because he *did* cheat? What if saying no was too hard?

While our school gives us sex ed lessons on how to use condoms to prevent pregnancy and disease, they don't prepare us at all for the emotional aspects of a relationship. I have no idea what's going on in terms of our love life.

"Come out with me to Goose Pond," Alex says.

"You know my curfew is eleven," I reply.

"It's ridiculous your parents won't let you stay out later," Alex complains. "You're sixteen now."

"I told you. I've asked them so many times," I argue. "Mom said I can stay out after midnight once I turn seventeen, but not before."

His parents don't care when he comes home, so long as he makes pizzas until the restaurant closes.

"You could always ask your parents to let you leave Niko's earlier."

"That's a nonstarter."

"So you expect me to convince my parents to change my curfew, but you won't talk to your parents about leaving work early? That's bullshit."

"We're a family business, and my family needs me."

"They let you off to watch the playoffs with Ryan, and to go on spring break. Why won't you ask for me?"

He sighs. "Lu, I just want to be with you."

"I want to be with you too. Come over."

"We always go to your place. Besides, we won't be alone

there. You always get distracted and worried when your parents are around."

"We won't be alone in Goose Pond either. Not with all those senior girls hanging around you. Are you going to do mystery shots again?"

He pauses. "You know I don't want those girls. You are all I need, Lu." His voice rumbles low, full of passion and want. "I want to continue our conversation we started last week. You know, about..."

Grace had told her boyfriend, Ben, she loved him after they slept together for the first time. Several months later, we found out he had cheated on her. When Grace heard, she cried so hard, she threw up in the bathroom at school.

I never want to feel that way. Max told me the locker room gossip he heard during gym class. All the boys wanted to know who was doing what with who, and they made fun of guys who weren't getting any. It seems like everyone is having sex.

But I'm not ready. Especially not after spring break. How could he even broach sex after the argument we had earlier today? Does he even notice how much he's hurting me?

We're not on the same page about anything.

"Alex," I start, my voice shaking, my heart shattering. "Maybe we're moving too fast. Maybe we need time apart."

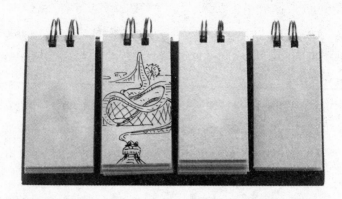

TODAY
SOPHOMORE CLASS TRIP

IF YOU HAVE A FEAR OF HEIGHTS, CONSIDER YOURSELF WARNED.

That is the sign displayed in front of the next ride Max wants to try. It's called Acrophobia, and it involves climbing a gazillion stairs to a two-hundred-foot-tall platform and then freefalling.

"Isn't acrophobia a fear of spiders?" Grace asks.

"No, that's arachnophobia," Max replies.

"Thank Christ. I thought this ride involved spiders."

I crane my neck back to stare at the platform that looks higher than the AT&T building in Nashville. "They should call this ride 'Acro-I'm-gonna-lose-my-shit,'" I say.

Caleb squints up at the platform. "Yeah, I think I'll sit this one out too."

"I thought you liked wild rides," I say.

"Yeah, but I don't want you to have to be by yourself again."

Max watches our exchange, as Grace waggles her eyebrows at me. Ugh, I love my cousin, but she does not know when to stop.

She and Max get in line for Acrophobia.

"Let's go drive go-karts," Caleb says.

I air my T-shirt out as we fall into line at the track. A song I like is playing over the loudspeakers, so I dance a little because there's nothing else to do while we wait. I glance over my shoulder. Alex is getting in line for go-karts too. He glares at Caleb.

"Shit," I mutter.

Caleb notices Alex in line behind us. "Is he following you around or something?"

"Who knows? I can't believe he drenched me like that. At least the sun is drying my shirt quickly."

Caleb glances down at me. "Oh, it's all wet."

This is the first time in the history of the universe a boy hasn't noticed the girl he's interested in is wearing a wet T-shirt. Either he's a total gentleman, or he's not into me. Maybe he's into Grace.

"Why'd Alex spray you?" Caleb asks.

"We were arguing..."

"I couldn't believe it when I heard you broke up. I thought you were so into each other."

We were... *We are*. "Just because two people are into each other doesn't mean they end up together." I look up at Caleb to find him giving me a sympathetic look. "I don't know why I told you that. I mean, I barely know you."

"I get what you're saying."

"You do?"

He fidgets with his cell phone.

"Are you dating anybody?" I ask.

He pauses for a moment, then shakes his head.

A bunch of go-karts skid to a halt. The previous riders, mostly middle schoolers, leave the track. The bored park employee's eyes never leave his phone screen as he opens the gate so we can enter. I choose a yellow kart. Caleb grabs a blue one. Alex, Ryan, Marcie, and Dana take karts behind us. I settle into my buggy, buckle my seat belt, and take the wheel.

"On your mark," a booming voice says. "Get set. Go!"

A loud bell rings. The race starts, and we take off. My kart's whiny engine sounds like it has a stuffed-up nose, but it's pretty fast. I zoom out ahead of everybody else from my school.

"Suckers!" I yell. All these years of playing *Mario Kart* are about to pay off.

Alex accelerates up next to me. "What the hell, Lu?"

"What's your problem?" I say over the noise of my kart.

"You gave me crap for holding hands with Marcie, and you're hanging out with Hernandez?"

I shoot Alex a look. "I'm not interested in him."

"If you say so."

Caleb cruises past both of us.

"Oh hell no," I say.

Alex speeds up and cuts off Caleb. Caleb swerves to avoid him. I push down on the gas to catch them. At the same time Marcie crashes her go-kart into mine, slamming me into the side rail.

Ow. I wish I had a red turtle shell like in *Mario Kart*. I'd totally hurl it at her. I imagine Marcie spinning wildly out of control with stars bursting from her head.

My foot becomes lead as I take off after her. I ram into the back of her kart.

"Ugh, you bitch," she shouts over her shoulder.

"You started it."

My little engine roars as I speed up to catch Alex. "I hope you know what you're getting into with Marcie. She tried to smash me up. She might secretly be Bowser."

"Lu, seriously." He drives faster, cutting me off.

I veer to the right, then cut up next to him and pass him again.

Alex and I are neck and neck as we turn the final corner and peel down the straightaway to the finish line. I glance over at him. Suddenly he's smiling at me, smiling like he's enjoying the race. With a grin, I stomp the pedal at the last second and push forward to beat him.

"Yes!" I scream, punching the air as my kart careens to a stop.

Alex climbs out of his seat with the biggest scowl I've ever seen. "I want a rematch."

"Don't be a sore loser," I say with a laugh.

Alex adjusts his ball cap and crosses his arms like a pouting little boy.

"Dear God," Caleb says, wiping a bead of sweat off his forehead. "Hanging out with Lulu is dangerous."

"Maybe you shouldn't then," Alex replies.

Caleb looks back and forth between us, then holds his hands up in surrender. "I'll meet you outside," he says to me.

Alex stalks him with eyes like a hunter, as Ryan, Marcie, and Dana appear at his side.

"You did great," Marcie tells him. "You won."

Alex sighs and fixes his cap again, even though it doesn't need fixing. "Actually, Lulu beat me."

He leans down to whisper in my ear, where only I can hear. "Can we talk later? Please?"

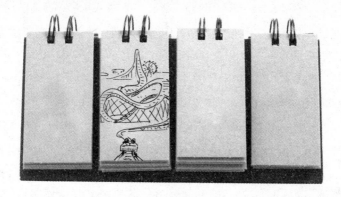

TODAY
SOPHOMORE CLASS TRIP

"Y'all," I say, fanning myself. It's noon and it feels like we're in the middle of Death Valley, not Atlanta. "I am seriously about to die from heat exposure. Can we please hit the water park now?"

"That's probably a good idea," Max replies. "The seats on the last ride were so hot they were sticking to my thighs."

"Me too," Caleb says. "I thought my thighs were glued to my go-kart."

"Right?" Max agrees, smiling at him. Max's gaze holds on Caleb's for a long moment. My friend seems really happy today. Caleb's light blue eyes must be hypnotizing him again.

"We're in too."

Alex and Ryan have appeared beside us. I agreed to talk to Alex later, but didn't specify a time because I'm not prepared for that conversation. I guess this means he'll be following me around until then. But where are the other baseball players and Marcie and Dana?

Did Ryan and Alex ditch them? Nothing sucks worse than getting ditched by your friends.

Grace and I grab our backpacks from the lockers and head to the bathrooms to change. After I struggle into my white bikini—which is basically like wrestling an alligator, I meet Grace outside the stalls. She's wearing a yellow halter top and matching bottoms that look great with her brown hair and skin. All she needs is a pink orchid above her ear and she'll look exactly like the pictures from when she visited her grandparents on Oahu last summer.

Hopefully none of the chaperones spot us in these bathing suits, think they're inappropriate, and want to make us change, because this is all I brought.

"You look hot, girl," I tell her.

"You too." We link arms together.

"Can you do me a favor? Don't leave my side, okay?"

She turns to look at me. "Why not?"

"Alex wants to talk."

She pauses. "That sounds like a good idea to me. You guys need to get it all out."

"What does that mean?"

"It means that the tension between y'all is off the charts, and if you don't deal with it, you are going to explode sooner or later."

"We're not combustible, you know."

"Are you sure about that?" Grace gives me a look. "You guys were so into each other. Are you sure you don't want to try again?"

"I want to, but I don't want to get hurt again," I say quietly.

"At first it was great, but toward the end, I felt like it was all about the physical for him, you know? It was like he only had time for me after he got through with everything else."

"And that's a bad thing?" Grace asks with a smirk. "God I miss it."

"Then why haven't you gotten a new boyfriend?"

She goes silent. As much as she tries to hide it with humor, I can tell she's still not over being cheated on by Ben.

Grace and I had drifted apart freshman year, but after she broke up with Ben, we became closer than ever before. We spent many nights hanging out together, sometimes talking, and sometimes not. With friends, I feel like I have to fill the silence, to keep everything moving. But with family, I can just be with them, no questions asked. When we became single, Grace and I needed that unquestionable support.

"If Alex had liked me as much as I liked him, he would've made more time for me," I say.

"He's a guy." Grace adjusts her tankini straps in the mirror. "Guys only think about a few things: sex, eating, and sports."

"I don't know if that's true. Some guys are into music too," I say, making my cousin laugh. But I know neither of us really believe guys are that simple.

Still, if Alex liked me as much as I liked him, he would've spent more of his free time with me.

If Alex truly loved me, he wouldn't have spent the entire spring break camping with his friends and other girls...the other girls he never said would be there.

I would've been more of a priority in his life.

"Our relationship felt one-sided," I tell Grace. "I've tried to explain it to Alex before, and he didn't understand what I was saying then, so why would he now?"

Grace shrugs. "Maybe he realized what he's missing."

When we meet back up with the guys, Max has shed his T-shirt, revealing his great set of abs. He never seems to gain weight no matter what he eats.

Grace is rocking that tankini. Ryan gives Grace a double take, and even after he looks away, I can tell he's studying her out of the corner of his eye.

Alex is staring at me.

Suddenly I feel uncomfortable because I realize Caleb's here too. I don't want to be so exposed in front of someone who might have a thing for me.

I peek at him, but find he's not even looking my way. Thank God. That's when I see what he's looking at. Not me. Not Grace.

He's zeroed in on a shirtless Max.

Max.

Holy crap, does Caleb have a thing for Max?

Does my friend know? Maybe this is why Max suddenly developed an interest in basketball.

For the first time all day, I grin for real. I am going to give Max and Caleb every opportunity to get together today if it's the last thing I do. I'd even ride the Mind Bender if I had to.

All of us lay our towels on the edge of the gigantic wave pool, where hundreds of people jump up and down through the crashing waves as music plays over the loudspeakers.

Alex strips off his T-shirt, revealing his tanned olive skin that would look right at home on Santorini, and takes a seat on the other side of Max.

Sitting on towels in their bathing suits, Ryan and Grace start playing that game where you try to smack each other's hands. He puts his hands out toward her, palms up. She places her hands on top of his. A few seconds later, he yanks his hands away and tries to smack the tops of her fingers, but she rips her hands back in the nick of time, laughing.

I reach into my backpack and pull out the latest novel in Cady James Morrison's *The Atlantis Clues* series. Even though they're graphic novels for little kids, Cady's intricate drawings inspire me to become better and better. I eagerly turn from page to page, studying not only the story line but her inking details as well. She's my favorite.

Once I'm sufficiently baked, I shut the book, ready to get in the water. Alex goes into the wave pool, so I decide to go in the opposite direction to the lazy river. I find a float shaped like a white unicorn and drape myself across it like I'm Cleopatra, Queen of the Six Flags lazy river.

After a couple of circuits around the lazy river, I pull myself out of the water and return to my towel. Now Grace is sitting on the edge of the wave pool, dangling her feet. Ryan is kicking water at her, flirting.

"Grace, want to go do the Flowrider with me?" I ask.

"No, thanks," she says. "I want to lie out more."

"I'll go," Max says.

Okaaay. I was trying to give him time alone with Caleb, but Max decides to cockblock himself. I didn't even know cockblocking yourself was possible.

While we're waiting in the long line, water misters spray us with a cool drizzle. Max drapes his arms around me, hugging me from behind. He rests his chin on the top of my head.

I open my mouth to ask him about Caleb, but decide to keep quiet. If they're interested in each other, they need to figure it out for themselves. I hate it when people try to tell me what Alex and I should or shouldn't do, as if they know our hearts and minds. I don't want to do the same thing to Max.

When we reach the front of the line, Max says, "Let me go first. I'll let you know if it'll make you sick to your stomach."

Max enters the Flowrider, where a continuous wave curves up and splashes down over and over again. He climbs on a boogie board and rides the wave like he's a California surfer. People watching from the line hoot for him, and even when the wave grows monstrous, he doesn't crash out. I clap when his turn is over and he steps back onto dry land.

"You'll be fine," Max calls out from the bottom, shaking the water from his hair. "You got this."

I choose a boogie board. "My turn."

The park worker opens the gate and ushers me in. Cool water laps at my ankles as I gingerly step into the Flowrider, careful not to slip in the never-ending wave. I set the boogie board down and step on top of it, taking a deep breath.

I bend my knees, urging my boogie board out of the pool at the top, then slide down to surf the wave. The water moves in a gentle rhythm. I'm doing pretty well, maintaining my balance enough to risk dancing to the music blaring over the loudspeakers a little bit. Then the wave grows. And grows again. Grows to something my amateur ass can't handle.

The board slips out from under me. I go down, slamming butt-first into the bottom. The wave flips me over twice.

And my bikini top gets ripped off.

It shoots away in the fast-flowing wave and disappears under the foamy water.

My hands fly to cover my chest. "I lost my top!" I cry, feeling around under the water with one hand, covering my boobs with the other.

"Oh shit!" a random guy cries.

"Damn, do you see that?!" yells another pervert.

I scramble back up the Flowrider to the pool at the top of the ride, ducking my body under the water, still covering my chest.

"You need to get out," the Six Flags worker guy says. "Your turn's over!"

No way in hell am I getting out of this water without a top. "Somebody give me a shirt!"

The Six Flags worker gapes at me. What, has this never happened before? Why isn't he doing something?

"Help me!"

Boys in the line are pointing and cracking up. Tears prick my eyes. Oh God, what do I do?

Right then, Alex jumps into the Flowrider pool out of nowhere. After he dunks his head several times, he emerges victorious with my bikini clutched in his fist.

I grab it from his hand, covering my boobs with the other. "Oh my God, thank you."

"I figured it probably flowed back up here with the wave," he says in a very professional voice.

Leering kids are cracking up.

"Nice rack!"

"I bet she did that on purpose."

My breathing races out of control. Covering my chest with one hand, I fling the bikini top with the other, trying to get it to unravel. The straps are all tangled!

Alex moves in front of me to block onlookers. "Turn around, you assholes," he calls out, and most of the oglers listen to him because he's a buff baseball player. He averts his own eyes, as I struggle into my bikini. It's hard enough putting swimsuits on when they're dry, but when they're wet? I deserve an award.

Once it's finally back on and covering everything, I find Alex's eyes. "Thanks. I didn't even know you were here."

He clears his throat. "I was in line."

Maybe Caleb was right. Maybe he is following me.

He reaches out to squeeze my shoulder. The touch of his smooth fingers makes me shiver. "C'mon, let's get you a towel."

Down at the bottom of the Flowrider, we meet Max, who won't look me in the face as he asks, "Uh, you okay?"

"I'm fine."

"Good. Great." He bites his bottom lip.

I want to laugh, because Max looks like he'd rather get the sex talk from his parents than be here right now after seeing my boobs, but I want to cry too. Losing my top sucked.

Max suddenly hops up and down on the pavement. "Listen, I need to go to the bathroom. I'll meet you back at the towels."

"Okay," I say as he speeds off, mortified out of his mind.

Alex walks me back to the pool area where I left my backpack, pulls out my towel, and wraps me up in it.

My cheeks are on fire as if sunburned. "Well, that wasn't embarrassing at all."

Alex's eyes twinkle. "I know how you feel."

"How could you possibly?"

"Remember that one baseball game?"

"Oh yeah!" I point at him and start laughing.

"I'm jealous," Alex says. "I mean, I'd rather a bunch of strangers see me than a bunch of moms." He cringes and shudders.

At bat during a game a few months ago, Alex bunted and sprinted for first base. He dove for the bag, and when he got up, he was safe, but his baseball pants were full of dirt. He unzipped his pants right there at first base, pulled them down a little, and started brushing off his underwear and legs. His teammates started catcalling from the dugout.

"Woo baby! You must work out."

"Are you from Tennessee? 'Cause you're the only ten I see!"

I smile at the memory. "What were you thinking?"

"I wasn't." Alex lifts a shoulder. "I only wanted the sand out of my underwear. That shit burned."

"You never told me you were embarrassed about that. You zipped your pants up and got ready for the next play like it was no big deal."

"I wanted to die, then. But now?" He wags his eyebrows at me. "When people ask about it, I tell them I was trying to impress you with my package."

"Oh stop, you do not."

He laughs. "Okay, okay. I don't tell people that. But it's true. I always wanted to impress you during my games."

Alex reaches into his backpack and pulls out a bottle of sunscreen, passing it over. "Get my back for me?"

He swivels on the chair to face the other direction. His olive tanned back is muscled and smooth before me. My fingers itch to trace his spine. My mind flashes back to an afternoon nap we took in my bed, when he sat up and the bedsheet fell down around his waist, revealing his perfect body. I got up on my knees behind him and kissed the spot between his shoulder blades. Then he sleepily looked over his shoulder at me and kissed my nose.

That was the first moment I ever thought, *I love this boy*.

My hand shakes as I squirt sunscreen onto my palm. I take a deep breath as I massage the lotion into his firm skin I know nearly as well as my own. I lick my lips, wishing I could press them to the back of his neck.

I jerk my hands away. "All done," I squeak before doing something I'll regret.

He turns to pick up the bottle. "You next."

I'm afraid if he touches me, I'll combust. "No, thanks. I'm good."

"Lu." Alex raises his eyebrows. "I don't want you to burn."

"Fine." I gather my long hair to one side, draping it over my shoulder.

"I've always liked this little braid," Alex says, touching the thin section of my hair. "It's sexy."

I clear my throat, and he goes back to the task of pouring sunscreen into his hand. When he begins to massage it into my upper back, I shiver at the tingly touch. His hands move down to above my bikini bottoms. I hear him begin to breathe more heavily, inhaling deeply through his nose.

I peek over my shoulder at him.

Out here under the sun, the sight of Alex smiling blinds me. Our eyes meet, and the smile slides from his face, turning serious, as we take each other in. The sunlight pounds down, heating the moment. Being with him is too much.

I pull my sunglasses down over my eyes and scoot over to my own chair.

With a sigh, Alex stretches out on the seat next to me, his tan legs on display in a pair of red swim trunks. My eyes follow his thighs up to his abs to his face, which is wearing a smirk.

"See something you like?" he asks.

Ugh, how did he know I was staring? I have on sunglasses.

I choose to ignore his remark and let out a yawn.

"Tired?" he asks.

"Exhausted. We had to get up so early—"

"And I imagine you stayed up late."

"Always."

Alex folds his hands behind his head.

Seeing him in his bathing suit reminds me of that afternoon nap in my bed again. My parents had traveled to Nashville for a real estate conference. The house was all mine, and as soon as the coast was clear, Alex came over. We kissed all the way up the stairs to my bed, where we made out in our underwear for hours. It was the first time anyone had ever seen me so exposed, but I felt safe the entire time. Anytime he moved his hands around my body, he looked me in the eyes and asked to make sure I was okay with it. And yes, it was very, very okay.

I need to stop thinking about him like this. "Where's Max? He should've been back by now."

Alex glances around. "Not sure."

"I'm gonna go find him." Without looking back, I stand and shed my towel.

I wait outside the nearest bathrooms for a bit and find no sign of Max. He's not at the water park snack area either. Did my friend ditch me? This day is not turning out like I thought it would. My stomach has motion sickness, even though I haven't ridden a single roller coaster.

I decide to go back to the lazy river to see if Max and Grace are there. I take care to ease myself into the water so as not to have Wardrobe Malfunction Part Two.

The water is warm, but shivers race up and down my body.

I'm sixteen years old. I've met a ton of boys, but no one has ever made me feel like Alex does. If I was sure he'd spend more time with me, if he'd make more of an effort to be with me and take more care with my feelings, I'd ask him out again in a heartbeat. If only he'd tell me he loves me, I'd give him anything he wants.

But then I remember he seems ready to move on with Marcie. And he went camping with other girls like it was no big deal. He yelled at me after his baseball game, after I had drawn a picture of him playing, which was me trying to show how much I cared about him.

Maybe there are some things you can't forget.

I drift down the lazy river on a float shaped like a flamingo, trying to get my feelings under control or at least in some sort of order, but my mind spins like a whirlpool.

A group of boys float by in bright yellow inner tubes. "Hey! It's the girl who flashed us."

"What's your name?" another one asks.

Ignoring these jerks, I paddle myself away, heading toward the waterfall up ahead. Looks like a cool, private place to be alone to collect my thoughts. I abandon my flamingo, swim behind the waterfall and pull myself up onto a ledge.

Where Max and Caleb are kissing each other's faces off!

"Oh my God," I squeal.

They break apart.

Caleb's eyes pop open wide. "Oh my God."

"Oh my God, I'm so happy for you," I say.

"Shit," Caleb says, slowly sitting on the rock. He covers his face with his hands.

Max's eyes are filled with hurt as he stares at Caleb.

The waterfall roars behind them.

"I'll go," I say to Max, pointing over my shoulder. "We can talk if you want, whenever you're ready. Or if you're not, that's okay too. Okay, see you later," I ramble.

Max takes my forearm. "Please don't tell."

"Never," I reply, hurt he thinks I'd tell his secrets. "I'm going to"—I pause to take a breath—"I'm going back to my towel to lie out in the sun."

Max gives me a curt nod, then turns his attention to Caleb, who hasn't moved or said a word.

I jump through the racing waterfall, belly flopping back into the river. I shove my arms in the water to move as quickly as I can with the current. To get away.

How long has Max been kissing Caleb? It didn't seem like a fumbling first kiss where you're getting to know the other person. It looked like they've known how to kiss each other for a while.

Why didn't Max say anything? We've always been so open with each other.

Why would my best friend keep this from me?

When I get back to our area on the pool deck, the chair Alex had occupied is empty. Grace is still gone too. Digging my phone out of my bag, I send her a quick text: Where are you?

I lie down on my towel and close my eyes behind my sunglasses as I wait for my phone to beep in response. But it doesn't. Great, first my best friend is freaking out behind the waterfall. Second, my cousin appears to be missing.

I wish I had my tablet with me, so I could work on my latest panel. Writing and drawing always help me calm down, and I could use that right now.

I decide to daydream about my book, to distract myself from the real world.

The biggest decision I need to make in my novel is whether Ander, my main guy character, lives or dies. The book would have more gravitas if Ander were to die and Nera had to learn to live without him on the desolate and destroyed surface of the Earth.

On the other hand, I love a happy ending. Romance readers will like the book more if it has a happily ever after.

I sigh. But how realistic is a happily ever after anyway?

When I wake up from my nap on the side of the wave pool, my throat is parched, my body stiff. I need to apply another coat of sunblock.

Alex is lying beside me again. Is this a dream?

He turns his head sideways to face me. "Sleepyhead's awake."

"Did Max come back yet?"

"No. Maybe he met a guy from another school or something."

I freeze up, envisioning Max and Caleb kissing.

I tap out a text to Max: I hope you're okay. Love you.

Staring at my phone, I wait for a response that doesn't come. "I have no idea where Max and Grace are. I've lost both of my buddies."

"Me too," Alex says, checking his phone. "I don't know where Ryan is."

I text Grace again: Seriously, are you okay? Why aren't you answering?

Her response arrives a few seconds later: I'm with Ryan.

Me: What!

Grace: We both feel like you and Alex need time alone to work stuff out.

Me: Work what out?!

Grace: Ryan says Alex is miserable without you. You're miserable too. Use today to fix things. Werk!

Alex's phone dings. He studies the screen. "Ryan is hanging out with Grace. He won't tell me where they are."

"Our friends are the best," I say sarcastically, standing to collect my things.

"Where are you going?"

"To find a cool place to sit and drink an iced coffee." *Someplace I can mope about how my friends abandoned me on a field trip.*

He gets to his feet too. "You can be my buddy."

I groan under my breath. "Alex, don't."

He gives me a little smirk. "What? I was thinking we could ride go-karts again. I need a rematch."

"You want to lose to me again?"

Alex holds out a hand. "C'mon, Lu. Hang out with me today?"

I stare at his outstretched fingers.

When I don't say anything, his hand drops to his side. "Okay, how about lunch? I saw somewhere on the map you'll probably like. The place just screams kale smoothies."

He knows the way to my heart is through my stomach.

This boy is dangerous.

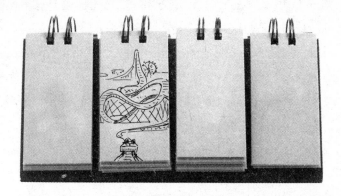

TODAY
SOPHOMORE CLASS TRIP

After Alex and I have changed back into regular clothes and stowed our backpacks in lockers, he chooses a sit-down restaurant called Daddy O's that has salads and fruit for me, and burgers and fries for him.

The hostess seats us under an umbrella on the deck.

Once we've ordered food and have drinks, Alex drums his fingers on the table as he stares out over the park. "Do you think the Worthington endowment is running out of money?"

"Oh God, yes," I exclaim. "Wait. As class president, don't you know how much is in the endowment?"

Alex shakes his head. "All I know is the law firm in charge of the endowment gives the school a check every year. And this year, it was only enough to pay for the good trips for the juniors and seniors."

"Grace and Max said I was being paranoid thinking the money was running out, but the endowment is supposed to allow us to travel to learn new things. What does Six Flags teach us?"

He folds his hands behind his head. "Today I learned you should never wear a bikini on the Flowrider."

I scowl at him as a bright smile breaks out across his face, a smile that makes me beam in return.

Alex leans toward me across the table, as he twists his cardboard straw. "How's your book coming?"

I wrap my hands around my water glass. "I've been thinking a lot about what you said after reading my previous draft. About how the scientific details were lacking?"

"Yeah."

"I've been doing lots of research trying to figure out how Nera and her family survived living underground for fifteen years. I'm incorporating details about how her father grows crops under giant heat lamps he installed before the asteroid hit."

My ex-boyfriend raises an eyebrow. "Is Lulu the Hater of Science becoming a scientist?"

I brush a lock of hair that fell out of my ponytail behind my ear. "Yeah, maybe."

"What other details have you added?"

I start speaking with my hands. "Ander is in love with Nera, but it would be better for his people if he joins forces with Clan Muir and hooks up with their leader, Alexa. She's the villain."

Alex's mouth falls open. "Did you name the girl villain after me?"

"You said to name a hot character after you. You did not specify it had to be a guy. She's very attractive, I promise." I move on. "So Nera needs to prove her value to Ander's clan. Clan Skene. I was thinking she could teach the clan how to make soap. Her dad had been making it in the Niagara Falls caves for years."

Alex gets excited. "Maybe we could try to make soap ourselves, with like, ingredients we find in the woods."

"You're such a geek."

"Then you'll be able to write about it from firsthand experience."

The server drops off our food. Bean salad and watermelon for me. A chicken sandwich and fries for him. I hate that he's eating that, but I keep my mouth shut, not wanting to disturb this peace we've found.

Alex pops a fry in his mouth and speaks as he chews. "I talked to a recruiter at our last game."

I open my eyes wide. "From what school?"

"Auburn."

I push my bean salad around on my plate. "Is that a good school for baseball?"

"Pretty good. I mean, it's an option."

"What do you want?"

Alex drags one of his fries around in the ketchup, making a swirl pattern. "Vanderbilt. I'm really excited about this weekend's game. A Vanderbilt scout is coming to watch. They're my best bet for getting out of Manchester."

I take a bite of watermelon. "So, you're gonna apply to Vanderbilt, then?"

"I like that it's only about an hour from my family, but there's no way I could afford it. Even with a scholarship, I don't know how I'd pay for living expenses."

"Could you get a job?"

"I won't have time for it. Not with school and practice."

"You manage okay now."

"College will be different, Lu."

"Maybe you should start saving more money now. Then you'll have savings when you get to college. You could use that for living expenses."

He drops his fry, abandoning it to sink in a glob of ketchup. "Listen, I need to tell you something," he says in a hard voice. "Mom's going to have another baby. In October."

Oh wow. A new baby would make six kids.

"Congratulations," I say gently, but his eyes close. It's clearly the last thing he wants to hear.

"My parents can barely support me and my sisters, and then they go and do this shit?" Alex covers his face with his fists. "I'm so pissed at them...but I'm not, you know?"

"'Cause you love your family."

He nods, then drops his hands as his face relaxes. "Hey, maybe it'll be a boy this time and I won't be so outnumbered by all those girls."

I laugh quietly. "Everything will be okay."

Alex pauses to eat a few fries. "But what if it's not? What if Papu and my parents can't handle the restaurant when I leave for college? What if I can't afford college anyhow?"

"When did you start working at Niko's? When you were in middle school?"

"Yeah."

"And the restaurant survived without you before. Niko's will keep going, even if you move on. I mean, you have the best pizza in town."

Alex grins a little. "Papu loves when you say that."

I feel my expression fall. I haven't seen his family in months.

"Yia Yia and Papu miss you." Alex slowly drags a fry through the ketchup, then leaves it to sink. "When he heard you broke up with me, he grabbed me by the ear and asked what I did wrong."

I don't know what to say to that. An awkward silence looms over the table.

Right then, some kids walk by beneath us and point up at me. "Hey, it's that girl! Flash us again, baby."

Without missing a beat, Alex lifts his glass and tosses the rest of his water down on them, and they scatter like ants at a picnic. We crack up together.

Alex turns back to me. "How about that rematch?"

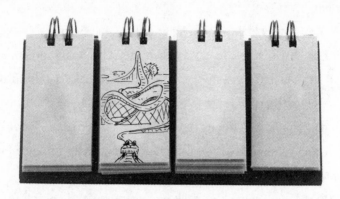

TODAY
SOPHOMORE CLASS TRIP

The rest of the afternoon, Alex and I one-up each other at everything the park has to offer.

I'm still not okay with the fact he was holding Marcie's hand earlier, but my need to beat him at games outweighs everything else I'm feeling.

We ram each other with bumper cars.

He beats me at this game where you kick soccer balls at a target.

And because I beat him at Skee-Ball, he has to ride the Ferris wheel and carousel with me. I can't stop laughing, watching him bob up and down on a horse. He even swivels an imaginary lasso above his head like he's a cowboy.

"The heat's making you delirious," I tell him.

"Yee-haw," he replies.

Next, we find this game where you climb-race up rope ladders. We scramble like spiders up to the top of a tower. He loses his footing and falls off the rope ladder momentarily, then pulls himself back on *American Ninja Warrior* style. I reach the top at the same time as him and thrust myself forward.

"I win!" I cry, landing on the inflated balloon, bouncing up and down.

Alex lands on top of me. I try to scramble away, but he secures an arm around my waist. "Do you have to win at everything?" he asks.

"I guess I could let you win one."

He props himself up on an elbow and gazes down at my face. His skin smells of chlorine and warm sunlight, but under that is the smell of him I know so well. A comforting smell, like warm, clean sheets.

Our eyes meet, and we start to smile, and my heart begins to rumble like a roller coaster going up, up, up, and then it happens. Alex starts tickling me.

"Ahhh!" I squeal, jerking away from him, but he keeps on tickling my sides.

I fight back, shoving him onto his back, and he flips me over.

"Hey, you! You kids!" My head pops up to find a park worker yelling at us. "No sex on the rides. It's Six Flags policy."

The warning doesn't stop Alex at all. He continues the tickle attack. "Wonder what happened that made them institute that no-sex-on-the-rides policy," Alex says, cracking me up.

My cell buzzes in my back pocket. I ease out from under him

to check my notifications. With a deep sigh, Alex rolls away from me, the float gently bobbing beneath us like the ocean.

Max texted: I need you.

I tap back: Where are you?

By the entrance near the bus.

I'm coming.

"I'm sorry," I tell Alex, carefully standing up on the unstable inflatable surface. "I have to go find Max. He needs me."

"Is he okay?"

My body lurches back and forth. "I'm not sure."

Alex lumbers from his knees to his feet, wobbling. "I can come with you."

"I think he needs to talk to me privately," I say.

Alex drags a hand through his hair. "Okay, I guess...text me when you find him, so I know you're safe."

Part of me thinks I should stay. On the other hand, I'm not sure what the tickling would've led to. Would I have the strength to say no? I glance over my shoulder at Alex as I descend the tower stairs, hoping he'll give me a smile, but he's already scrolling on his phone.

I walk as quickly as I can through the park, the heat so thick it's like a rain forest. My damp T-shirt sticks to my skin. At the park entrance, I find Max sitting alone on a bench, absently clutching his phone.

I sit, wincing as the bench's hot surface burns my legs, and hug Max, holding him as close as possible. "You okay?"

"No," he says with a sob.

Max has sunglasses on, but I can tell he's been crying because a tear streaks his cheek. "I told him we could trust you. That it would be okay to let you know about us."

"Of course. I'd never tell anybody unless you asked me to." I rest a hand on his shoulder.

"I wanted Caleb to hang out with you today. I figured he might be open to telling you about us if he only got to know you."

"Okay."

"Instead, he broke it off."

I never meant to mess things up for Max. How was I supposed to know they'd be behind that waterfall? If I could go back in time, I'd stay parked on the side of the wave pool, baking myself to a crisp.

"Does anyone else know?" I ask.

Max shakes his head. "Caleb isn't ready to come out to his teammates yet, or his parents, and I understand. But I wanted my best friend to know. I mean, half the fun in having a boyfriend is getting to talk to your friends about him."

"Right?" I laugh softly.

"You finding out spooked him, and now he's gone."

I hug Max, holding him tight. He gently pats my back, then eases away. "It's too hot out here for hugging, Lu." He fans his face with a hand.

"Your face is all red. I'll get you some water."

I walk over to a snack stand to buy Max a bottle. While I'm standing in line, I check notifications on my phone. Nothing from Grace. But there is a text from Alex.

Alex: Did you find Max?

Me: Yes, we're good.

145

As I wait for the people in front of me to pay, I shove my phone in the back pocket of my jean shorts. Things with Alex were going surprisingly well over lunch. It felt so natural, like it was in the beginning, when we first got together and things weren't so physical between us. It was more like being good friends. Maybe that's what we're meant to be. Friends.

But none of my friends make my heart race. None make my skin blaze with a single touch.

I buy two overpriced waters, and as I'm walking away, Caleb comes out of the bathroom. My feet stop moving. I suck in a breath.

As he pushes a finger beneath his sunglasses, wiping his eye, he looks up, sees me, and stops in his tracks.

I wave at him with a bottle of water.

He dabs under his sunglasses again. Is he crying too?

"I was grabbing some waters for me and Max," I say.

"Could I have a sip?"

I pass him a cool bottle. He quickly opens it and takes a long chug, drinking nearly half of it in one go. "Thanks. I lost my wallet earlier and can't find it anywhere. I've been backtracking my steps, but I'm sure it's gone for good. This day can't get any worse." He gives me a sad, nervous smile.

I reach into my pocket and pull out the money Dad gave me this morning, separating a twenty-dollar bill from the other cash, and passing it to Caleb. "Here."

He steps back from me. "Oh, no, I couldn't take your money."

This must be a pride thing for him. "Pay me back at school Monday."

With a grateful nod, he takes the cash.

I start to leave, to return to Max, when Caleb reaches for my elbow. "Is he okay?"

"Not really, no. He's upset."

Caleb deflates.

"This is a sucky day for everyone," I say.

"You're having a bad day too?"

"You would not believe what happened to me earlier." Deciding to cheer him up, I put on a little show, playing up what happened to me in the Flowrider. "My bikini top flew off and I was basically naked in front of everybody, including my ex-boyfriend."

Caleb throws his head back and laughs. "No."

"It's true. You wouldn't believe some of the gross stuff guys yelled at me. Anyway...that's why I came behind the waterfall."

"To hide?" His skin takes on a rosy hue again.

"Yeah, I needed a moment by myself...I didn't mean to, um, interrupt you and Max. I promise I won't say anything."

Caleb pushes his sunglasses up on top of his head, then rubs his red eyes. "I fucked things up with Max."

"Lulu?" a voice says from behind me.

I turn around to find my best friend.

"You were taking a long time with the water," Max says to me, his voice cracking like he's freaked out. "I came to find you. What are you doing?" Does he worry I'm messing this up for him?

"Lulu loaned me some money," Caleb says. "I lost my wallet. I think it fell off when we went upside down on the Scream Machine. Maybe I'll look under there."

"No!" Max and I shout at the same time.

"You'll get decapitated," I add, and Max nods sagely.

Then Caleb and Max turn to stare at each other. They stare so long, I might as well be invisible.

"I'm sorry I messed everything up," Caleb says quietly.

Max pauses. "You didn't. Well, you sort of did, but not for good, you know? I mean, I want you to be friends with my best friend."

Caleb takes a deep breath. "I can do that, but I'm not ready to tell my parents or anyone else about us yet."

Max reaches out a hand toward him, but pulls it back at the last second. "I understand that. I can wait."

Caleb closes his eyes and pulls his sunglasses down.

I feel a twinge of jealousy. Max has been out for years, and I can't imagine how difficult it would be to have a secret boyfriend, but he's willing to wait for Caleb to be ready.

If Alex truly wants me back, wouldn't he wait for me? Would he be willing to work through our problems? He said he wanted to talk...maybe that means he is ready to sort things out. To have a relationship where everything isn't one-sided.

The sun is starting to melt into a rosy gold horizon. I check the time on my phone. We have forty-five minutes before we need to meet back at the buses to go home.

"Guys, I have to go," I say, and take off into the park.

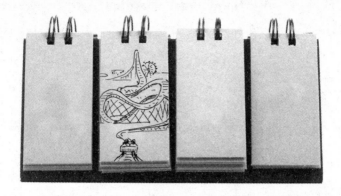

TODAY
SOPHOMORE CLASS TRIP

Where are you?

When I text Alex, he doesn't answer at first.

Fifteen minutes later, he writes back: Just got off the Dare Devil Dive. Going to the Mind Bender.

No way will I ride that, but I could wait for him at the exit. On the way there, I stop in the bathroom to check my appearance. I dab the sweat off my sunburned forehead, try to air out my T-shirt, and tame my frizzy blond ponytail with some water. It's the best I can do.

Back outside, I walk quickly to the Mind Bender exit, where I lean across the wooden fence, taking a deep breath.

I watch the roller coaster dip and loop above me. Screams pierce the evening sky every time it goes upside down. The coaster rolls to a stop and riders begin to file out. I stand on tiptoes, searching for Alex until his head appears above the crowd. At over six feet tall, he towers above most of the other riders. As he gets closer, I discover he's not alone.

He's with Marcie.

I can't believe he went back to her.

As he walks my way, his smile begins to grow. When she sees me, Marcie's face falls.

"You came back," he says when he reaches me. "Is Max okay?"

"He's good. I wanted to see if we could have that conversation now."

Marcie steps up next to me. "Alex, I've barely seen you at all. You promised me we'd spend the day together," she says matter-of-factly.

He did? He averts his eyes, and nervously scrubs a hand through his hair. "I'm sorry, I know I did. But I need to talk to Lu."

So, he had planned to spend the day with Marcie. An uneasy feeling begins to fill my body.

Alex puts on his hat. "Let's go for a walk, Lu."

Marcie sets a hand on her hip. "Did you even get to ride any of the rides you were interested in?"

"I had a good day," he says slowly, his eyes darting back and forth between us two girls.

"You spent practically the whole bus ride here talking about riding the Goliath. Did you?"

He looks up at the skyline where a roller coaster peeks out over the trees. Desire fills his eyes. Not for Marcie, but to ride that roller coaster. Even after everything that's happened between us, I want him to be happy, and if that means riding a dangerous contraption that probably has more g-force than the space shuttle, then fine.

"I don't care if you ride the Goliath," I say. "Go for it. We can talk after."

"Let's go!" Marcie says excitedly, taking his hand to pull him away from me. He drops her hand and looks over his shoulder at me as they walk away.

I don't want Marcie to be alone with him again. I hurry after them. I can do this. I can ride one ride. One ride won't hurt. "Wait," I call. "I'm coming too."

Alex slows down to wait for me. "Don't you get motion sickness?"

"I haven't ridden a roller coaster in a long time. Maybe I'm better now."

Marcie smirks at me, which makes me want to do this even more. No roller coaster is the boss of me.

While we wait in line, Marcie scrolls on her phone.

"Did you ever find Ryan?" I ask Alex. "I haven't heard from Grace in hours."

"No, it's like they disappeared." Alex pulls his phone out of his pocket and thumbs on the screen, shaking his head. "They really wanted us to talk, I guess. We can after we ride the Goliath."

Marcie peeks up from her phone at Alex, eyes full of hurt. If he told her they'd spend time together today, I can understand how she'd be pissed.

The line rapidly begins to move. As I shuffle forward, I check out the signs describing the ride.

AT 250 FEET HIGH, GOLIATH IS A HYPERCOASTER!

YOU'RE ABOUT TO HIT 4 GS!

READY TO FREE-FALL 12 STORIES?

My stomach lurches at the words. I reach out to Alex, grabbing his arm. His hand closes over mine. Marcie watches us, then swivels around to face forward, bowing her head.

As we move closer to the front of the line, the ground shakes every time the roller coaster roars past, full of people screaming their lungs out.

When the roller coaster careens to a stop, kids excitedly exit the ride. A few people are touching their foreheads, as if they have a headache. One man zigzags his way out, looking like he completed a dizzy bat challenge.

Once the Goliath is empty, a park worker opens a gate for us to enter. I reluctantly approach the ride as a worker ushers me into a bucket seat with no floor beneath my feet. My legs dangle in the wind. Oh hell, what if my legs get cut off?! I bite down on my lip and let out a little whine.

Alex takes his cap off, folds it, and stuffs it in his front pocket, then takes the seat beside mine, giving me a worried look. I breathe deeply through my nose, out through my mouth. *In through the nose, out through the mouth*.

Alex touches my wrist. "It's not too late. You can still get off the ride, Lu."

I shake my head. I can do this. "I'm fine."

The bars come down over our chests, locking us into our seats. *Click.*

A high-pitched noise that sounds like an airplane begins.

"You ready to experience Goliath?" an announcer exclaims, and everyone else yells "Yeah!"

I squeak, "Okay."

The roller coaster edges out of the gate and slowly begins to climb toward the pink and purple sky. This isn't too bad. The roller coaster chugs to the top of a hill, almost to the point where we're vertical. Then it slips over the hump and we plummet.

"Oh my gawwwwwwwwwwd," I yell as the wind hits my face. The roller coaster zooms upside down in a loop. With my legs freestyling below me, I feel like I'm flying. Cautiously, I stretch my arms out as if I'm Supergirl.

"Woooo!" I yell along with everyone else as we go upside down like a thousand times in two minutes. The ride careens to a stop.

My body lunges forward. My eyes are squeezed shut.

I cautiously open them to look sideways at Alex. "I survived."

He grins. "Yeah, you did."

The restraining bars over our chests lift, and Alex stands up on the platform, reaching down a hand to help me. When I rise, the blood rushes to my head. A slick, slimy sensation trickles across my skin. The ground spins. *Don't throw up. Don't throw up.*

"Need to sit. I need...water. Medicine." I let out a low moan, nuzzling Alex's chest.

Alex wraps an arm around my waist, ushering me to the exit. "There's gotta be a first aid stand around here. Let's find a map."

"Alex," Marcie says. "We need to go. We're supposed to be at the bus in five minutes."

"Lulu and I'll be there as soon as we can," Alex replies.

"C'mon," Marcie says. "This is ridiculous. You're going to get in trouble."

"Would you tell Coach where we are? I'm sure he'll understand."

I peek up from Alex's chest to see her rushing off.

After asking a park worker how to find a nurse's station, Alex keeps a firm arm around me as we make our way there. When we arrive, he tells the nurse, "She has motion sickness. Can you help?"

The nurse escorts me to a room with a wooden exam table covered with white crinkly paper and jars full of cotton balls and a defibrillator on the wall.

A woman with a Six Flags ID lanyard brings an ice pack for the back of my neck. Alex presses a cold compress to my forehead. I sit still with my eyes shut and catch my breath.

"How you feeling?" Alex asks a few minutes later, pulling the compress away.

"Better, thanks." I lift the ice pack off my neck. "Sorry for the trouble."

"No problem. I'm used to it with you," he jokes, and I playfully push him away.

"Can you believe it?" I say. "I rode a real ride and didn't throw up. Wooo!"

Alex laughs.

I push myself off the table, then begin to stand. A sudden heat wave rushes through my body. I touch my forehead, feeling dizzy.

Alex helps me to sit back down. "Don't overdo it."

"I feel better than I did. We should get back to the bus, like Marcie said."

I groan, remembering how he had planned to spend the day with her.

"What's wrong? Need to lie down again?"

"No...I'm confused. You said earlier you wanted to talk to me, but you had planned to spend the day with Marcie."

"I know. But you and I need to sort out some things."

The next words out of my mouth are a whisper: "Please don't date Marcie."

He moves to stand between my knees, pressing his forehead to mine. "Lu, all you have to do is say the word, and you've got me."

Maybe it's adrenaline from the roller coaster. Maybe I'm delirious from the heat.

Maybe it's the smell of him.

I reach out, grip the front of his gray V-neck shirt and yank him to me. Our lips meet, warm and familiar and right. His tongue sweeps into my mouth. I've missed this. I've missed him so much.

In less than a minute, he takes me from zero to sixty. One hand is up my shirt while the other plays with the button on my jean shorts.

"Oh God," he mumbles. "You feel perfect."

I gasp into the warm, smooth skin of his throat as he takes me back to all those late nights. Words sit on the edge of my lips: *I love you, I love you, I love you.* But I stay silent, except for my sighs of pleasure. The more his hands touch me, the more I unravel.

The door swings open. Alex yanks his hand away from me. I cover myself.

The nurse glares at us. "Seems like everyone's feeling better. I'll give you a minute to get ready to leave." The door slams shut.

"Oh my God, that was so embarrassing," I cry. A stranger saw me with my shorts unbuttoned. A stranger saw me doing—doing *that.* And after the bikini incident earlier today! "I'm going to go die now."

Alex wraps his arms around me. "So, we got a little carried away. It's no big deal."

I stiffen, leaning away from him. "It *is* a big deal."

My cell phone chimes. A text from Max reads: Where are you? You're in deep shit with the chaperones.

I type back: Got sick. On my way.

I hop off the table and onto my feet, still feeling wobbly after the roller coaster. Or is it because of Alex?

We dart out of the nurse's office saying, "Thank you," over our shoulders, but I don't meet anyone's eyes because it mortifies me we got caught.

We jog through the park. I'm not in as good of shape as Alex, and I still don't feel my best, but somehow manage to stay on his heels as we dart around little kids and their parents.

We stop by the locker to grab our backpacks. That's when he takes my elbow, stopping me. I turn to face him. Lights from the Ferris wheel shine down on his face, the face I just peppered with kisses.

He licks his lips. "Are we back together?"

I close my eyes. "I'm not sure. Just because we had one day together doesn't mean our problems are solved."

"I don't get it. Today you acted totally jealous of Marcie."

"That's because I am jealous."

"You and me? We're good together," he says, looking from my lips to my eyes.

"Yeah," I say with a sigh. "But things were moving too fast, and we weren't on the same page in general."

Alex gently caresses my arm. "I'm sorry you felt pressured.

I never meant for you to feel that way. I would've waited. I never would've forced you."

"I know you'd never hurt me, or any girl..."

He tilts his head to the side. "What went wrong, Lu? I want to fix this."

"I tried to talk to you so many times. You don't listen."

He squeezes my hand. "Talk to me now. Whatever you need to tell me, I'm listening."

"You went camping on spring break, and there were girls there, and you didn't tell me they were coming. You said it was a guys' trip, but Marcie was there—"

"I've told you—I wanted to spend time with Ryan, not those girls."

"But you still went, and I barely heard from you for a week. What if something had happened with Marcie?"

"But nothing did happen, because I liked *you*. You were my girlfriend." He lets out a huff, as if he can't be bothered about my concerns.

"I wish you had texted me back. I kept wondering what you were doing, and it was making me so upset, and I felt left behind... God, I sound desperate."

"You could've asked to come camping with me."

"My parents never would've let me go."

"Did you even ask them?"

I shake my head. "They wouldn't have agreed. Besides, you told me it was a guys' thing. I would've looked desperate if I tried to tag along. Plus, I needed to stay home to work on my book."

"This is ridiculous. You want me to change how I act, but

you won't change for me either. So many nights I asked you to come out to Goose Pond with me and the guys, and you said you had to work on your book. How many times did I ask you to take a break?"

"You knew I couldn't stay out past eleven, but you expected me to anyway!"

We're talking past each other, like we always do. I'm listening to the same song on repeat. Still, I try to get through to him: "I want to see you more often. I felt like I only saw you at school and late at night when you'd sneak over. I want to go to movies on Saturday night, or out to dinner, or hell, bowling. Something other than Goose Pond. *Something*."

"I have to help out at Niko's on weekends, you know that. We're a family business. We need another line cook on weekends, but my grandfather can't afford to bring somebody else on." He takes his ball cap off and runs a hand through his hair, scratching his head. "You're lucky you don't have to work."

Did he imply I'm spoiled? I play with the hem of my shirt, fidgeting.

"So, can we try to work through these things?" he asks. "Was there something else?"

I inhale sharply. "We were getting so physical, and it scared me—"

"I'm sorry you felt that way, Lu," he says softly.

"I wanted to sleep with you."

His brown eyes grow wide. They glisten excitedly under the bright lights. "Okay, there is absolutely nothing wrong with that," he says with a nervous laugh. "We can do it tonight if you want."

I clench my eyes shut. "You don't get it."

"What don't I get?"

I wanted him to tell me he loves me first. But what I didn't realize is if I can't tell a guy I love him, I shouldn't be in bed with him. It's the twenty-first century. Girls can say "I love you" first. And if I'm going to be with him, he needs to know how I feel. How serious I am about him.

So I decide right then and there to do it.

"I love you."

A roller coaster flies by above us with cars full of screaming kids.

Alex doesn't say the words back. Instead, he looks at me as if I told him he could never play baseball again.

Then his eyebrows pinch together as his eyes narrow. "You broke up with me, then you get jealous of me hanging out with Marcie, but you don't want to get back together with me." He shakes his head, biting his lower lip. "And now you tell me you love me?"

"Is that all you have to say?" I ask quietly, waiting to hear the words back.

His Adam's apple shifts as he swallows. "Uh, thank you."

Thank you?

Thank you?

I turn and dash toward the lot where the bus is parked.

"Lu!" Alex calls out behind me. "Lu, wait up!"

Tears burn my eyes as I jog, my backpack banging against my back.

Right then, a voice booms over a loudspeaker like the announcer in *The Hunger Games*. "Alex Rouvelis and Lulu Wells, your teachers are searching for you. Report to your bus at once.

Attention! Alex Rouvelis and Lulu Wells, return to your school bus at once."

Okay, that's not mortifying at all.

"Lu!" Alex shouts behind me.

I reach the bus a few moments before him. Kids start yelling out the windows.

"Those assholes, making us wait for them."

"Do you know how hot it is on this bus without air conditioning, Rouvelis?"

"I told you they were screwing."

Coach Rice is standing there clutching his phone, glaring at us.

"Where have you been?" he scolds us. "And why weren't you answering my texts, Rouvelis?"

Alex drags a hand through his hair, catching his breath. "Didn't Marcie tell you? Lulu needed to go to the nurse. She got sick on a ride."

"No, Marcie didn't say anything. You missed the curfew by half an hour! Everybody's been waiting for you. We had no idea where you were." He turns to one of the chaperones behind him. "Leslie, can you go tell the park officials we found them?"

"I'm sorry, Coach. Really," Alex says, out of breath.

"Me too. You knew the curfew. Nobody could find you because you weren't answering your phones."

My face burns with humiliation. I wasn't paying attention to my phone because I was fooling around with Alex.

"You can check with the nurse's station if you want," Alex says. "They'll tell you we were there."

I shoot daggers at Alex. If Coach Rice calls, the nurse will tell him we were hooking up, and then Coach Rice could tell my parents, and nobody wants to get the don't-hook-up-in-public-places lecture.

"Missing curfew could affect your future field trips," Coach Rice warns. "The school may not let you go next year."

"Nooo," Alex says as I cry, "But junior year's when the field trips start getting good."

"You should've thought of that before being late and not calling a chaperone."

"Ask Marcie!" I say.

"We told Marcie to tell you," Alex adds, but Coach Rice shakes his head.

"Lulu, you have a week's worth of detention. Alex, I'm sorry, but you can't play in the next game."

Alex stumbles back as if someone punched him. "But it's the last game of the season, Coach. The Vanderbilt scout is coming!"

"I have no choice, son. I don't think you understand how serious this is. You're benched. Time to get on the bus. We're leaving as soon as Leslie gets back from talking to the park officials."

Coach Rice walks up the steps, as the engine roars to life, its rumbling drowning out the voices pouring from the windows.

Alex looks like he might cry. "I won't get to play in the last game."

All the pain and humiliation I'm feeling from the last ten minutes swells into an ugly bubble in my throat. "It's only one game," I spit. "No big deal."

"No big deal?" Alex blows up at me. "It's the last game of the season! College scouts come to our games, and I need every chance I can get. You gotta get your head out of your ass, Lu. Just because something isn't important to you doesn't mean it's not important to me."

"You're right—"

"You know that camping trip I went on? The one you keep giving me shit for? Ryan was having a tough time, and I needed to be there for him." Alex's voice falls to a yell-whisper. "His mom had told him she was divorcing his dad for some guy she met online in Florida, and she was going to move there, and all you cared about was that I wasn't texting you every five minutes."

Oh my God—poor Ryan. I had no idea about Mrs. McDowell. I open my mouth to respond, to tell him I understand, but Alex keeps on ranting, "Tonight was all your fault. Why'd you have to ride the Goliath anyway?"

"I'm sorry, Alex—"

"If it's not something you care about, like your novel or your garden, then you don't think it's important. Join the goddamn real world already."

He storms up the bus steps, leaving me alone in the night.

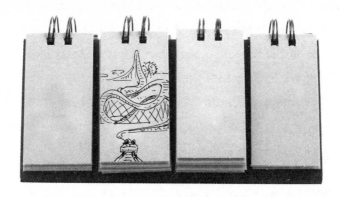

TODAY
SOPHOMORE CLASS TRIP

I climb slowly onto the bus.

Tears fill my eyes, but I don't let them fall. Instead, they leak down the back of my throat, burning, giving me the urge to cough.

Alex took an empty seat toward the front of the bus, but he's glaring out the window, so I move past him to see if there's another free spot. I overhear a guy whisper, "She banged him so long she missed curfew by thirty minutes? Damn."

I gasp, and stumble over my feet, grabbing the back of a seat to stay upright.

Other kids stare at me, whispering to each other. Did anyone hear the mean things Alex said to me? I swallow a sob. No one has ever treated me that way. No one. How could he? My heart physically hurts so bad that pain shoots up my left arm.

Max is sitting with Grace, who's fast asleep against the window. Caleb is across the aisle from Max. They are both laughing and playing a game on their phones, oblivious to the fact that Alex just broke my heart. I manage a wobbly smile for Max. He lifts his eyebrows, looking concerned.

Not wanting to disturb Max and Caleb's seating arrangement, I find an open spot beside Mrs. Schmidt, the teacher who warned us to make good life choices.

My choices today were unthinkably bad.

The inside of the bus is dark except for the glow of cell phones, but it's light enough that I can see Marcie duck out of her seat and move up front to sit with Alex. The top of his head turns toward her. Marcie stays with him as the bus drives toward home. Back to reality.

I never should've kissed him today. I should've trusted my first instinct—that even though Alex and I are attracted to each other, he doesn't want the things I want. He doesn't need the things I need.

We don't belong together.

PART III

MAY 7,
JUNIOR CLASS TRIP

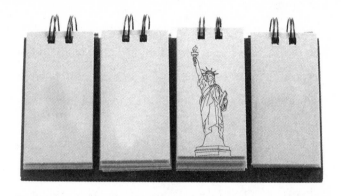

TODAY
JUNIOR CLASS TRIP

Somebody knocks on our hotel room door.

A quick peek at the alarm clock says it's one o'clock in the morning. The lights are out. I'm already under the covers in my pajamas, on the verge of sleep.

Our class arrived in Hoboken, New Jersey, a few hours ago and checked into the hotel. When the chaperones confirmed we were in our rooms before bed, they put pieces of scotch tape into the creases of our doorframes. If the tape is broken or missing in the morning, they'll know we opened the door or snuck out. And voilà, the chaperones will send us home before our field trip to Manhattan even starts.

The knock sounds again. With a groan, Grace climbs out of bed.

"Who is it?" I mumble into my pillow. The thirteen-hour bus ride here was so exhausting, I fell into bed immediately.

Grace peeks out the peephole. "Lulu, it's your boyfriend."

I sit up straight.

"I can't open the door," Grace tells him. "The tape!"

After last year's fiasco when I missed curfew, the school put a written warning in my record and said if I ever misbehave on a field trip again, I won't be allowed on future trips. I'm lucky they let me come this year.

Thank God they did. New York is the literary capital of the world! I'm about to board my mothership.

I climb out of bed to speak through the door. "You better not get me sent home, Nick. I'm not letting you in."

"Trust me. You can," he calls out.

Against my better judgment, I turn the knob and open the door to reveal my boyfriend. A slow smile appears on his cute face.

I smile back and simultaneously cross my arms across my chest. I'm wearing a thin tank top to bed, and while we've made out a few times, I'm not ready to give him a show yet.

"I paid one of the bellboys to help us out," Nick says. "He'll retape our doors once we're finished."

"Finished with what?"

Nick leads me out into the hallway, checking both directions. "Come to my room."

"Where's Caleb?"

"Checking out the hot tub downstairs."

Does the scotch tape stop anybody?

Nick pulls me into his hotel room and shuts the door, then pushes me up against the wall, kissing my neck. Oh God, he's such a good kisser.

For the first time ever, his hands shimmy under my tank top to caress my waist. As we kiss, his fingers move higher and higher, but I ease them back down to my hips. I feel a ticklish aversion to his hands, a need to push them away.

Part of me wants to go further, but something is stopping me. Maybe we need to spend more time together?

Maybe I need to kiss him more?

I lean forward to press my lips harder against his.

JUNE
SUMMER BETWEEN
SOPHOMORE AND JUNIOR YEARS

"Promise me you'll be careful," Lila says, clutching the backpack full of contraband to her chest. The contraband being wine coolers she agreed to buy for Grace, Max, and me.

I bounce on my tiptoes like a little girl. "I promise."

"You won't do anything stupid?"

"What, like strip down and roll in a mud puddle?"

"Yeah. Or talk to older men, or get in a fight."

"None of that sounds like stuff I'd do."

My sister gives me a long look.

Since before I was born, Manchester has hosted a music festival called Bonnaroo.

Manchester is halfway between Nashville and Chattanooga,

halfway between Memphis and Knoxville, halfway between Atlanta and Louisville.

The town is near a U.S. Air Force base and has a bunch of fast food restaurants and hotels, but hardly anything ever happens. Except for in the summer. People travel from all over the United States—and the world—to set up camp, drink tons of beer, smoke weed, and listen to music, all on a huge piece of farmland only a few miles from Dad's dental practice.

Bonnaroo attracts plenty of older acts my parents love (they went bonkers when Elton John was here), but also younger musicians like Lorde and The Weeknd.

Bonnaroo is a big deal.

Now that we've turned sixteen, Grace, Max, and I are finally allowed to attend by ourselves.

My cousin hugs me from behind. "Lu!" Then she gives Lila a big hug too.

Lila looks up at Max, who's wearing a white tee, green cargo shorts, and a pair of yellow suspenders meant to look like a tape measure. "You keep getting taller and more handsome! Guys are gonna be all over you here."

Max grins politely, but I'm sure he's secretly thinking about Caleb, who's here somewhere with his friends. Maybe we'll run into them later tonight. Caleb probably won't go out of his way to find Max, because they haven't told anyone else they're together.

"Y'all take care of each other tonight, okay?" Lila says. "And text if you need me. I'm meeting up with some high school friends."

Max, Grace, and I hurry off with the contraband backpack,

excitedly looking for a place to sit. Not too close to the main stage, but not too far away either. We wave at people from school and around town. The sun is beginning to set, and pretty soon, it'll be difficult to see the ground.

Groups of people have already staked out spots on the grass and are eating, drinking, and passing around joints. All I can smell is weed and manure.

Some police and security are here, but so far no one has confronted the pot smokers.

As soon as we pick our spot, we spread out a picnic blanket. Then Grace and I ditch our T-shirts we left home in, revealing the super cute strapless halter tops our parents would never have allowed us to wear. We take a selfie together, making kissy faces. Max squeezes between us for a group picture, sticking his tongue out.

After a quick look around for (1) police officers and (2) Mom's church lady friends, we crack open the wine coolers Lila bought us.

"Cheers," we say, clinking our bottles together.

A single guitar chord rings out in the night. We jump up and down, cheering and dancing.

Max throws a fist in the air. "Wooo!"

Large bonfires fill the air with smoke. Drums begin to play. The guitarist goes wild.

Grace and I dance our asses off, my hair swinging around my body. I feel alive.

And that's when it happens.

Dana Jenkins appears and dances her way over to me. "Lulu, you got moves!" Dana shouts over the music. "Grace, why didn't you ever tell us she can dance?"

"She's my cousin, of course she dances," Grace shouts back.

If Dana's here, then that means Marcie isn't far behind. And if Dana and Marcie are here...I begin to lose the beat. My body starts to slow—

Ryan appears, carrying a six-pack.

And Alex strolls up behind him, one hand deep in his shorts pocket, the other holding a dark brown glass bottle.

We haven't spoken in a while. Not since he chewed me out at Six Flags. I stopped by his locker the morning after the field trip to apologize for getting him in trouble, but he slammed his locker door and stalked off like he didn't hear me.

Two more times, I tried again to say I was sorry. Each time he looked right through me like I wasn't there. Then he stopped liking my posts online.

He never apologized.

I'd given this boy ten months of my life, and either he didn't understand how badly he'd hurt my heart, or he didn't care.

At Bonnaroo, my anger simmers like a volcano fixing to erupt.

Ryan comes up behind Grace, places a hand on her hip, and speaks over shoulder. "Dance with me?"

She takes his free hand and they begin to dance, as he takes a sip of his beer. They've been friends a long time, but ever since they'd disappeared at Six Flags together, they seem to be getting closer and closer. Every time I ask what's going on with them, though, Grace waves a dismissive hand and says, "We're having fun. Nothing serious."

Grace and Ryan move farther and farther from Max and me, drifting away. Soon they're dancing right beside Alex and Marcie.

Dana, Marcie, and Grace are on the dance team together, so

they start matching one another's moves and laughing. Alex and Ryan join in.

When Marcie and Alex start getting handsy, I feel like I'm going to be sick.

My feet stop dancing. I never knew anything could make me feel this bad. "God, I hate him."

Max shoots him a dirty look. "Me too, but we're not letting him ruin Bonnaroo for us, okay? You've got to let him go."

Easier said than done. I hate being the friend who's always down in the dumps, but right now, it's hard to be anything but. My first boyfriend—my first love—is dancing in front of me with another girl.

When Marcie sees me staring at their naughty moves, she pulls away from Alex and whispers in his ear. I can't hear what she said— the music is thumping so loudly, but he looks up at me, appearing a little sheepish. As she looks into my eyes, her forehead scrunches up in apology. Alex points the other direction over his shoulder and takes her hand, and Marcie begins to follow him away.

Which is worse? Seeing them together in front of me, or wondering what they're doing all alone? Does he take her to his favorite bridge overlooking the interstate and slow dance along to his truck radio like we used to?

A guitar hits a piercing high note.

Ryan walks after Alex and Marcie, tugging Grace with him, but Grace shakes her head, gesturing in my direction.

"C'mon, Lu," Ryan calls out over the loud music, swaying back and forth. "Why can't you and Alex get over yourselves and hang out together? It sucks that we're all stuck between you."

"Yeah, it does suck," I snap. "But I'm not gonna be miserable just so everyone else can have a good time." The crowd cheers as the band finishes its song. "Y'all can do whatever you want, but I'm gonna stay right here and enjoy the music."

"And drink these shitty wine coolers," Grace adds, draping an arm around me. I feel a surge of love for my cousin. A couple of years ago, she would've abandoned me for him. She's changed so much.

"Fine, whatever," Ryan says. "Grace, text me if you change your mind."

He jogs after Alex, nearly tripping in a dirt divot. How many beers has he drunk?

I chug from my bottle, wishing wine coolers were stronger. Wafting bonfire smoke stings my eyes.

"I'm so mad," I say to my friends. "This night was supposed to be fun. Why can't I start over?"

"Because you loved him," Max says.

Loved. Love? I don't know. "I wish I hadn't told him," I say through tears. "I wasted those words."

Grace gnaws at her fingernails, like she does when nervous.

"What is it?" I say.

"Lu, I have something to tell you, but it's going to upset you. Still, you deserve to know."

I hold my breath.

"Ryan told me...he said that when you told Alex you loved him, it freaked him out. Alex is so dead set on getting out of this town, to go play baseball somewhere, he couldn't handle the idea of settling down."

I bite my lip. "He thought my saying 'I love you' would make him have to settle down?"

It's a hot summer evening, but I'm shivering. I put my T-shirt back on over my halter top. "I'm glad I told him I loved him and got it out there. Otherwise I'd probably still be wasting my time with him, waiting for him to say it first."

Max cuddles me against his chest. "I want you to be happy. Whatever that means. But you're so much more than Alex's girlfriend. You're everything, you know?"

"I know."

"Alex is not worth you being depressed. He's the one missing out. You are too much of a badass to let this get to you."

"You're my favorite cousin," Grace says.

"And my best friend," Max adds.

"A great writer."

"A lover of animals!"

I point my wine cooler up toward the night sky. "The garden girl!"

"Wooo!" Max screams as the crowd roars.

The three of us collapse onto the picnic blanket, and Grace and I snuggle against Max's shoulders. Tears pool in my eyes, and I swipe them away.

I do everything I can to push thoughts of Alex and Marcie out of my mind. I concentrate on the deafening drum beat. Watch smoke drift in patterns across the sky. Search for answers in the stars.

The band's lead singer starts singing lyrics about loving yourself.

I need to do that more.

I don't tell my friends this, but I decide something right then and there: love hurts too much.

I never want to experience this pain again.

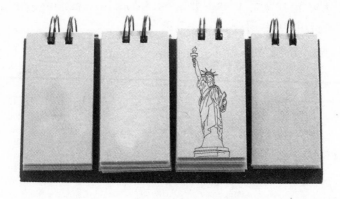

TODAY
JUNIOR CLASS TRIP

A few hours after I sneak back to my hotel room, I wake up at six o'clock to get ready for my big day in New York.

I decide to wear my comfortable black tunic dress and white sneakers. Our room is so tiny, I keep crashing into the end of my twin bed as I'm ambling around sleepily. The hotel's dark maroon wallpaper makes it feel like it's still the middle of the night.

After I finish doing my makeup, I check my purse to make sure I have Mom's credit card, money, and phone.

Grace is simultaneously watching an online makeup tutorial on her phone and carefully applying green eyeliner. She looks stunning, as always.

I yawn. "Ready to go?"

"I need a few more minutes." She points at her mouth. "I need to do my lippy."

"I told Nick I'd meet him for breakfast, since we won't get to see each other all day."

She flashes me a knowing grin. "See you downstairs."

I leave our hotel room and ride the elevator down to the lobby.

Finally, a school field trip that truly excites me. I've always wanted to visit New York. I've never been here before, but I think about this city every day because this is where nearly all of the literary agents and publishers work.

If I don't find a literary agent who can sell my book to a publisher, *Here Comes the Sun* will never be published. I've sent twelve query letters to agents, asking them to read my graphic novel and to consider representing me. No bites yet. I'm hoping being in New York will give me some good publishing karma.

I meet Nick at the hotel Starbucks. He stands, rising up to his full six feet, handing me a cup. "Good morning. It's green tea. Careful, it's hot."

"Good morning," I reply, giving him a quick kiss before taking a sip of my much-needed caffeine.

I like that he remembers my Starbucks order. Also, he's ruggedly handsome and tan with cropped brown hair. He plays on the basketball team with Caleb, who set us up a couple of months ago. He looks and dresses as if he's in one of those *Fast and the Furious* movies I secretly adore (white T-shirts, jeans, boots), but he's a dork at heart. And boy do I like watching him run up and down the basketball court. Just like Max, a basketball player hypnotized me and now I'm suddenly a fan.

The chaperones told us to meet by Starbucks at seven o'clock in the morning to catch the train into Manhattan. They want to pack as much sightseeing into one day as humanly possible.

"I wish they'd turn us loose," I say to Nick. "I mean, we're seventeen. Don't they trust us to walk around?"

"No," Nick says with a grin. "I have all sorts of ideas how to spend this trip, and none of them are teacher-approved."

"Oh yeah? Like what?"

He leans closer, nuzzling his face against my hair. "Most of my ideas involve us staying here in your room."

Okay, number one. We're in New York City. How could he give up this opportunity to see the city to stay here and fool around? Number two, we haven't gone that far yet.

Grace has already slept with two guys—her first boyfriend freshman year, and she's been sleeping with Ryan McDowell off and on since last year, even though she doesn't want to date him seriously because that "would give him all the power." Her words, not mine. And I'm the only one who knows Max and Caleb started doing it in October before homecoming.

Meanwhile, I feel like the world's last seventeen-year-old virgin. Everyone says your first time isn't perfect, and I don't expect mine to be, but I at least want to feel comfortable with the guy.

"Let's pretend we have food poisoning so we'll have to stay back at the hotel," Nick whispers. "We'll say we ate bad cheese burritos at the gas station on the turnpike."

"No way, that's gross," I reply, making a face. "And like anyone would believe I'd eat a cheese burrito. Besides, I can't wait to see Central Park and the MOMA," I ramble. "And I hear the vegan pizza is to die for. And Dad said he'd disown me if I leave without trying a pretzel."

Nick gives me an easy smile, playing with a lock of my hair. "Want to hang out again tonight?"

"Okay," I say, even though I'm not 100 percent sure I want to. I like Nick a lot—he's a great guy—but it was hard to relax with him last night, because when he slid his hands beneath my tank top, that ticklish feeling overwhelmed me. I wasn't totally feeling it with him physically.

On the other hand, maybe that's safer for me emotionally.

I can't handle another broken heart.

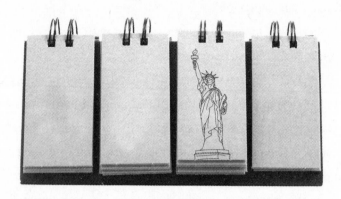

TODAY
JUNIOR CLASS TRIP

For this class trip, the school gave us two options.

Both choices include the main attractions like the Empire State Building and the Statue of Liberty, which we're doing tomorrow. For today, however, track one has the Museum of Modern Art (MOMA), a walk-through of Rockefeller Center and Times Square, lunch involving pizza and pretzels, an afternoon at the Met, and an art installation in Central Park. Track two has the Intrepid Sea, Air, and Space Museum and a Yankees game before they meet back up with us in Central Park.

I'm doing track one with Grace and Max, while Nick and Caleb chose track two. At first it made me sad I wouldn't be hanging out with my boyfriend today, but it's not like we have to do everything together. If I want to talk to him, he's only a text away.

Kids from school begin pouring into the lobby, swarming the Starbucks like zombies. At this hour, everybody needs a caffeine fix. I wave at Grace, who accepts a cup of coffee from the barista. She blows into the lid to cool it, as she walks my way. Grace looks super cute wearing a white tank top and a pair of denim overalls featuring cropped short shorts. Totally going to steal those tomorrow.

Grace joins me on the couch. "I am so excited."

Max and Caleb plop down across from me with large iced coffees. Max rests the cup on his thigh, closes his eyes, and leans his head back, his camera nestled safely against his stomach. He's not awake yet. Caleb smiles at him sideways.

Mr. Sanderson, the chemistry teacher, and Coach Rice appear. Coach Rice brought his trusty bullhorn. He clearly does not care if he wakes up other hotel guests.

"Okay!" Coach Rice shouts into the bullhorn, startling Max awake. His coffee starts to tip over, but he catches it. "We're going to split you up into your tracks. Bob is leading track one," he says, pointing to Mr. Sanderson. "I'm taking track two. Wooo, Yankees!"

"Booo," a bunch of his baseball players say. Being from Tennessee, we're all Braves fans.

"Track two, follow me," Coach Rice says, and nearly all of the boys and a couple of girls, including Marcie and Dana—who are wearing cute baseball caps—rise to follow him. Caleb squeezes Max's knee before joining the track two group, looking over his shoulder to smile at Max.

Nick leans over and gives me a quick kiss goodbye.

"Take lots of selfies for me," he says, winking.

Max, Grace, and I are all smiles as we follow Mr. Sanderson

out of the hotel with our drinks in hand, but my smile disappears when I see that one other guy decided to take the museum track: Alex.

OCTOBER
JUNIOR YEAR

Grace, Max, and I are one another's dates to the homecoming dance.

Music is blaring as we walk into the dark gym. It's decorated with balloons and streamers in our school colors, red and black. I wore a tight black dress I found at the back of Grace's closet, and she chose a sparkly pink one from mine. Max looks like a million bucks, wearing black pants and a navy blue vest over a fitted black T-shirt.

"Shoes off," says Coach Donovan, the basketball coach. "I don't want anyone scuffing up my floor."

Grace and I slip off our heels and set them alongside the gym wall with all the other shoes.

"This is so uncivilized," Max says, taking off his black loafers that shine like a new car. "It totally smells like feet in here."

"You mean, like it does every day?" Grace retorts.

It's almost like Ryan knows Grace's every move, because he appears next to her within seconds of our arrival. He looks like a British spy with his gelled auburn hair and perfectly fitted dark blue suit and black tie.

"Gracey," he says. "Look at my new socks." He lifts his suit pants leg to reveal a red sock that says GOD BLESS GIRL POWER.

Grace rolls her eyes so hard, I worry they'll pop out.

"You know you love them," Ryan says, throwing an arm around her. She can deny her attraction to him all she wants, but I know how their evening will end: doing it in her basement rec room, unbeknownst to Uncle James and Aunt Lilibeth upstairs binge-watching whatever TV show they discovered this week.

As Grace and Ryan talk quietly off to the side, Max scans the gym. I follow his eyes to find Caleb hanging out with the basketball team. Those goofballs actually have a ball and are shooting free throws in the middle of the dance.

Max lets out a long breath of air, staring across the gym at Caleb.

"You okay, bud?" I ask. "You seem down in the dumps tonight."

"All I want is one dance with him."

I loop my arm around Max's elbow. "You'll dance with me, right?"

He pats my hand.

The music suddenly changes to classical organ music. It sounds majestic and royal wedding-ish and totally ridiculous in our smelly gym where I did Zumba this morning.

The homecoming court begins to file into the gym, wearing long ball gowns and tuxedos and plastic tiaras. In addition to the homecoming queen and king, who are seniors, each class elected a prince and princess to the court.

First the two freshmen walk in. I have no idea who they are. Max yawns and doesn't even raise his camera to capture the moment.

I elbow him. "If you don't document this for the yearbook, then it didn't happen, and how will they tell their grandkids?" I hiss.

Max laughs at me before moving to snap some candids of kids from our class standing in a group nearby.

Jaylen Morris, the sophomore star running back of the football team, looks ridiculously hot escorting the sophomore class princess, Andrea Edelman, a talented soprano in the school show choir. They look like movie stars. Or at least future contestants on *The Bachelor*. I cheer for them, because *holy hotness*.

Next, it's time for my class. The juniors. Dana Jenkins sails in wearing a sparkly long red gown as if she's on her way to the Miss Teen USA pageant.

With a huge grin on his face, Alex comes in next, his movements fluid like he's riding a moving walkway at the airport. I suck in a breath. He's dressed in a tuxedo with his hair slicked back, looking so good. I clap politely.

Along with the rest of the homecoming court, he escorts Dana to the center of the gym to massive applause. When all eight of the Coffee County royalty are there, they do a choreographed dance.

"Is this a Disney musical?" I ask Max over the music.

Grace reappears next to me. "It is. It really, really is."

Alex, who is *not* a dancer, is a step off the beat and gets lost behind everyone else. Grace and I start giggling at him, and because we're incapable of standing still during a fast song, we learn the group dance. The moves aren't that difficult to pick up.

"Me and you, Lulu," Grace says as she dances, not even out of breath. "Next year. We'll be homecoming king and queen, and we'll choreograph the sickest dance this school has ever seen."

I dance up against my cousin. "Okay, but I get to be king."

Grace watches me move. "You should try out for the dance team senior year."

I give her a look that says *what?*

"We think we have a good shot of going to state championships next year, but we need a few really good new girls."

"You know I love dancing, but Marcie and Dana hate me."

Grace shakes her head. "After they saw you dance at Bonnaroo, they want you on the team. They think you're hot!"

"You do have moves, Lucifer," Ryan interjects. "Just like your cousin," he adds, patting Grace's butt.

She playfully pokes him in the chest with a pointer finger. "Keep your hands to yourself, McDowell."

He winks. "I get it. Not now. Later."

A slow song comes on, and members of the homecoming court move toward each other for a dance.

Instead of watching, I check my phone to see if I have any notifications. Anyone who would contact me is at the dance, but pretending to check messages is better than watching Alex. No matter how much I try not to care, seeing him with other girls will never stop hurting. As the song ends, I can't help it. I peek away from my screen to see what he's doing.

I look up in time to see him give Dana two tiny pecks on the lips.

My stomach lurches, and I turn away. Marcie Wallace looks over at me, sticks a finger in her mouth, and mouths "gag me." She and Alex only dated for a couple of months before he moved on. I get how Marcie feels and give her a small smile in return.

Being here in the gym brings back all sorts of memories.

As my first real boyfriend, pictures of Alex and me used to cover the bulletin board in my bedroom. My favorite was a candid taken at the sophomore homecoming dance. After Alex and I had our formal, staged picture taken in front of red and black balloons that matched the football uniforms, Max snapped a picture of us dancing in a dark corner of the gym, unable to keep our hands off each other. A dark suit intensified Alex's hotness, and he smelled like fresh mint. I wore a short, sparkly silver dress that left little to the imagination.

"I love that dress, babe," he had whispered in my ear, his arms locked around my waist. "You're driving me wild."

Junior year homecoming is a whole other story.

I want to move on with my life, but how can I do that when I see Alex all the time? I wish high school were over already. Maybe I can apply to be an exchange student in Switzerland.

I glance around for the nearest exit, wondering how pissed Max would be if I made a run for it. There's a romantic comedy about rival neighborhood dog walkers on Netflix that has my name on it.

That's when Caleb comes up.

"Want to dance?" he asks me, and Max's face falls. He stalks off toward the bleachers and slumps down on a bench.

"Sure, I guess," I reply quietly, stretching my arms around Caleb.

About halfway through the song, Caleb's best friend Nick Johannsen walks up. He gives me a quick smile, then focuses on Caleb.

"Dude, what are you doing?" Nick asks under his breath.

"Dancing."

Nick pointedly looks between Caleb and Max, who've been glancing at each other all night, but you'd never know unless you knew what to look for.

Caleb stands up straight, his back muscles going rigid beneath my hands.

"You know you're my friend no matter what, right?" Nick asks him. "I'll be here for you."

Caleb nods, and Nick pats his shoulder.

"Save a dance for me, okay, Lulu?" Nick asks before walking off.

"What was that all about?" I ask.

"He knows about Max," Caleb whispers.

"Did you tell him?"

Caleb shakes his head. "He brought it up to me. Said he could just tell. He could see it in my eyes or some shit."

I tighten my arms around Caleb. "He's not wrong. I can see it in your eyes too." I blink at him dramatically, giving him a playful, sultry look.

That's when I come into Alex's sights. His jaw hardens as he quickly averts his gaze to focus on another group of kids.

"You okay?" Caleb asks me, watching Alex.

"Memories hurt is all."

As Caleb and I spin around again, we see Max watching us

from his seat on the bleachers. His camera sits beside him on the bench. He's only taken a few shots since we entered the dance. Max folds his hands together and stares down at his socked feet.

"He's hurting too," Caleb suddenly says.

"Yeah, he is."

"I can't do this anymore."

"Do what?" I say with a panic-filled voice. He's about to ditch Max. "Not tonight. Don't leave him tonight at homecoming. Please. Whenever he thinks about school dances, he'll remember getting his heart broken. And it would suck. Don't."

Caleb gives me a slow grin. "I'm not dumping him. I need to make things right with us."

The slow song isn't over, but Caleb says, "Will you excuse me?" and rubs his hands together, leaving me standing alone in the middle of the dance floor. Some couples swaying next to me notice I'm all alone and follow my eyes across the gym. Caleb beelines over to the bleachers and sits beside Max. So close their thighs touch. Caleb takes Max's hand in his.

My mouth falls open.

I find Grace, who's standing with Ryan. Her jaw drops at the sight of Max and Caleb together. She starts bouncing on her toes excitedly. Ryan raises his eyebrows.

People in the gym start to notice. A few guys and girls shriek, "What?"

"Max and *Caleb*?"

"How cute!" a girl says.

"I knew it," says another girl, who probably had never thought about Max and Caleb until this moment.

Some people aren't so nice in their comments. I want to punch something when I hear some of the words people use to describe them. My heart gallops away with fear for my friends. Maybe Caleb shouldn't have declared his feelings for Max in front of the whole school.

That's when Nick Johannsen leads some of the basketball players across the gym to join Caleb. Nick's support brings tears to my eyes.

Max appears totally stunned at all the attention.

I scurry over in my bare feet and squeeze in beside him. Grace gives him a huge hug. "I'm so happy for you," she squeals. "And you'd better give me all the details later."

Max returns her embrace.

Alex comes toward the bleachers too, adjusting the junior class prince crown perched on his head. My pulse pounds. My hands shake. He hasn't spoken to me in so long... Does he miss me at all?

He walks right past me, to stick out his hand to fist bump Caleb and Max. "I'm glad for you guys."

Boys from the baseball team and Grace's dance team sit down next.

I overhear Caleb whisper to Max, "Come home with me after this? I need to introduce you to my parents."

As I sit there leaning against Max, incredibly excited for my best friend—so excited it helps to dull the pain in my chest, Nick takes a seat on the other side of me.

Would Caleb have ever come out if Nick hadn't encouraged him? "Thank you," I tell Nick, wiping a tear from my eye. "Thank you so much."

He smiles. "Still saving that dance for me?"

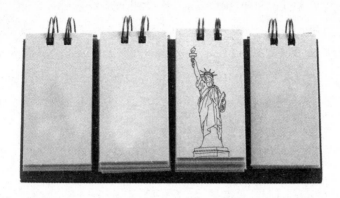

TODAY
JUNIOR CLASS TRIP

Alex is skipping the Yankees game to visit MOMA and the Met.

He is skipping a baseball game—baseball, the love of his life—
to do artsy activities. Okaaay.

"Have fun at the museum, Rouvelis," Ryan calls to Alex, making
a jerking-off motion. "I'll text you pictures from Yankee Stadium."

Alex waves as if unconcerned, then sips from the straw of his
Frappuccino. He pulls the plastic lid off to scoop whipped cream
into his mouth.

Nick sees what's happening and narrows his eyes at Alex. He
comes back over and whispers, "Let's stay here, Lulu."

I place a hand on his chest, hardly believing he wants to skip
New York City to stay in bed all day. "I'm not skipping the Met or
MOMA. I'm not missing any of this. Not for anything."

"Okay," he answers quietly, glaring at Alex. "Text me, all right?"

We kiss quickly before he takes off with the other guys.

Outside the hotel, the sun is already up. The air is humid. Today will be a scorcher. Our group of about fifty kids walks down the sidewalk to the PATH train station, where we get tickets for the trip into Manhattan. I press buttons on the machine, working to figure it out.

"How much money are you putting on your ticket?" I ask Max.

"I guess ten dollars?"

I choose the same amount. Then I have to figure out how the turnstile works. Men wearing down vests and dress pants and carrying briefcases, and women in colorful dresses rush to make their train. Do any of them work in publishing?

I imagine sitting next to a fancy editor lady on the train. I would be doodling on my sketchpad, and she'd look over my shoulder at my panel and gasp, "Why, you're writing the next big thing. The next *Harry Potter*! Here, sign this book contract right now."

In reality, the train is packed with commuters, so I stand gripping a metal pole for dear life. We sway back and forth as the train car speeds down the tracks. I bend my knees and widen my stance so I don't lose my balance.

I study the New York City map posted on the wall to see where Union Square station is located. Cady James Morrison is having a book event near there this afternoon at three o'clock after school lets out.

I would love to hear her speak, and maybe even get a book signed, but it's not happening. Our class won't be anywhere near

Union Square at three o'clock. We'll be at the Met, which looks to be like—I squint at the map—seventy blocks away. Might as well be a zillion.

When the train pulls into Herald Square station, people rush to squeeze off the train. The air smells like coffee, perfume, and dirty metal. Mr. Sanderson stops in the middle of the platform and examines the exit signs for different streets. New Yorkers slam into us, jostling our backpacks. What a bad place to stand.

Mr. Sanderson looks down at the map in his hands, then back up at the signs. He narrows his eyes.

"It's this way!" Grace calls out, taking charge, and we follow her up a staircase and out into bright sunlight.

I look left and right. Drivers honk their horns and pedestrians crowd the sidewalks, pushing past us. Up here, the air smells like fried dough and car exhaust. Tall buildings soar above my head. There are probably more people on this one street than in all of Coffee County back home.

I smile up at the blue peeking between skyscrapers.

I already love New York.

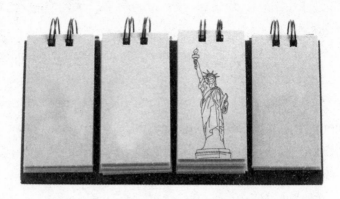

TODAY
JUNIOR CLASS TRIP

Our plan for today is this:

First, we're walking up through Times Square on the way to Rockefeller Center before heading even farther uptown to MOMA. I'm glad I wore my comfy white Converse.

Max is in his element, snapping pictures left and right.

Grace is power walking ahead of everyone in her sandals because she didn't hit the gym this morning and needs to get her cardio fix. Her words, not mine.

Me? I walk leisurely along, trying not to miss a thing. When I go clothes shopping back in Tennessee, pictures of models fill the store windows. Here? TV screens show videos of the models as they leisurely stroll across green meadows under the sun. This city feels like magic.

Alex falls into step beside me, adjusting his backpack. "You doing okay, Lu?"

I'm still not used to him talking to me again. "Huh?"

"You looked like you were lost in another world on the subway."

"Oh, I was. I was imagining someone discovering me on the train and deciding I was the next J.K. Rowling."

He laughs. "That's a good daydream. I wouldn't mind it if someone saw me on the train and decided I'm the next Derek Jeter."

"Guess what? You're the next Derek Jeter," I announce in a deep, booming voice as if I'm a game show host.

He laughs, squinting as he cranes his neck back to stare up at the buildings towering above us. "I can't believe I'm in New York," Alex says. "My yia yia still talks about how every time she visits New York, she sees it in a new way. Like, it looks different from the last time she came."

"That makes sense. It's so big, it must be impossible to see everything. Hey, do you think I'll be able to find vegan pizza?"

Alex nudges me with his elbow. "Oh, Lu. Never change. I'll stay on the lookout for some."

I begin to slow my pace, carefully considering his words. *Never change.* A year ago, he told me to join the goddamned real world. I cringe. It still hurts, thinking of the conversation that broke my heart.

Alex increases his speed to walk beside Grace, chatting with her.

"I can't believe he chose this track," I whisper to Max.

My best friend carefully lays his Nikon camera against his chest. "Of course he took this track. Alex is totally into you."

"Stop."

"Lu, he's skipping a Yankees game for you."

"Because he's a Braves fan."

Max gives me a withering look. "Because he wants you back. That's why he's with us."

"I have a boyfriend."

"Look, I like Nick a lot," Max says. "I love that you and I are dating two best friends. It's like we're in a romantic comedy. But what if, like..."

"What?"

"What if you and Alex are meant for each other?"

I scoff. "Have you been sniffing glue? Did you forget about how you told me to get over him? That he wasn't worth it?"

"Do you want him back?" Max asks. "After what he did, I'd take him back."

I still can't believe what Alex did. It landed him, Ryan, and the entire varsity baseball team in a week of detention.

Max swoons. "It was like, the most romantic gesture in history. He risked so much to show you he wants you back."

I mean, Max isn't wrong. What Alex did last month was super romantic—and so risky that Coach Rice threatened to take away Alex's captaincy of the baseball team unless he put everything back to rights.

But Max doesn't get it.

He and his first serious boyfriend are going strong. He's never had his heart totally broken. He's never apologized profusely, only to be ignored for months.

He doesn't know what it's like to wake up in the morning and wish your alarm clock for school had never gone off, because it means you have to see the person you love...who doesn't love you back.

MARCH
JUNIOR YEAR

Nick walks me to my front door after our second double date with Max and Caleb.

It's the first warm night we've had after a long, frigid Tennessee winter. Tree branches are beginning to bud, and I can smell spring in the air.

Nick gently sets a hand on my lower back to usher me up the stairs. "I had a really good time tonight. Even though you beat me."

"I didn't beat you," I reply. "I obliterated you."

He grins and shoves his hands in his pockets. "I guess my basketball skills don't translate to mini golf."

"I guess not," I tease.

"How'd you get so good at mini golf anyway?"

"Many, many vacations to Florida with my family."

We fall into silence as we climb my front porch steps. "We've been having fun, right?" he asks.

I pull my house keys from my purse. "Yeah."

"Can I take you out again? Like, just me and you?"

I inhale a sharp breath. I agreed to hang out because he's Caleb's best friend, and we've been talking off and on since homecoming, but honestly? I haven't thought about anything beyond one round of mini golf.

I swipe a lock of hair behind my ear. "You already want a rematch?"

He playfully bumps his arm against mine. "No more golf. I just want to hang out. We could get food or see a movie or whatever." He peeks at me sideways with a nervous smile.

He's sweet and cute, and he's been nice to me so far. I haven't had a boyfriend in a year. I haven't wanted one because it took a long time to move on from Alex. Only lately have I felt like it might be time to try something new.

Alex seemed to move on just fine from me. To Marcie, to Dana, to God knows who else. I tried not to imagine him with another girl, but it's hard not to when photos of him and other girls hanging out at Goose Pond show up in your Insta feed without warning.

Then one night a couple of months ago, I opened his profile and pushed the *Unfollow* button. One step forward.

Maybe it's time for me to take a tiny step forward again.

"How about a movie?" I say.

Nick leans down and softly kisses my cheek, then after a quick peek into my eyes, he pecks my lips. "Next Friday?"

"Okay." I touch my lips. The kiss felt different from other kisses I've had. Different, but still nice. Warm.

Once I'm safely inside the doorway, Nick waves goodbye to me with a big smile on his face.

As I close the front door, Dad calls out, "Lulu? Come see me, please."

I follow his voice to the den, where he's watching TV and working on his laptop. When he sees me, he shuts the computer and takes off his glasses.

"Is everything okay?" I ask.

"One of my patients told me something today, and I thought you should know. Alex's grandfather passed away last night."

"Papu?"

Dad nodded. "I heard it was a massive heart attack. They couldn't save him."

"Oh my God," I whisper. "Poor Alex. And his grandmother."

"The funeral service is tomorrow. I'm planning to drop by. Do you want to come?"

Hot tears burn my eyes. Papu and Yia Yia were always so nice to me when I was dating Alex. But we're not anymore. Alex doesn't even speak to me. What if my being there pisses him off?

"I don't know, Dad."

"Think about it and let me know, okay?"

Alex and I broke up a year ago, but I knew how much his grandfather meant to him. He adored Papu. He must've been hurting so hard, to know that he would never see his grandfather again and absolutely nothing could change that.

Papu bought Alex his first baseball glove in kindergarten. He ate breakfast one-on-one with Alex at the Waffle House at least once a month, which was a big deal for a kid with four sisters and a baby brother. Alex's life would never be the same.

I decide to go to the funeral.

The next day, my parents and I walk into the crowded funeral parlor to find Alex in his black suit, sitting with Yia Yia and comforting her as people pay their respects. Alex's mom is cradling the new baby boy against her chest as he whines. Mr. Rouvelis is shaking hands with everyone, ducking his head frequently. He keeps pushing his glasses up on his nose, as if they weigh a thousand pounds.

Ryan and Coach Rice stand in the long line of those waiting to greet Alex's family.

When I reach Alex, his eyes are bleary and red. "Hey, Lu."

Stretching up onto tiptoes, I tentatively hug him. "I'm so sorry. This sucks."

His arms tighten around me. "Thanks. I'm glad you came."

"Of course. Your papu was the best. Remember the first time I came to his house? He said, 'Alex! Is this the famous girlfriend who doesn't eat meat? She's missing out on my meatball sauce.' I should've tried it to make your papu happy."

Alex gives me a small smile.

"I drew you this," I say, passing him a note. It's been forever since I've given him one of my doodles, but once this particular vision came to mind, I couldn't stop sketching.

Alex unfolds my drawing of Papu with his bushy mustache, wearing a dark suit and holding up his pointer finger. The voice bubble reads: *Back in my day, we took the girl to dinner and then necked in the car.*

Alex bursts out laughing at the sketch, drawing gasps and stares from funeral goers.

Then he slowly begins to cry. I give him another long hug. When he pulls back, his teary brown eyes catch mine. I swallow the lump in my throat.

He returns to sit with his grandmother, wiping away his tears, he carefully slides my note into his breast pocket and pats it. He looks up, staring at me like he would an opposing team's pitcher, totally focused.

Deep down inside, his gaze jump-starts my broken heart.

I immediately tamp it back down by remembering the bad times. Like how Alex never said anything to me last fall when I won the county fair art contest, even though I congratulated him for winning the school district's athlete of the year.

Yes, I would come to the funeral to pay my respects, but I'll be damned if my heart felt any sort of hope about Alex.

———————————

During study hall a few days later, I'm sitting with Nick, who has his arm around the back of my chair. I catch Alex looking my way. He waves, and after the shock wears off, I wave back.

Nick sees this exchange and his eyebrows furrow. "What's up with that?"

"It's nothing. I went to his grandfather's funeral, and he's probably saying thanks."

"You went to your ex's grandfather's funeral? That's kind of weird."

I give Nick a look. "His grandfather was always very nice to me. I liked him a lot."

Nick squeezes my shoulder, tugging me closer. "I'm sorry to hear he died. You think Alex would mind if I said something? Gave my condolences?"

"No, he'd probably appreciate that," I reply, leaning against Nick.

After his grandfather's funeral, Alex starts nodding and smiling at me in the halls. More often than not, if I peek his way in the cafeteria or library during study hall, he'll glance away as if he hadn't been staring at me.

We don't really speak, except to say "hello" and "how are you?" I'm good with that. I wouldn't mind asking for his thoughts on the latest draft of *Here Comes the Sun*, and I could use his feedback on my query letter to potential literary agents, but being around Alex is still painful, like a lingering muscle strain that flares every time I stretch.

I ask Grace, "Does the pain ever stop?"

She looks down at her hands. "I don't know."

And then one day at school, everything changes.

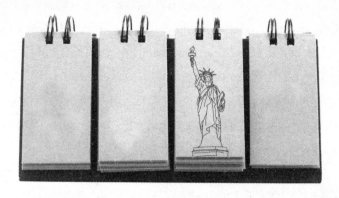

TODAY
JUNIOR CLASS TRIP

One time Mom and Dad showed me a video they took during their honeymoon to Japan.

In Tokyo, there is an intersection called Shibuya Crossing, where more than a thousand people cross the street at a time. Mom and Dad said that if you went into a coffee shop above the crossing, you could watch the massive crowds move in unison across the street. As I studied the video, I wondered if aliens were watching us from space, and if they were, did they think the people crossing Shibuya in unison were all part of one collective being?

As our group approaches Times Square, the crowds begin to overwhelm me. I start to feel insignificant. Like a tiny automaton of a collective whole. Like a bug.

People pack the sidewalks. Some walk by me, smiling, while

others rush by panicked as if they're late for an appointment. One man is muttering to himself, shaking his head. A woman stares straight ahead, looking at nothing. Another woman wearing a hijab strolls by holding hands with her young son. A bunch of people are playing with their phones or listening to headphones.

Bright billboards and screens flash with ads for Coke, the Gap, and the new George Clooney movie. Cars on the side streets honk. Street performers busk on every corner.

Why does such a bright place make me feel so dark inside? So alone?

I loop my arm through Max's to stay close to him. Some of my classmates buy *I heart New York* T-shirts from a street vendor, but Alex and Grace walk by. As town sheriff, Uncle James doesn't make much money. I imagine Grace is saving her cash for a great souvenir. Alex probably won't buy any souvenirs at all.

"I want to have my picture taken with Elmo," Max says, stopping beside a group of people dressed as Sesame Street characters. They wave their large furry arms, welcoming Max into their circle. I snap a photo.

Grace is hanging all over some buff guy dressed up as Spiderman, and I record the whole thing on my phone to post online.

Meanwhile, Alex is posing with Nintendo characters, including Mario, Luigi, and Princess Peach, while a girl from our class takes his picture.

Max nudges me. "Mr. Sanderson is going to have a stroke."

Our chemistry teacher is standing there wide-eyed, as strangers walking by jostle him. He gulps. One of the mom chaperones tugs on his shirt. "Bob, Bob! Let's keep on walking. Tell the kids it's time to go."

I decide not to take any pictures with the Times Square tourist traps, and instead, simply look around at the hundreds of people. Here, nobody knows me. Does anybody know anybody here?

How lonely.

It kind of reminds me how I feel at school sometimes. How even though I have a boyfriend and great friends, something still feels missing, like I'm not totally whole.

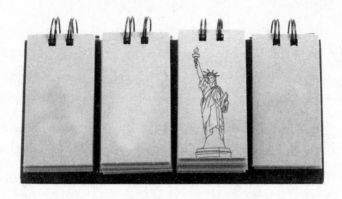

TODAY
JUNIOR CLASS TRIP

The lobby of the Museum of Modern Art is bright and airy and quiet.

With its big open windows that remind me of the Nashville airport, MOMA is a dream. After the bustling Times Square and crowded Rockefeller Center, this is more my speed.

Mr. Sanderson calls out for us to gather around him. "You all are free to explore. Stay with someone from our school at all times. Be back here in two hours. And if you're going to be late"—Mr. Sanderson stops to pointedly stare at Alex and me, causing me to blush—"Make sure to call or text me. Understand?"

Everybody nods and breaks off into groups to explore the museum. Mr. Sanderson opens up a pamphlet and walks away squinting at it.

"Do y'all mind if I find a place to sketch?" I ask Grace and Max.

"No problem," Grace says. "Text us where you are, and we'll come find you in a little while."

After wandering around for a few minutes, I find the perfect place. The exhibit I choose features nude statues of various shapes and sizes meant to show the human body in all its forms: tiny, big, wrinkly, smooth, medium, black, white, brown, tired.

I wish we had museums like this in Tennessee. This kind of inspiration would help me with my own work. I love drawing people, but my details need more specificity—more interesting elements that readers won't find in other people's work.

I take a seat on a bench in front of a statue of a middle-aged naked man lounging on the floor, resting his face on a fist. The statue is so lifelike, it shows every wrinkle, every dimple. His collarbone is pronounced, sticking out from above his chest. The man appears exhausted and overwhelmed.

I pull my tablet out of my backpack, turn it on, and open to a blank sheet. After popping a Jolly Rancher in my mouth, I begin to sketch the outline of the man. His protruding collarbone is my favorite aspect. Maybe I should give my character Ander a noticeable collarbone. It would demonstrate his strength, and also could show that he's hungry—

"Ryan's going to be sorry he missed this exhibit."

Alex has appeared above me, gazing at some of the sculptures of athletic, younger people. He then looks down at my tablet.

"Moved on to nudes, have you?" he teases me.

"You should see all the nude sketches I have of you," I fire back, joking.

Alex's jaw drops. "You drew nudes of me?"

"Of course not. But I could." I point my stylus at him. "Don't cross me, or I'll campaign against you for senior class president with a bunch of naked Alex pics. But instead of like, sexy nudes, you'll be doing stuff like mowing the lawn or flossing your teeth."

He grins. "You're running against me again?"

"It's a tradition. I don't want to let anybody down."

Plus, I've gotten to know my classmates by this point. I spend more time listening to what they want. They know I won't stop fighting for them.

And I have a secret plan this time. I giggle evilly to myself.

I pull my legs up to the side of me on the bench, getting comfy, and continue to sketch the old man statue.

Alex sits at the other end of the bench to stare at the old man. He looks so relaxed and comfortable with himself in his distressed jeans and white T-shirt, I'm tempted to sketch him instead of the statute. Seeing his toned baseball player arms gives me ideas for improving my drawings of Ander.

In silence, I sketch the man's bald head, taking care to get the shape of his ears and skull just right. Out of the corner of my eye, I see Alex stare down at his watch. Is he bored?

"Wishing you were at the Intrepid with the other guys?" I ask.

He looks up from his watch, surprised. "Not really. I'm right where I want to be."

"Alex, what are you doing?" I ask with a huff.

"Visiting a museum."

"No, I mean, why are you hanging around me?"

"We're friends, right?"

I twist my stylus pen, anxious to change the subject, even though I'm the one who started the conversation. "Where'd you get that watch anyway?"

"It was Papu's. When he died, Yia Yia gave me his watch and his old Air Force dress uniform. The watch was his father's—my great-grandfather's. It's from the 1920s."

"Wow. Can I see it?"

He holds out his wrist. The strap is brown leather, the face dark green, the hands bright gold.

"It's beautiful," I say, and begin a quick sketch of his wrist and the watch. I show it to Alex when I'm finished.

"Hey, that's pretty good," he says.

"If I don't make it as a graphic novelist, maybe I can be a watch designer," I joke. I turn my attention back to sketching the old man.

Alex and I sit in silence as I work until Max and Grace stroll into the exhibit.

Max spins in a slow circle, examining the statues. He whistles. "Oh man, the guys'll be sorry they missed this."

"That's what I said," Alex replies, as Max lifts his Nikon and snaps a picture of us.

Grace sits right between Alex and me, staring at a statue of a young male athlete. "Dayum."

Max peeks over my shoulder at my sketchpad. "Oh, Lu. Gross."

"What?"

"Of all the amazing stuff in this museum to sketch, you choose naked Prince Charles over there?"

"That is *not* naked Prince Charles," I say.

211

"If that's what you say." Max's expression turns dubious.

He pulls out his phone and swipes it on. "We still have another half an hour before we have to be back in the lobby. There's an exhibit on immigration I want to check out. C'mon, Grace."

"I'm good here," she says, totally creeping on the young athlete flexing his butt muscles.

"Grace!" Max pointedly looks at my cousin. "Let's go."

"Oh, fine."

My friends take off, looking over their shoulders at me and whispering as they leave. What conniving busybodies.

Alex leans over onto his knees and begins to laugh silently.

"What now?" I say.

"Max and Grace crack me up."

My phone buzzes with a text from Nick. He sent me a picture of the sun gleaming on the Hudson River. I grin and mischievously take a picture of the naked Prince Charles to send back.

Nick replies with the blushing face emoji and the eggplant emoji.

I giggle as I send back the screaming face emoji.

Alex watches me out of the corner of his eye, letting out a deep breath.

"What have you been working on lately?" he asks.

"I finished my third draft of *Here Comes the Sun*, and I'm putting finishing touches on some of my panels, to make them the best they can be. I'm also trying to find a literary agent now. I've queried twelve agents, but no one has responded to my emails so far."

"When did you send them out?"

"About two weeks ago."

"That's not long at all. I'm sure you'll hear back soon."

"I hope so. Most agents say that if they are interested, they'll respond within a month or two. Waiting sucks so bad."

"I know what you mean. Coach helped me apply to attend this baseball camp at Duke this summer. It's a big deal. Only like, fifty guys from the entire country are accepted."

"That sounds incredible. What kind of application did you have to do?"

"I sent in my stats from the past three years, plus a few videos."

"Did you send the one of your triple play against Franklin County?"

He beams. "You saw that?"

The Franklin County batter hit a line drive to first base. Alex caught it, tagged the first base runner out, then hurled the ball to second. The second base runner was sprinting back to tag up but didn't make it in time.

Not wanting to admit I watched the YouTube clip like, five times, I shrug. "Yeah. It was a good play. When do you find out if you get to go to this camp?"

"Any day now."

"I wish you had told me this morning. I would've thrown my change into the fountain at Rockefeller Center and made a wish for you."

His smile is radiant. "Thanks, Lu."

"So you'd be gone all summer? To North Carolina?"

"It's a six-week program. It's super expensive, but Yia Yia said she would help pay, you know, since it might help me get a scholarship."

"What about Niko's? I mean, don't you have to work this summer?"

"Stamatia's sixteen now. She said she's ready to make pizzas if it means I can go to this camp." Alex's face hardens. "And I told my father that I'll need the time off. He wasn't happy. I'm sure I'll have to spend the rest of the summer working double time trash duty. But I don't care. If I get into this camp, I'm going."

"Good for you," I say quietly. "I'm a little surprised, though. What made you stand up to him?"

Alex scrubs a hand through his hair. It's so long now, it curls around his ears. "Lately, I've been thinking about what's important."

He lifts his eyes to take in my face.

I jerk my gaze away, inhaling sharply.

For a long moment, we sit in silence before he rises to his feet. "We better get back to the lobby before Mr. Sanderson flips out on us."

I stow my tablet in my backpack, sad—and relieved—this conversation is over.

MARCH
JUNIOR YEAR

I decide to scale back my proposal for a garden.

All the studies I've read say it would take a massive garden to fully sustain a cafeteria our size. Still, even with a small garden, we could create a gardening club, or a healthy lifestyle group, but it seems like all my school cares about is sports. I want the school to care about those of us not-so-athletically-inclined kids as well.

And deep down, I admit part of me kept up the crusade as a big eff-you to Alex.

Most days at lunch, I sit near the doors to the cafeteria, holding a sign. This week it says: RESISTANCE IS FERTILE. Next week's will read: GARDENING FOREVER, HOMEWORK WHENEVER.

Everyone, including the teachers, has to navigate around me to get inside the cafeteria. Plenty of people weren't happy about it.

"Get out of my way, Garden Girl."

"Fucking weirdo."

Max plops down next to me. "Don't worry about them. They've never had an original thought in their lives." He holds out a container to me. "Grape?"

It isn't unusual for Max to join my protests, but I gasp when Alex squats beside me a few days after I attended Papu's funeral.

"How's it going?" Alex asks.

"The school board put me on the agenda for their next meeting. I'm gonna try to convince them again. I have a better plan this time."

"When's the meeting?"

I give him the date and time, figuring he's being nice, but not actually interested. It shocks the hell out of me when Alex shows up at the school board meeting.

He sits in the back with Grace and Max. Nick and Caleb had an away basketball game that night, so they weren't able to make it.

When my spot on the agenda comes up, the chairman of the board pulls his eyeglasses off and sighs. "Back again, Ms. Wells?"

"Yes, sir. First, I'd like to thank you and the board for agreeing to implement a Styrofoam-free policy in all Coffee County schools."

The chairman gives me a quick nod. I wore them down on one point at least.

"I have a petition to build the garden, signed by ninety percent of the students and nearly all of the faculty of Coffee County High. Blair's Construction has offered to do all of the digging and framing for free, and two local nurseries have agreed to donate all the seeds we need. It won't cost taxpayers a thing."

The chairman rubs his eyes. "It still doesn't solve the problem of land. There's nowhere to put a garden."

It was true. Residential developments surrounded the school property. Unless someone agreed to give up their backyard, no land was available.

"I've been thinking. The parking lot is huge. If we could give up about forty spots, I think there'd be enough room for a garden."

"Then where would those forty people park their cars?"

"Er, they could bike to school? It would be better for the environment. And we could get more busses?"

"Taxpayers would have to pay for those busses. And many of our students live way out at the edges of our county, some over twenty-five miles away. You want them to bike to school in twenty-degree weather in January? In the snow? What if they don't own a bike?"

I don't have answers to his questions. Why didn't I think of this before I came up with this idea?

"Let's take a vote," the chairman says. "All in favor of Ms. Wells's proposal to dig up the parking lot for a school garden, say aye."

Of the twelve members, one man and two women say aye. The rest vote no.

The school board votes down my request. Again.

I cover my eyes with a hand.

"Sir?"

I drop my hand to see Alex standing up from his seat in the back.

Everyone in the room turns to stare.

Alex scans all the adults, then swallows. "I play first base for

217

Coffee County. We need the school garden, so we can have healthier options for lunch."

"Thank you for playing baseball and making our town proud," the chairman says. "I'm sorry, son, but we simply don't have the land for a garden."

Alex gives me a shrug and a sad smile. I nod gratefully, happy that he even tried.

After the school board meeting ends, I walk outside into the brisk March air. Alex makes his way over to me. I tug my jacket closely around my body, and he puts his hands in the pockets of his puffy jacket.

"Thanks for doing that," I say.

"Sucks it didn't work."

We stand there staring at each other. The wind gently fluffs his hair, which has been growing out. Last time I went to Niko's for dinner and saw him through the glass kitchen wall, his hair was pushed back away from his face with a headband. He looked older, more sure of himself.

"Why'd you come?" I ask.

"I know how important this is to you."

I don't get it. Hadn't he told me to "join the goddamned real world"? The memory still makes me cringe. It still makes my eyes water.

Now he's standing up for me in front of the school board? What's changed?

"I better go," I say finally.

"Me too. See you tomorrow."

Grace gives me a ride home from the school board meeting.

218

I scroll through her iPhone to choose a song. "I can't believe Alex showed up."

She nervously raps her hands on the steering wheel. "Listen, I need to tell you something...Ryan came over the other night."

"To bone?"

"I wish you would stop saying that word, Lu. It's gross."

"You're the one boning him."

She waves a manicured hand, dismissing me. "Ryan told me something Alex said." She looks over at me with sad eyes. "Alex said he misses you."

"He's the one who stopped talking to me," I exclaim. "I tried to apologize."

"Believe me, I know. I just thought you should know what Alex said."

"Okay, thanks," I said, trying to decide how I feel about this.

Being with Nick was safe. I wasn't about to risk falling for Alex a second time, even though my heart nearly exploded out of my chest when he stood in front of the school board asking for a garden.

The next day at school, I take my garden protest poster out of my locker before lunch. On my way to the cafeteria, Max jogs up with his camera, out of breath. "Outside. Come outside."

I hustle after him down the hall, past the trophy cases to the school entrance. Max shoves the glass doors open. I follow him out into the sunlight.

Alex is standing in the middle of the front lawn with Ryan and a bunch of baseball players. The guys are using shovels to dig up the grass. Big piles of dirt dot the front lawn.

What?

They're digging up the grass!

I rush over to Alex. "What are you doing?"

He uses his T-shirt to wipe the sweat off his face. His big brown eyes find mine.

"I'm digging your garden."

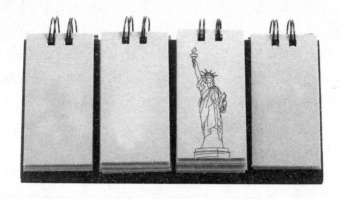

TODAY
JUNIOR CLASS TRIP

Next up, we're grabbing lunch nearby before taking the subway up thirty blocks to the Met.

Mr. Sanderson gives us permission to find someplace to eat, as long as we stay within a three-block radius of MOMA. I have some almonds and a soy protein bar in case I can't find something to eat, but I really hope we do.

Max, Grace, Alex, and I discover a pizza parlor with a brick facade. The booths are green, the floors brown tile. It smells like grease and olive oil, sort of like Niko's.

Plenty of cafes in Tennessee are decorated like this, but when you walk into a place like Davy Crockett's in Manchester, you know everybody and they know you.

This New York pizza parlor is very different. I want to know who these people are and where they came from. I imagine some are tourists, but others dressed in suits and dresses appear to be on a lunch break from a law firm or hedge fund. Other people wear plumber and electrician uniforms. I spot a few New York City cops and bus drivers too. Back in Manchester, it feels like almost everyone is white or Latino. New York is far more diverse.

A sign on the wall says: GO EVERYWHERE, TALK TO EVERYONE, EAT EVERYTHING.

We walk up to a counter, where I count ten different kinds of pizza. Two men are behind the counter taking orders and reheating slices once people have made their selections.

"Do you have vegan pizza?" Alex asks.

The worker nods. "Coming right up." He goes into the back and comes back with a single slice, which he slips into the oven to heat up.

"Yay, Alex," I say, dancing in place. "Yay, Alex. Vegan pizza. Yay, Alex."

This makes him laugh. "I remember when you used to do a celebratory dance for just about everything I did."

"Oh yeah? What was your favorite?"

"Probably that time I found a parking spot right in front of the school, so you did a cheer for me. Or wait, what about the time Mom gave me that black Polo hoodie I had been wanting? You did a dance for that too."

"If you get into your baseball camp, I'll do a dance."

"Now I really can't wait." Alex's infectious grin makes me giddy.

Max clears his throat behind me. "Lu, your food is ready."

The worker passes me a slice of pizza on a super flimsy plate.

Grease seeps through the paper onto my hand as I make my way over to the register to pay.

Once we all have pizza, the four of us sit in a cushy booth.

With one hand, Max holds his slice of cheese. With the other, he is snapping pictures of us on his phone.

We're digging into our pizza when Max's phone dings. "Aw, Caleb sent a picture from down by the Hudson." He flips his phone around to show a photo of Caleb and Nick in front of the Intrepid aircraft carrier, squinting in the sunlight.

The caption reads: *We miss you!!*

I smile at the screen. My boyfriend is very cute.

But he hasn't texted since he sent the blushing emoji and eggplant emoji, which was at least an hour ago. This worries me. But come to think of it, I haven't texted him either. Under the table, I type a text to Nick with a kissy face emoji, to make sure he knows I'm thinking of him.

I bite my bottom lip, feeling guilty about spending time with Alex. And for enjoying it.

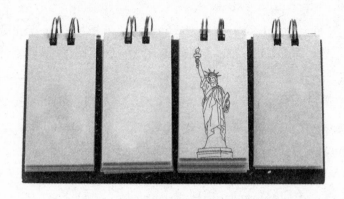

TODAY
JUNIOR CLASS TRIP

We ride the subway up to the Met.

On the way, my phone buzzes. The notification bar reads: RE:
Young adult graphic novel query.

With a shaking hand, I swipe my phone screen on and open
the email, holding my breath. It's a response from Jessica Hollis at
Writers Incorporated, one of my top choices for a literary agent.
Over the years, she's sold several of my favorite graphic novels. My
eyes scan down to the message.

Dear Ms. Wells: Thank you for your query. Unfortunately,
your work does not seem like the right fit for my list.
I wish you all the best in your publishing endeavors. —JH

A hot wave rushes up my body and settles in my stomach. It feels like someone placed a searing brick on my chest.

She rejected me.

She rejected me with a form letter.

I mean, I know everyone faces rejection at some point—plenty of people turned down even J.K. Rowling herself—but my body feels deflated. And did it have to happen while I was here in New York?

What if this is only the first rejection? What if I'm not good enough? When we leave the subway, I walk behind the rest of the class in case I start to lose it. My stomach hurts.

Mr. Sanderson leads the group up to the stairs to the Met. We all take a seat on the steps to listen to his lecture. Max sits in front of me, and I lean against him, resting my chin on his shoulder. Tears make my eyes go blurry.

"It's two o'clock now," Mr. Sanderson says. "You have until five o'clock to enjoy the museum. Stay with a partner at all times. No horsing around, got it?"

Grace, Max, and Alex stand and begin to head inside.

"Guys," I say. "I'm going to call Nick real quick. I'll come find you." They nod, and I swipe my phone on.

My boyfriend picks up on the second ring. "Hi. How's your day so far?"

I pull my knees to my chest to wrap an arm around my shins. "Not the best. I got a rejection letter from an agent."

"Oh, that sucks, babe. You'll be fine, though. Your book is great."

That's all Nick ever says about it. That it's great. I wish he'd criticize it, or at least tell me which parts he likes more than others.

"Besides that, how are you enjoying New York?" he asks.

"It's good. I had pizza for lunch, and now I'm about to go to the Met."

"I had a hot dog from a street cart. It was better than one of my dad's cooked over a campfire." I cringe about the poor pig who had to die for that hot dog. "We're on our way to the Yankees game. Listen, I know you're upset about the agent, but try to enjoy today. You can query more agents."

"Thanks."

"Hey, um, Caleb showed me a picture Max sent of y'all at lunch. You were with Alex?"

I cringe, not realizing Max had sent pictures.

"Yeah," I say, taking a deep breath. "We all wanted some pizza. It was no big deal."

"I didn't realize you guys were hanging out again."

I decide to be honest. It's not like I'd do anything with Alex, and I really don't want to hurt Nick. "We were at MOMA together and had lunch after. That's it."

Nick pauses for a long moment. "Oh. We'll see each other tonight, right?"

"Yeah, at the park." I smile into the phone. "Can't wait."

We hang up, and I walk inside the museum to find my friends waiting for me in the lobby.

Grace hurries to my side. "What's wrong, Lu?"

"I'm okay."

"No, you're not," Max says. "What's going on?"

I swipe my phone on and open the email with the rejection, showing it to my friends. They all agree it sucks big time.

"And on top of that," I say, "Cady James Morrison is doing a signing downtown today, and I'm missing it."

"Oh wow, she's your favorite," Alex interjects.

Alex remembers my favorite childhood author? That gives me a warm feeling inside.

"Yeah, she is. But I'm also interested in Cady's career. There's a question and answer section at the signing, and I wish I could ask how she got started. How long did she have to wait to get published? Does she have any advice for aspiring authors?"

"Where's the signing?" Alex asks. "Maybe a teacher might let you leave the Met for a few minutes."

"It's at a bookstore down near Union Square, which is a long way from here. Like seventy blocks."

His mouth forms an *O*.

He glances around. Looks down at his grandfather's watch. "We have three hours to spend here."

"Yeah, and it doesn't seem like enough." I gaze up at the expansive ceiling. "You could spend weeks in this museum."

"No, you're misunderstanding me. This place is huge. Who's gonna know we're not here? Let's sneak out and go to the book signing."

My mouth falls open. "You want to leave?"

He nods encouragingly.

Grace is wide-eyed. "What if y'all get caught?"

"We'll get kicked off the senior year trip next year," I say.

"I've heard they're thinking of Paris or Rome," Max says.

Alex turns to me. "It's worth it, right? What if you learn something at this signing that helps you find an agent?"

I've always wanted to go overseas, but right now, this book

signing is more important for me. "You don't need to go, Alex. Grace can come with me."

She stares down at her strappy wedge sandals. "I'm getting a blister. There's no way I could walk fast enough."

"Or I could go," Max says, but he shuffles from one foot to the other. He looks down at his phone and with a small voice says, "But I wouldn't know how to get around or anything. Um..."

Alex shakes his head. "I'm going."

Coach Rice didn't allow Alex to play in the last game of the season—a game in front of college scouts—because we were half an hour late at Six Flags. I can't even imagine the amount of trouble Alex would be in if he ran off in New York City. What if Coach didn't let him play the rest of the season? Or part of next year's? Alex would be risking everything for me.

"I can't let you do this," I tell him.

His eyes bore into mine. "It's my decision. I'm going to the bookstore whether you go or not."

My body is shaking like I'm about to ride a roller coaster. But the idea of meeting my favorite author outweighs all the risks. "Okay," I say before I lose my nerve. "Okay, let's go."

Max gapes at me. "Holy shit, you rebel."

Alex checks his watch again. "We need to go now if we want to make it back in time."

Grace says, "Max and I'll cover for you with Mr. Sanderson. But, please be careful? Text me when you're there."

"When anyone asks where you are, I'll say you're using the bathroom because of the pizza from the diner," Max says dramatically as Alex cracks up.

"You're both disgusting," I say. What is it with boys and bathroom humor anyway?

"And if Nick asks what you did this afternoon?" Grace says under her breath.

I swallow hard as Alex takes off his ball cap and scrubs a hand through his long hair.

"I'll tell Nick myself," I say. "This book signing is important to me."

After giving Max and Grace quick hugs, Alex and I sneak out the entrance. He swipes on his phone and begins googling the best way to get to Union Square. "This way," he says. "We need to find the subway. Line number four."

Alex begins to jog down the street, dodging people. I follow on his heels. At the subway, we add more money to our passes and jog to the train platform just in time to see a train pulling away.

"Shit," I say, peering down the dark tunnel searching for train headlights. "How long do you think we'll have to wait?"

Alex looks around at the platform, which is steadily filling up with people. "Probably not long."

I bounce on my tiptoes, trying to stay calm. I'm about to go to my first-ever book signing. I might get to meet Cady James Morrison.

Yay, yay, yay! Oh…hell.

If the chaperones find out we left the Met, the school will send us home and definitely won't let us go on next year's trip. Which wouldn't be the end of the world for me.

But what if Coach Rice kicks Alex off the team? The horrible memory of Alex yelling at me at Six Flags pops into my mind. *Join the goddamned real world already.*

Blood rushes to my head. I cover my eyes and sway to the side. "Oh God, what are we doing?"

"Whoa, whoa," Alex says, putting an arm around me, to hold me up. "You're all right."

"I don't want to get you in trouble again. What if we get caught and Coach Rice won't let you play? It's important. For your future. What if you get into the Duke baseball camp but aren't allowed to go? We're going back to the Met."

As I turn to leave the subway, Alex reaches out to take my elbow.

"Going to this book signing is important for your future too, Lu," he says quietly. "We're doing this."

Bright headlights flash through the tunnel as our train roars into the station.

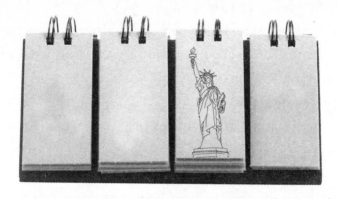

TODAY
JUNIOR CLASS TRIP

We jog up the subway steps into Union Square.

My first impression is that it's very green and not as busy as Times Square. There are lots of shops and restaurants. Groups of people lounge on benches in a park that runs through the center of the square. A street performer plays the guitar. This is the New York I always pictured in my mind.

Alex scrolls through the map on his phone. "This way."

We run down the street, dodging people, our backpacks banging against our backs. At Fifth Avenue, Alex puts an arm out in front of my stomach, stopping me from crossing the street. We're forced to wait many long seconds for traffic to stop. I glare at the

DON'T WALK sign, begging it to change. It turns to WALK, and Alex and I begin to sprint again.

We make it to the bookstore with two minutes to spare. Outside the entrance, I take a moment to dab the sweat off my forehead and smooth down my hair.

"How do I look?" I ask.

Alex scans my face and black tunic dress. "Like a gorgeous mess."

I playfully smack his shoulder.

Elementary school kids and their parents crowd the bookstore. Every seat is filled and kids sit cross-legged in the aisles. Alex and I find a place to stand near the back. The store is so packed, I have to lean against him to stay upright. My face is right next to his tanned bicep, which impressively stretches his white T-shirt.

A bookstore worker wearing a badge and vest comes out onto a dais where a table and microphone are set up. "If you could all please silence your cell phones and lower your voices." The noise falls to hushed, excited whispers.

"I'd like to introduce the author of over thirty books—your favorite mystery author, Cady James Morrison!"

She walks out to massive applause. Cady looks a lot like the photo at the back of her book, only a bit older. Long brown hair, square glasses, fashionable scarf. She's wearing a T-shirt that says *Muggle*.

"I wish I were her," I whisper to Alex. "She's so cool."

Cady talks for about five minutes, giving us an overview of her latest book about a girl on an archaeological dig who discovers a new type of dinosaur fossil, but bad guys conspire to take the credit for her find.

"Dicks," I murmur to Alex, who stifles a laugh.

Next, Cady answers questions from the crowd. She is lovely and gracious the entire time, even when people ask questions they could learn the answers to by reading the latest novel in the series.

Nobody asks her questions about her career or writing craft, though, and even though I keep raising my hand, the moderator hasn't pointed at me yet. I know she sees me waving my hand back here, but she keeps calling on the little kids. She probably thinks I'm too old for this event. This is like how people discriminate against teenagers who trick or treat on Halloween.

"This is absurd," I whisper to Alex. "No one's even asked her what's her Hogwarts house."

"It's obvious she's a Gryffindor," Alex whispers back. "Like you."

His words take my breath away. This boy knows me so well. I place a hand over my heart, trying to still it.

"We have time for one more question," the bookstore worker says, and proceeds to call on a girl from the front row.

"Shit," I say, and two small boys turn around to gape at my language.

Alex purses his lips to keep from laughing.

By the time she's ready to sign books, Alex and I only have an hour and fifteen minutes to get back to the Met.

"If everyone could calmly form a line in front of me," the worker says.

"I'll go buy you a book so that she can sign it," Alex says.

"Let me give you some money," I say, reaching into my purse.

"Pay me back later. Hurry, get in line!"

Everyone rushes toward the worker managing the crowd. Secretly I consider bowling these kids over and sprinting to the front, but in reality, I speed walk over and get up on tiptoes to see how many people are in front of me. About twenty people.

"Shit," I say again.

This time a perturbed mother shoots daggers at me.

Cady James Morrison is taking time to chat with everybody, which is good news for me in that she might be willing to answer some questions, but bad news because we're running out of time. Some kids are carrying tote bags full of her books, and she's willing to sign each and every one of them.

Alex hurries over with a copy of her first book, *The Atlantis Clues*, which he hands to me.

I run my fingers over the embossed cover. "I read this book a hundred times when I was little."

"We're the oldest people in the line. I should've asked for a senior citizens' discount."

"Hush."

I keep checking the time on my phone. The line slowly inches forward. A bunch of kids want their picture taken with her, which takes even longer.

By the time I near the front of the line, we only have forty minutes left to get back to the Met, and I can't stand still.

The kid in front of me pulls out like twenty copies of her books. Some appear to be foreign language editions. Is that Russian?

"Oh my God, you've got to be kidding me," I mutter to Alex, who had been acting carefree about ditching the field trip, but is now glancing at his watch every two seconds.

It takes Cady James Morrison ten minutes to sign the boy's books with a shiny purple sharpie and snap a picture with him.

We only have thirty minutes left to return uptown. My armpits and forehead are damp.

"You're next," the bookstore worker says to us.

Alex and I approach her table, and I hold out my book with shaking hands.

"I have all of your books at home, but I couldn't bring them because I'm on a school trip," I ramble.

She smiles up at me, taking the book and opening it to the title page. "Thank you. What's your name?"

"Lulu."

"Oh, I love that name," she says. "I might have to use it in a book, if that's okay."

"That would be the best thing ever. You're my favorite author."

"Thank you, sweetie." She autographs the book with her purple sharpie. "I love your accent. Where are you from?"

"Tennessee."

I feel faint. Alex puts a steadying hand on my back, for which I'm grateful.

"I'm glad you stopped by my signing during your trip," she says.

"I've never been to a signing before. It was great."

"Maybe my publisher will send me to Tennessee one day. We'll see!"

Alex nudges me. "Didn't you have a question, Lu?"

My voice cracks. "Is it okay if I ask you a question?"

"Shoot."

"Do you have any advice for aspiring writers?"

She puts the cap back on her purple sharpie. "I guess I would say, if you want to write, read, read, read. Read everything you can get your hands on. And don't ever give up."

"Like, even if you get a bunch of rejections?"

"Especially then." She adjusts her glasses. "The first book I wrote went out to over fifty editors, and everyone rejected it. For *The Atlantis Clues*, over twenty editors rejected it, but one made an offer. It only takes one."

"It only takes one," I repeat.

"Write the book you want to read, Lulu, and I guarantee someone else will want to read it too. You just have to get it into the right hands."

In a way, maybe her advice goes beyond books.

Be the person you want to be, and everything else will fall into place.

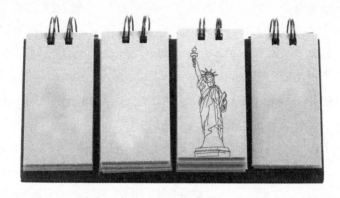

TODAY
JUNIOR CLASS TRIP

Alex and I wait impatiently for the subway to take us back uptown.

We're supposed to be back in the Met lobby in fifteen minutes and we're seventy blocks away. We might as well be at the North Pole.

"Maybe we should get out and take a cab," I say, bouncing on my toes.

Alex scrolls on his phone. "Looks like that would take longer. We can't risk getting stuck in traffic. I think this is our best bet."

Based on the trip downtown, going back will take at least ten minutes. Then we'll need to sprint to the Met.

I text Max.

Me: Emergency, emergency! We're going to be late. Can you stall?
Max: On it.

The floor begins to shake and subway headlights finally appear. "Oh thank you sweet Jesus," I say as the train slows to a stop.

We rush aboard, snagging two open seats in the middle of the car. I place my backpack on the floor between my legs.

Now that I'm on the subway and the car is moving, I relax a little. "That was the best thing that's ever happened," I squeal to Alex. "Thank you for taking me."

He smiles at me sideways. "You're welcome."

The guy to my right is manspreading, taking up part of my seat, so I scooch closer to Alex. Our thighs touch. The subway is mostly quiet, except for the car rocking through the tunnel.

"Can I ask you something?" Alex says under his breath.

My back stiffens. I grip my knees. "Uh, sure."

"Does Grace say much about Ryan?"

"Yeah, I mean, she's worried about him since his mom moved... part of her thinks he should go be with her in Florida, but none of us want him to leave. I heard he's living with his grandparents for now?"

"Yeah." Alex is silent for a minute. "But does Grace say anything about *them*? You know, together?"

"You mean, other than the fact they bone all the time, even though they pretend they barely know each other in public?"

"Yeah, besides that."

"What exactly are you asking?"

Alex musses his dark hair. "He wants to go out with her. He wants her to come to prom with him."

A vision of my cousin with Ryan at prom fills my head. Their prom photos would look so cute, with her sweet smile and glamorous looks, and his red hair, freckles, and sexy grin.

"She's not planning to go to prom," I tell Alex.

"What about a date, then?"

"I don't think she wants anything serious, you know? She thinks Ryan is cute and likes hanging out with him, but he's kind of wild…"

"He is that," Alex agrees. "But I think he'd be serious about Grace, if she wants to be serious about him."

I adjust my purse strap nervously. "We should let them figure this out."

"We could help them."

I give him a look. "Would you want anyone helping you with a relationship? Butting in trying to meddle or fix things?"

"Oh. Yeah, I get it." The subway slows to a stop at the Fifty-Ninth Street station. "Except…didn't Caleb set you up with Nick?"

"You know about that?"

He shrugs. "I heard about it from Ryan, who heard from Grace."

People exit the train and more climb onboard, passing by us. "Caleb set me up on a date with Nick, yeah. But introducing two people is different from meddling in an already complicated relationship."

He clears his throat. "You and Nick seem pretty close."

"I like him," I hedge, as the train begins to move again. "But it's not totally serious yet."

Alex swivels his head to look at me. "You, uh, you haven't—?"

Whether or not I've slept with Nick is none of his business. But I've always told him the truth. I shake my head in response.

Alex's eyes pop open wide. He turns to look out of the speeding train at the dark tunnel.

"Me neither," he says quietly.

I let out a deep sigh. Considering how popular and cute he is, and given that he's dated at least three girls since our relationship, I figured he was screwing around with whomever he wanted. Especially since he had been so interested in sleeping with me.

"That's, um, surprising," I say carefully, which makes him chuckle.

"It hasn't felt right. Not like, you know…"

I find his brown eyes. "For me either."

What if the reason I can't get comfortable fooling around with Nick isn't the actual fooling around part? What if it's my partner? But how does that make sense? Nick is cute and sweet. I like kissing him. Shouldn't attraction be enough to trigger the passion I need so bad?

"Do you love Nick?" Alex asks.

I inhale sharply, keeping my eyes fixed on a subway ad for cheap flights to Paris. "I don't know yet."

"You don't?"

"I mean, I'm not saying I couldn't, but I don't. Not yet, I mean." I scrape my hair behind my ears. "Those words aren't something I say just whenever."

He blows air out of his mouth. "I'm sorry, Lu. For everything I said that night. You know, at Six Flags?"

"I'm sorry too. About causing you to miss your baseball game, and saying it was no big deal you wouldn't get to play. I know how important it is to you."

He waves a hand. "It's important, yeah, but I lost something that night that was a whole hell of a lot more important than baseball. I lost the girl who loved me."

I clench my eyes shut. "You didn't love me back."

"I was a stupid dick who didn't understand what was important in life. And now, lately, I've been starting to understand what's
more important than anything."

I spring out of my seat, grabbing a subway pole to hold on
tight. The train rocks back and forth. This is too much.

Slowly, he stands beside me as the train pulls into the 86th
Street station, brakes squeaking as we come to a stop.

"This is us," I say, and we exit the train.

Alex quickly checks the time. "We need to jet. You okay to jog?"

I run. "Go, go, go!"

We speed up the stairs out of the subway station and sprint down
the sidewalk toward the Met. I lose my breath, and I'm panting and
huffing. Blisters sting my heels where my sneakers rub against raw
skin. Max texts me, warning us to come in on the right side of the
lobby, because he'll distract Mr. Sanderson on the other side.

Alex leads me up the steps of the museum. I welcome the blast
of cool air-conditioning as we hustle to the lobby, sidling up to the
rest of our group at 5:03.

Three minutes late.

Everybody is staring at us, some giving us knowing looks,
while others roll their eyes. Given our disheveled appearance, who
knows what they think we've been doing.

Our chemistry teacher appears in front of us with his trusty
clipboard. "Are you two okay?" Mr. Sanderson examines my
sweaty face and leans over to whisper, "Max told me you ate some
questionable pizza."

I am going to kill Max.

"It wasn't Niko's pizza, that's for sure," Alex says in a snooty voice.

241

I bite down on my lips to control my laughter.

"I love Niko's," Mr. Sanderson says wistfully.

"Next time you're there, I'll make you my special bruschetta," Alex says, patting the teacher's back, and Mr. Sanderson's eyes light up.

Mr. Sanderson walks away to lead the front of our group.

Alex turns to me. "We did it. I can't believe we got away with that." He pulls me into a hug and lifts me off the ground, swinging me around. The hug feels warm and familiar and not at all tingly in a bad way. It does things to my body I haven't felt in a year. Things I shouldn't be thinking about.

I push against his chest, to get him to let me go. "Alex, stop. I can't."

Alex immediately lets go of me and steps back, his face falling. "I'm sorry. I was excited, is all."

With trembling hands, I straighten my dress. "Thanks again for taking me." I clear my throat, then move to stand with Max and Grace, who both want to know how it went. I show them my signed copy of *The Atlantis Clues* and tell them about Cady's advice.

Max studies Cady's signature and her note that says, *Tell your story, Lulu!*

"Seems like it was totally worth the risk to ditch the Met," Max says, touching the autograph.

Grace's phone beeps; she swipes it on. "Ryan says I need to look at Instagram." Her thumb slides over the screen. "Uh, Lulu, you gotta see this."

She shows me Marcie's Insta story featuring Alex sweeping me into his arms. The video has been edited to be in black and white slow-mo, as if we're in some sort of old timey movie.

Alex hugged me less than two minutes ago.

242

"Ugh, Marcie's not even with us today," I say. "How'd she get this video?"

Grace peers around at our classmates, many of whom are chatting and glancing our way. "Someone here must've sent it to her. She must still be mad that Alex dumped her."

Two seconds later my phone pings with a text from Nick. I saw the video.

Me: It was a hug, nothing more. I told him to let me go.

Him: Is he bothering you?

Me: No. It was no big deal.

Him: Okay, if you say so. But it didn't look that way.

I turn off my phone screen and stare at the pavement, finding it difficult to breathe. I feel awful. Nick must be totally pissed.

"Okay, everyone," Mr. Sanderson calls. "We're heading over to Central Park now. Stay together."

Our group begins to walk, but I fall behind, my thoughts and feelings a jumbled tumbleweed.

Alex slows to wait for me. "Ryan sent me a text about that video of us. He said it was some Oscar-worthy shit."

Alex thinks this is funny? "I can't believe this."

"It's all good."

"Nick doesn't think so."

Alex adjusts his backpack. "I'm sorry, Lu. I shouldn't have hugged you like that...I couldn't help it." He places a hand on my arm, stopping me on the sidewalk. "I know you have a boyfriend, but I wanted you to know I'm here. I can wait."

A bus driving down the street lays on its brakes, screeching. "That's not fair, and you know it, to put that kind of pressure on me."

"I wanted to tell you the truth," he says.

"Alex, I told you I loved you. You didn't talk to me for months and months, and now you show up and want me to take you back?"

A taxi cab honks loudly.

"I was a dick. I know it. I was stupid, and I've grown up a lot since then."

"I know you have," I say quietly, thinking of how he stood up for me in front of the school board. And dug up the school's front lawn for me, which landed him, Ryan, and the baseball team with detention. Not to mention, they had to fill all the holes back in with dirt.

He put me first.

"It was hard for me to move on from you," I say as busy strangers sidestep around us. "In some ways, I'm still not over you. I don't know if I ever will be. But you were so mean to me after Six Flags, Alex. And you didn't listen to what I had to say before we broke up. When we were together, you never had time for me."

"I've changed. I can show you."

"You already have," I cry, covering my face with my hands. He reaches out to touch my shoulder, and I pull away from him. "But this is all overwhelming, and I need to go."

Alex's expression falls again. "Lulu—"

"I'm not doing this, okay?"

I jog up through the other students to walk with my friends, trying to remember how to breathe.

Alex shattered everything with one hug and a few words.

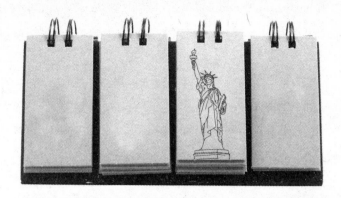

TODAY
JUNIOR CLASS TRIP

Once we reach Central Park and aren't so closely surrounded by our classmates, Max, Grace, and I sit down to talk beside the Bethesda Fountain.

Max pulls out his phone to check it. "Caleb says Nick is upset."

"Is he mad?" I ask softly.

Max shrugs. "More like, sad."

The thought of seeing Nick sends shivers up my spine. He's going to be pissed.

Nick has been so good to me since we started dating. He calls when he says he will. He takes me out on weekend nights to do all sorts of things. Even like, bowling. He never leaves me hanging.

"Alex wants me back."

Grace squeals. "I knew it."

"What are you going to do?" Max asks.

"I have a boyfriend."

"That's not an answer," Max says gently. "Do you still love Alex?"

I pull my knees to my chest, wrapping my arms around them. "I always will, I think. But it doesn't matter. When I was with him before, it hurt too much. It sucked. I don't want to feel that way again."

Grace and Max give each other a look. She gestures at him, and with a roll of his eyes, he shrugs as if saying, *Fine, if I must.*

"You're scared," Max says. "Like Alex was when you said you loved him."

I rest my forehead on my knees. Isn't being scared better than my heart breaking into a billion pieces again? Better than crying myself to sleep at night?

I mean, I have my friends, family, working on my book, my political causes...I don't want an all-encompassing love that takes over my whole life. I need a relationship that fits into it just right.

As the sun begins to set into a red-orange haze, the rest of our class joins us in the park to explore an art installation featuring flags fluttering colorfully in the wind. My fingers itch to draw the reds, blues, greens, and yellows waving like ribbons. Once night falls, we will watch a light show.

Max and Caleb meet with a quick kiss.

Normally when Nick greets me, he kisses my cheek or lips. This time he gives me a side hug, staring ahead at the dark purple flags, not meeting my eyes. Oh shit. Max was right: Nick is sad.

Alex reunites with Ryan and his baseball team. A few of

the guys bought Yankees caps, and Alex is playfully shouting, "Traitors!" at them.

Coach Rice turns on his bullhorn. "The light show starts in half an hour. You can grab some dinner from a street vendor or a café, but don't go farther than three blocks, understand?"

Ryan appears next to Grace, and plays with a lock of her hair, then whispers in her ear.

She nods up at him. "We're gonna take a walk and see what we find to eat."

I raise my eyebrows at her. Something tells me they have different plans in mind for dinner.

"I want another hot dog," Nick says, and I'm tempted to discuss my hatred of hot dogs, but I'm already in enough trouble with my boyfriend.

"I'll meet you back here?" I say, and he walks off, sliding his hands in his pockets without another word. I let out a deep breath, relieved that Nick hasn't blown up at me.

Glad for a moment to myself, I find a pretzel vendor whose cart is parked beneath a tree. I order a plain pretzel, and as I'm waiting, a voice says, "Make that two please."

I turn to find Caleb Hernandez. Ever the gentleman, he insists on paying for both of our pretzels.

"Thank you," I tell Caleb, taking mine from the vendor's hands.

I bite into the hot, salty pretzel and groan. "I'm going to marry this pretzel."

Caleb laughs, but it doesn't reach his eyes.

"You doing okay?" I ask, licking grease off my thumb.

He rips into his pretzel, taking a big bite. "What's going on with you, Lulu? Are you cheating on Nick?"

I choke on my pretzel, coughing. "No, I would never."

"Max told me you spent a lot of the day with Alex."

"As friends, nothing more."

Caleb chews another bite. "You hurt Nick. I don't introduce my friends to just anyone. I thought you and Nick would be good together, though."

"We are."

"Then why are you hanging out with your ex?"

It's hard to explain. I have a connection with Alex. Always will. "He's my friend, okay?"

Caleb stops chewing. His jaw hardens. Then I see why: Alex is standing behind me, appearing sheepish.

"I'm sorry if I messed things up for you, Lu." He leans down, whispering where only I can hear. "All I want is for you to be happy. Whatever that means, okay? You deserve it."

I breathe in sharply, inhaling his scent and all the memories between us. Why wasn't he like this when we were dating? Is it for real, or an act? My pulse pounds beneath my skin, saying: *You know it's real.*

As Alex walks away, he passes Nick, stopping to say something to him before moving on. I watch Alex's black backpack disappear into the crowd.

Nick and Max, with hot dogs in hand, join us then.

"What did Alex say to you?" Caleb asks Nick.

My boyfriend doesn't respond for several seconds. "He said not to be mad at Lulu 'cause the video was his fault."

"It was," Max agrees. "Now can we eat? My hot dog is getting cold."

"Let's sit over there," Nick says, choosing a spot away from our group. The sky is now a harsh purple and dusty haze, streaked with ashy clouds.

Nick and I sit on the grass and tell each other about our days. It seems like an evening in Central Park would normally be incredibly romantic. Tonight, though, a tense undercurrent runs between us. Every time we touch, I hold my breath. I feel terrible for embarrassing him in front of our class and hurting his feelings.

Will he want to talk more about the Insta video? Or will he let it go?

Later, as the light show begins, Nick leans over, pressing his lips to mine. "I'm sorry I was mad earlier."

Only Nick would apologize for getting upset about something he has every right to be mad about.

"I'm sorry about the video," I say, trying to forget how Caleb asked if I was cheating. "It was embarrassing for both of us."

Nick smiles, brushing a lock of my hair behind an ear. "We were bound to have our first argument sometime, right?"

He kisses me again, and I kiss him back, enjoying how good he is at it, but waiting for the spark. Waiting for anything. All I feel is warm softness, but no electricity.

My cousin's wrong. I'm not scared. *I'm terrified*.

I felt more in that one hug with Alex than any kiss from Nick. It felt smoldering and comfortable.

Comfortable like your most cozy clothes fitting exactly right.

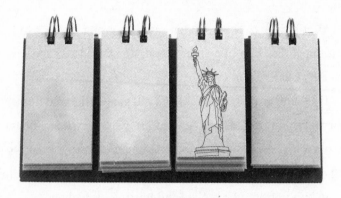

TODAY
JUNIOR CLASS TRIP

Back at the hotel, the chaperones give us permission to stay in the lobby and pool area until midnight. They won't be taping our doors because "they trust us to act like adults."

In reality, last night's tape trick didn't work.

Not only did the bellboy make a shitload of cash by retaping the doors of half our class, several kids told Coach Rice they had to leave their rooms to buy water from the vending machine. What was Coach supposed to say? Hydration is not allowed? Drink the Jersey tap water?

Tonight, everyone is planning to head down to the indoor pool and hot tub.

Grace and I put on our bathing suits, then meet up with Max to ride the elevator to the lobby. "Alex told me Ryan wants to ask you to prom," I tell her.

She grins to herself. "I might say yes."

"Realllly?" Max asks. "Did he hypnotize you?"

Grace gives us a smug look. "He does love to go down."

"Ugh, nobody wants to hear about that," I say.

"Speak for yourself," Max replies.

I playfully push Max out of the way. "For real, what made you change your mind?"

She adjusts her bikini top strap. "I don't know. I guess it's getting harder to stay away from him, when being with him is so easy."

"You think being with Ryan McDowell is easy?" I exclaim. "The first thing that boy does every morning is take a shirtless mirror selfie and post it online."

"He's good to me...and I don't mind the selfies so much."

"I don't either," Max replies. "I declare that the shirtless selfies may continue."

"Gross, y'all."

The hotel pool area reminds me of one of our high school dances, only everyone is in bathing suits. Someone set up wireless speakers, which blare a pop song I hear about a zillion times a day. Everyone is here. Everyone but Alex.

Nick takes my hand and leads me into the hot tub. We cuddle on the steps. His hands caress my waist and legs. I feel that ticklish feeling, the need to pull away, a need to protect myself. It doesn't make sense, because I feel safe with Nick—he won't hurt me, but his hands don't feel good either.

I glance over at Caleb and Max. They're sitting comfortably together on a pool chair, almost as if they're one person. When Grace joins Ryan, they can't keep their hands off each other.

All I can think about is keeping Nick's hands off my bare waist. I hate that weird tingly feeling.

What am I doing here? I wanted to protect my heart from getting hurt again, but everything feels gray, like an overcast beach without sunshine. With Alex, our very first kiss was fireworks on the Fourth of July. With Nick, I'm still waiting. Will I have to wait forever?

And if things don't work out with Nick and I move on to someone else, will those kisses feel wrong too?

What is the point in dating someone you're not deeply attracted to? Dating someone you're truly into is scary—like jumping off a cliff without knowing how deep the water is. You face a greater risk of having your heart broken. But when it's right, it's right.

As I'm sitting in the hot tub with Nick, and not feeling it at all, the risks of love seem to far outweigh the uncomfortable tingles. The aversion. That ticklish feeling that's been trying to tell me all along that Nick is a good friend and nothing more.

"Nick," I whisper. "We need to talk."

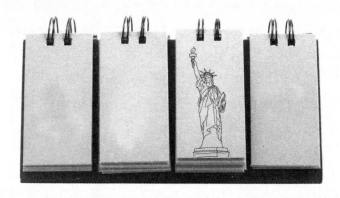

TODAY
JUNIOR CLASS TRIP

Once we're in Nick's hotel room, he runs a hand through his hair.

I sit down on the bed with him. "I'm so, so sorry. You're a great guy and I enjoy being with you—"

His voice cracks. "You're breaking up with me?"

My heart pounds like a loud drum. "I think we're better off as friends."

Nick leans over and places his head in his hands. "This is about Alex, right?"

I grip the bedspread, bunching it in my fists, carefully choosing my words. "I'd be lying if I said no. But it's more than that. You deserve to be with someone who can't keep her hands off you. I like you, but—"

"You like Alex more?"

Hot tears fill my eyes. Nick is such a nice guy. Am I doing the right thing? "It's not about Alex, I promise. You deserve to be with someone who can love you."

He drops his hands from his eyes, surprised.

I bite down on my lip. "This doesn't feel right to me. I'm so sorry."

"This sucks," he mutters. "This really sucks."

"I didn't cheat on you, I swear." My words come out as a cry.

He gently lays his hand on top of mine. "I know, Lulu. You're a great girl. I appreciate you telling me the truth." He squeezes my hand, his voice cracking. "I'm sorry I'm not the right guy for you."

"Me too."

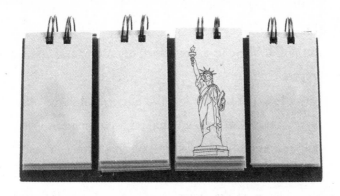

TODAY
JUNIOR CLASS TRIP

I return to my hotel room, eyes burning with tears and shame.

Caleb's never going to forgive me for hurting his friend. What if it affects his relationship with Max? What if Max is mad at me too? Nick was so understanding about this, it almost would've been easier if he'd yelled and ranted. Maybe that means I didn't break his heart. A broken heart is the worst. How could I do that to someone, after it had been done to me?

I let out a sob.

I send Grace a text: Can we talk?

After a minute of waiting for a response and receiving none, I decide to go look for her. But first, I wipe my eyes using tissues from the bathroom.

My phone beeps. A text from Nick. No hard feelings, okay?

Me: You shouldn't be so nice to me.

Nick: But we're friends, right?

Me: Always.

I turn off my phone screen, leave my room, and climb aboard the elevator.

A lot of my classmates left the pool, so now it's only stragglers. Grace and Ryan are cuddling on a pool chair together, her black hair and his red weaving together like flames. They smile as they talk. She playfully slaps his wrist after he says something that's most likely inappropriate. Then they join their hands again, intertwining their fingers. He kisses her knuckles.

I watch them, wondering why they haven't made it official when it's so clear they belong together. Maybe she's ready to stop pushing him away.

Which is what Alex has been doing: trying to fix things between us. To fit into my life, to better consider my wants and feelings.

Ever since we first met, we've had very little in common. Except the spark. Now I know what matters is the spark. The spark and the mutual respect. Maybe we didn't have that in the past, but we do now.

"Where's Alex?" I ask Ryan, startling him. He shifts his weight on the beach chair he's sharing with Grace.

"In our room. Number 568."

"Thanks," I say, then spin on my heels.

"Wait, what's going on?" Ryan calls out behind me.

"Oh my God," Grace squeaks.

But I don't stop for them.

I hop on the elevator, then rapidly push the button for the fifth floor, slapping it several times. *C'mon, c'mon, go up already.*

The elevator opens.

My feet take off running.

I dart past a clock chiming midnight.

Without hesitation I knock on the door to room 568.

Inside, a loud TV goes silent. Footsteps pad across the floor. The door swings open to reveal a barefoot Alex in a pair of track pants and a white T-shirt. He pulled his long hair back into a half ponytail. I swallow hard.

When he sees me, his eyebrows pop up. And even though I'm wearing a sheer cover-up over my bikini, his big brown eyes don't leave mine.

"Can we talk?" I ask, and he takes a step back, inviting me in.

PART IV

MAY 7,
SENIOR YEAR

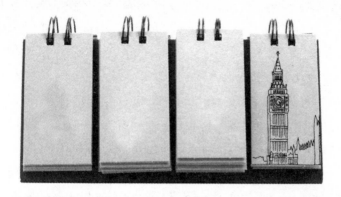

TODAY
SENIOR CLASS TRIP

The plane is dark.

Dim lights illuminate the aisles and a few people are watching movies, but most people are passed out asleep. It's the middle of the night on our flight to London, but I'm too amped up to rest.

In five hours, our class will land at Heathrow. Today we'll go to Big Ben and see Buckingham Palace. I can't believe that for the next five days, I'll be exploring London, holding hands with my boyfriend. I glance to my left. He's leaning against my shoulder, dozing, snoring slightly, probably drooling on my shirt. I kiss the top of his head, then turn back to my Wacom tablet in my lap.

The blank screen glows up at me. I've been brainstorming new ideas, but I haven't come up with anything yet. My agent, Peter, says that while *Here Comes the Sun* is out on submission to publishers, I need to stay busy, to keep my mind off waiting to hear back from editors.

He said, "I always tell my clients to go out and drink plenty of wine."

"I'm only eighteen," I replied.

"Oh. Well. Write another book, then."

Here Comes the Sun has been out on sub to editors for three weeks now. Some writers sell their books in a day. For some, though, it takes years. By the time I sell my story, I may very well be of legal age to drink wine. If I haven't sold by then, I will need lots of it.

But I keep telling myself I've made it this far. Getting an agent is huge. I just have to keep working hard and never give up, like Cady James Morrison.

Last August, I had queried Peter and he rejected me with the nicest note ever:

Lulu—One of the things I like best about your story is the science, and that your main character has used it to survive. I can tell you know what you're talking about. Your book will spur girls to pursue careers in science and technology fields. Your illustrations are beautiful and your world-building rocks. But you need to work on your pacing. As is, the story moves a bit too fast. Give me more time with these characters. Show me who they are. Please revise and resubmit.

After six months of revising, I signed with Peter in February, and after even more revisions, Peter thought it was ready to send to publishers. Mom must've told every single person in Manchester that her daughter, Lulu Wells, had a fancy New York literary agent. Even though I wasn't all that active at our church, the women's fellowship threw a potluck to congratulate me.

Mom told me I should call him Mr. Shepherd, but Peter said that made him feel like an old man. And I get why. He's only like, thirty.

I'm keeping my fingers crossed that when we land, I'll turn on my phone and find an email from Peter announcing we have an offer.

I pop a cherry Jolly Rancher in my mouth, then open the London guidebook I've been studying obsessively. Mom bought it for me when she heard we were going to London. The book is bulky, weighs a few pounds, and takes up tons of room in my carry-on. When I asked why I couldn't simply use travel websites on my phone, Mom said, "Those sites are all paid for by big companies who want you to spend money. A book like this will tell you about all the little-known things."

I turn it to the page about Big Ben and use my stylus pen to doodle a picture of the famous clock tower. Maybe I could set a new story in London. I've been working for so long on *Here Comes the Sun*, it's hard to imagine writing anything else.

My boyfriend stirs beside me. "Couldn't sleep?"

"Nope. Too excited."

"Happy anniversary," Alex whispers in my ear.

"You too." I nuzzle my face against his jaw, his stubble rough against my skin. "I love you."

"I love you too." He kisses me gently, then presses his forehead against mine.

He sits up to stretch his arms above his head, knocking his knuckles on the ceiling in the process. Coach seats are cramped for everybody, but especially for him.

"I have a very special anniversary surprise," he says.

"Oh yeah?"

"I know what you've been longing for your whole life," he flirts.

"What's that?"

"We're gonna join the mile-high club."

"Alex!" I hiss, then burst out laughing.

"Shhhh!" another passenger says.

Alex unbuckles his seat belt, stands up, ducking his head to avoid hitting the luggage compartment above us, and puts out a hand. "C'mon."

Oh my God, he's serious. I barely have a second to set my tablet down and unbuckle my belt before he tugs me out of my seat to the lavatories at the back of the plane.

"Yuck," I whisper-yell at him. "It stinks so bad in those things."

"Just hold your breath," Alex says, trying to control his laughter.

"Let me get this straight. You want me to suffocate while we're doing it in a smelly lavatory. Are you trying to kill me?"

"Never." He leans down to kiss my lips, and my body reacts instantly. I mold my torso to his. He pulls me toward the lavatory, and I playfully push against him.

"The mile-high club? Really?"

"C'mon, Lu, live dangerously," he teases, kissing me again. I will never get sick of his kisses.

"Young man!" We break apart to find a flight attendant sporting a severe bun. "What do you think you're doing?"

"Uhh," Alex starts, "We came back to ask for another beverage."

She purses her lips, crossing her arms. "That's not what it looked like to me."

"I promise," Alex says, faking a cough. "I'm parched. May I have a ginger ale?"

The flight attendant shakes her head as if exasperated, but crooks a finger for Alex to follow her. When her back is turned, he points at the lavatory and silently mouths, "Later!"

I laugh at him as I carefully walk back down the aisle, gripping seat backs to stay steady in case we hit turbulence.

Once he's back at my side with his ginger ale in hand, I lean against his shoulder.

He gestures at my sketchpad. "How's it coming?"

"No ideas yet."

"You'll get there."

I snuggle closer to him. "Did you really want to join the mile-high club?"

"Naah. Not today anyway. Gotta save some excitement for the flight home, right?"

He kisses me with lips tasting of crisp ginger ale, then starts playing with the TV screen on the back of the seat in front of him.

I love him.

I love him so much, and don't want to leave him, but I have to.

I haven't told him that I got accepted by RISD.

The Rhode Island School of Design.

A school that could change everything for me.

MAY
JUNIOR YEAR

The Saturday after we returned from New York, Alex appears at my front door in the early afternoon, dressed neatly in a pair of navy shorts, a gray T-shirt, and a Braves cap turned around backwards, his long hair poking out from beneath.

I wasn't expecting him, so while I showered this morning, I'm not exactly ready for company. My long blond hair is a frizzy mess, and I'm wearing my old Mickey Mouse pajamas. But I'm so happy to see him, it doesn't matter what I look like.

"Hi," I say.

He grins. "Hi."

With a reusable grocery bag in hand, he follows me inside.

"What's that?" I ask.

"I have two surprises."

It reminds me of sophomore year, how we met each other

every morning with a present. Did he bring me an apple from the farmer's market? A tomato from his yia yia's garden?

"Here's your first surprise." He passes me a folded piece of paper. Even though I wrote him notes all the time in the past, he never wrote me. I unfold it to find a drawing of a stick figure wearing a Braves cap like the one on his head. A voice bubble reads, *I like you a lot.*

I begin to smile and get up on tiptoes to hug Alex. "I like you a lot too," I whisper.

Out of respect for Nick, I kept my distance from Alex while sightseeing in New York, but we talked a lot at night. Now that we're home, my body zings with excitement.

Alex and I stand like that for what feels like forever, just holding each other, until the sound of someone clearing their throat interrupts us.

I pull back from Alex to find Dad standing there holding the comics section of the newspaper. My father studies us like a math problem he can't work out.

Alex sticks out a hand. "Mr. Wells, it's nice to see you, sir."

Dad shakes it. "Alex, how's your grandmother doing?"

"She's good. Thanks for asking."

Then Dad turns to me. "What's going on? Where's Nick?"

"We broke up."

"And you're back with Alex?"

"I'm trying, sir," Alex says. "But I have some work to do to win her back."

Dad takes off his glasses and chuckles. "What'd you have in mind?"

Alex holds up his grocery bag. "I figured I'd make her some chocolate-covered strawberries and see if she wants to go to a movie or dinner with me later."

I lift an eyebrow. "Don't you work on Saturday nights?"

"I talked to my dad. I'm taking off two Saturdays a month now. I have to work doubles on Sundays, but you're worth it."

I jump into his arms. If Dad weren't here, I'd wrap my legs around his waist and kiss him for the first time in forever.

Mom finds us a good pan to use for melting the chocolate, then leaves. When we were younger, she would've found excuses to putter around the kitchen. Today, however, Alex and I spend an hour in the kitchen alone, chatting and laughing and dipping red, juicy strawberries into melted chocolate. He feeds me one, his thumb catching on my lower lip, and we stare at each other.

The tension nearly burns the house down.

We take the cooled strawberries down to the basement, where we sit on the couch to eat and leisurely flick through the TV channels. His hair's gotten so long, he constantly has to push it out of his eyes. I want to do it for him.

Without thinking, I climb onto his lap, straddling him like I did when we were younger. My knees cradle his thighs as I run my hands through his hair. Alex moans.

My chest presses to his. Our hips rock together. His hooded eyes meet mine, and even though we haven't officially agreed to get back together, I can't wait to kiss him. I have to. My lips were made for his.

I lean in, but he pulls back, and I give him a bratty little whine that makes him chuckle.

Out of breath, his hands grip my waist, his thumbs making circles on my hip bones. "Lu, wait. I need to say something."

"Okay," I say, "but make it quick. I need to kiss you or I'm going to literally die."

His hands caress up from my hips to my back. "I don't ever want you to feel pressured, okay? We're moving at your pace. You tell me what you want and when you want it. Got it?"

"Got it. Now, it's quiet time," I say, diving in to kiss him. He smiles against my teeth as our mouths move together. I cling to him as his kisses grow more intense, more demanding, begging me for more, more, more. Being with him again is an electric shock to my soul.

I begin to grind my hips against his. Beneath me he feels strong and rock hard. One of his hands drifts downward to rest on my hip, the other on my butt, and the way he moves against me is the sexiest thing ever.

Our eyes meet before his lips capture mine in a long, deep kiss, our tongues twining as if neither of us can get enough. His body molds against mine, driving me wild.

Even fully clothed, he has me groaning his name in less than two minutes as tremors shock my body. I bury my face in his neck.

"Nobody's like you, Lu," he says, out of breath. "Nobody."

He wraps his arms around me for another long hug, holding me as we relax together on the couch. With wandering fingers, I lift his shirt and touch his stomach, making him gasp with pleasure. Since the last time I was with him, he grew a tantalizing strip of hair that points from his belly button to beneath his boxer briefs. I want to touch it with my tongue.

Right as I unbutton his shorts, his phone begins to ring.

With a sigh, Alex sits up, takes one look at the screen, and swipes it to answer. "Coach?"

As he listens to whatever Coach Rice is saying he starts to smile, and even though I didn't know what's going on, I smile too.

When Alex hangs up, he makes a celebratory fist. "I got into the Duke baseball camp."

"Congratulations! You deserve it so much. You've worked so hard." I hold him tight.

His face scrunches up. "The camp lasts a month and a half, Lu."

My heart lurches in my chest.

"Maybe it's best for me to stay here this summer, to be with you," he says.

I shake my head. "Absolutely not. We're talking about your future here. You're going. No matter what."

"But I just got you back, Lu. I can't lose you again." He kisses me long and intensely, weaving his hands in my hair.

"I'll be right here, okay?" I say. "We'll FaceTime every day if you want. I'm not going anywhere."

He brushes my hair away from my face. "I'm not going anywhere either."

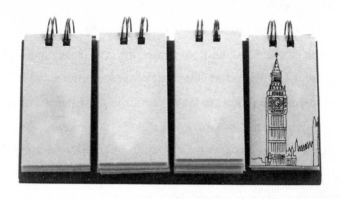

TODAY
SENIOR CLASS TRIP

As the plane prepares to land in London, I grip the armrests of my seat.

Alex and I made it through a month and a half apart last summer.

When I go to school in Rhode Island, we may not see each other for an entire semester. How in the world will we make it months at a time, over and over and over again for four years?

A few months ago, we learned Vanderbilt was awarding him a substantial scholarship to play baseball. It won't cover everything, so he'll have to get a work-study job and take out a loan, but the scholarship wasn't something he could turn down.

I didn't tell my friends or family I applied to the Rhode Island School of Design. Truth be told, I applied on a whim to see if I had the talent to get in. Maybe I could tell potential publishers that I was accepted.

I had been planning to go to Middle Tennessee State University, about half an hour from Alex. We'd see each other all the time. As adults, I'd be able to stay over at his dorm or he'd sleep at mine. I couldn't wait to wake up in the morning to his smiling face.

Last month, I received an email from RISD, admitting me to their illustration program this fall. I screamed my head off and did a celebratory dance, but still didn't tell my parents or friends. It didn't matter; I was going to MTSU.

When I brought it up to my literary agent a few weeks ago, to see if he wanted to brag to editors about my acceptance, he was like, "If you have the means, you should *actually* go to RISD. It would be good for your future. You're already a great writer and a fantastic artist, and formal instruction will only help your craft. It could take you to that next level."

Deposits were due May 1, and I didn't have much time left to decide. But the more I thought about what Peter said, how it would be good for my future, I considered how I always pushed Alex to do what was best for him.

Why wasn't I saying the same thing to myself?

After I told my parents, they were concerned I hadn't fully considered how much my life would change. That I would have to leave my friends. Leave my boyfriend, Alex, who I love more than anything.

But being an author is my goal, and all my hard work is paying off. Shouldn't pursuing my dreams outweigh all else?

So I did it. We paid the deposit.

All I have to do is leave the boy I love.

I want to cry.

"You okay?" Alex asks, glancing down at my hands gripping the armrests. My knuckles are white.

I tell him a white lie: "I hate flying."

He pries my fingers loose and takes my hand in his. "We're almost there."

I'm excited, but also sad. This is the last time I'm going on a field trip with my friends. We graduate in two weeks. Then we're all starting different lives.

Max is going to University of Tennessee at Knoxville, a few hours away, and Caleb is staying nearby at Lipscomb University.

Ryan is going to the University of Georgia, and Grace will be an hour and a half away from him at Georgia Tech in Atlanta, but first they plan to road trip across the country this summer.

Alex reports to Vanderbilt for weight lifting in July.

I have less than three months left with my boyfriend. What if he wants to break up before I leave?

I'll tell him after this trip. I don't want to ruin London for us by telling him I'm leaving. I need to spend this time with him. Depending on how he takes my news, this could be the last trip we ever take together.

The plane hits the tarmac, bumping up and down, rushing headlong against the wind.

As soon as the fasten seat belt sign is off, Ryan begins cheering. "London, I am in you!" he yells, and our entire class erupts with applause.

Alex rises from his seat and opens the overhead compartment to pull out his backpack. I carefully store my tablet in the front flap of my purse. People jostle us as they squeeze down the aisle. Alex holds me close as we shuffle off the plane, kissing the top of my head.

Our group moves through the terminal excitedly. Most of us, including me, have never been to another country before.

Ryan shifts his backpack on his shoulder. "Okay, here's the plan. As soon as we can ditch the chaperones, we're hitting up a pub."

"Yessss," Max agrees.

"We can order like, real cocktails," Grace squeals. "I'm getting a mojito."

"Is that the drink with mint?" Marcie asks. "I love mint."

"Me too, but I need to try a strawberry daiquiri first," I say.

"That's sacrilege, Lucifer," Ryan says. "You can't get a frou-frou drink in a pub."

"He's right. You have to order a pint of ale, Lu," Alex pipes up, as if we're in the *Lord of the Rings*.

"So it's settled, then," Max says to me, ignoring Alex. "We're getting strawberry daiquiris."

"With little umbrellas," I add.

We go through customs, where an immigration officer stamps my passport and says, "Welcome to the United Kingdom," in the most British accent I've ever heard. It's my own personal episode of *Downton Abbey*.

After his passport is stamped, Ryan adopts an exaggerated British accent. "Oh, Gracey, give me a snog, dahh-ling."

She pushes him away.

Mom gave me her credit card because it doesn't have any foreign transaction fees, but I still need to have some spending money. A bunch of us exchange dollars for pounds at the currency exchange.

While waiting at baggage claim, I turn on my phone and anxiously wait for it to find a signal. Messages start pouring in. Texts from Mom, Dad, and my sister, Lila, making sure I arrived in one piece. No new emails from my agent.

I sigh, stowing my phone away. "Nothing from Peter."

Alex drapes his arms around me from behind and kisses my cheek. "I'm sorry, babe. It's only a matter of time."

"I hope so."

"You need to email your agent and ask if he's heard anything," Marcie says.

I shake my head. "I don't want to waste his time."

"You're not wasting his time," Marcie replies. "He never would've taken you on if he didn't believe in you."

"If I haven't heard from him by the end of today New York time, I'll think about it."

It is taking forever for our luggage to arrive. Alex stands right up next to the chute where our suitcases will pop out. He's blocking everybody else and it's kind of embarrassing, to be honest.

"Alex," I call. "Come over here. It'll be easier to get our bags where it's not so crowded."

"No, this is the best spot," he assures me.

"Come stand by me," I say again.

"No," Alex grumbles, and I roll my eyes at my boyfriend.

"You two are like an old married couple," Caleb says.

"Just like you and Max," Ryan jokes.

My suitcase has a rainbow ribbon on it. When it appears, Alex has no time to react because he's standing right in front of the chute. He lunges for it and misses, and has to dodge a bunch of people to get it off the conveyer belt. This is not easy for a six-foot-three Hulk of a first baseman.

"You were right," Alex says sheepishly. "I shouldn't have stood there."

Once everybody has their suitcase from the baggage carousel, Mrs. Schmidt announces that everyone needs to follow her to meet our tour group. Four huge tour busses idle outside the terminal.

Coach Rice blows his whistle, which draws stares from several perturbed English women. "Settle down, everybody," he says, even though none of us are acting up. We're adults now; it's not like we're still annoying freshmen.

"I want to introduce you to Lawrence, our tour guide."

A man dressed in a sport coat gives us all a smile and a wave. "It's nice to meet you all. On behalf of the Queen's Tours, I would like to welcome you to England." His accent is crisp and defined. "We have two different schools traveling with us on our tour of London: Coffee County High from Tennessee in the United States." Ryan hoots again like he did on the plane, and a bunch of baseball players join in cheering. "And the Cicognini Boarding School from Tuscany, Italy."

The Italians don't cheer for themselves like we do. They stay silent. Our class stares at them. They stare at us.

The Italians all are dressed in chic leather jackets and distressed jeans and ripped T-shirts. One girl looks exceptionally cool in a white fedora.

"Do I need a fedora?" I ask Max quietly.

"You do. You really, really do."

"Oh my God, who is that?" Marcie says under her breath. She stares at a tall, trim boy with olive skin and jet-black hair—a human chess board with his white Henley, black jeans, and black boots.

"He's probably a professional model," I say, practically drooling. "I think I saw him in a magazine once."

"Hey, hey, I'm right here," Alex fake pouts.

"Don't worry, I'm looking on Marcie's behalf. My interest is purely scientific."

Max cranes his head to get a better view. "Mine too."

Marcie clutches my elbow. "Do you think we'll get to hang out with the Italian group?"

I shrug. "Maybe. I mean, if they're staying at the same hotel and traveling with us, I bet we'll see them a lot."

Some of the Italian kids, including Sexy McSexerson, board the same bus as me and my friends. We choose seats in the middle of the bus, far away from the stinky restrooms in the back. Max sits across the aisle from me with Caleb.

I giggle to myself when I see Jonah Zotter pass by, trailing the Fedora girl like a groupie. I haven't thought about my crush on Jonah in forever.

"This is a nice upgrade from the shitty school busses back in Manchester," I say. "We've come a long way since our freshman year trip."

"Remember when you threw gum in my hair on the bus?" Alex jokes.

"That was not me," I say, tickling my boyfriend's side. "It was Max."

"If you say so."

The memory makes me laugh. Things are so different now. Most of us are eighteen. Nobody is yelling. The bus doesn't smell like farts.

"Nobody's mooning anybody this time," I say.

"I could fix that," Ryan pipes up in his fake accent, but he doesn't make any move to moon us in front of the chic Italians. He's too busy cuddling with Grace.

My ex, Nick Johannsen, and Dana Jenkins pass by to get seats toward the back. "Hi, Lulu, hi, Alex," Dana says with a bounce to her step. Nick nods at us with a big grin.

Alex had suggested they might like each other, and he was right. They are reeeeeally into each other. Like, *can't keep their hands off each other at school/not safe for work* into each other.

Of course, Max had to comment when he found out they're dating: "Good for Nick. Another recipient of one of her world-famous hand jobs."

"She's nice, bud." This past year, Dana and I actually became okay friends since I joined the dance team.

"Just sayin'. A good hand job is nothing to scoff at."

Marcie sits in front of us with Paige, another girl from our team. Marcie leans out into the aisle to talk to me, but glances over my shoulder at the Italian model boy.

"It's official," she says. "I have to get a piece of that. Shit, why don't I know Italian? Do you think he speaks English?"

"I dunno. Talk to him," I whisper back. "What do you have to lose?"

Marcie glances at him again, biting her lip.

Alex stares out the bus window. "It's so weird driving on the other side of the road. I don't know if I'd be able to train my mind to do that."

"Maybe I'd be better at driving on the left side of the road. You know how bad I am at driving on the right side of the road."

Alex rests his palm on my thigh. "You'll have to practice driving for this fall, when you come visit me in Nashville." He leans closer to me, whispering in my ear, "I can't wait until we can have sleepovers whenever we want."

I suck in a deep breath of air.

Alex's forehead wrinkles with concern. "You okay?"

"Yeah," I lie.

"Lu, what's wrong?"

Could I be any more obvious? What am I going to do? Now is not the time to tell him I'm moving to Rhode Island. What if he yells? What if he cries...? This needs to wait until we get home.

"I didn't sleep at all on the plane," I say. "I'm worried I'll crash."

"I wonder if they sell any of that 5-hour Energy stuff over here. We can check at the hotel. See if they have a store."

Out of the corner of my eye, I see Max giving me a pointed look.

Other than my family and agent, Max is the only person I've told about getting into RISD. I told him a couple of days ago. He cried at the news: my best friend is both happy I'll be studying art at the best design school in the country, and devastated I'm leaving.

Part of me is devastated too. I wish I had a transporter like in *Star Trek*, so I could go to school in Rhode Island during the day and beam home at night.

Max leans across the aisle to whisper, "Lu, you gotta tell him."

I'm not looking at Alex, but I know him so well, I can feel his body tensing up next to mine.

He heard what Max said.

EARLY AUGUST
BEFORE SENIOR YEAR

Alex has been gone for six weeks to the elite Duke baseball camp.

Over that summer, we speak every single day on the phone or FaceTime, but it isn't enough. I can't wait to see him again. Only a few more days.

One night, he video chats me before he goes to sleep. His image pops up on my phone screen. He's lounging in his dorm room bed, his face super tanned from being out in the sun all day, every day. Bags hang under his eyes, but otherwise, he looks happy and content. Baseball's his whole life, after all.

"Hey, Lu-babe," he says, yawning.

"Hi."

"Did you hear from any literary agents today?"

I shake my head. "Sent out a few more query letters, though."

"Keep at it. I know people will love your book." He pauses to stare at me. "You look really pretty tonight."

"I took a shower for our video call."

He grins over the screen. "Wow, a shower. I'm a lucky guy."

I blow him a kiss and he returns it. Part of me wishes I had the guts to do more than pretend kiss him over the phone. Grace says I should proposition him with video chat sex, but considering we haven't done it in real life yet, asking for it over the phone seems unthinkable, like riding a unicorn.

Instead of offering video sex, I ask, "What are you up to?"

"I have a really big game this weekend. We're playing a team from the Dominican Republic in front of a bunch of college and pro scouts. The Dominicans are flying here."

"That sounds great. You'll beat the crap out of them, I'm sure."

Alex scratches the scruff on his cheek. "I dunno. From what I hear, these guys from the DR are better than us. They have a pitcher who can throw a hundred-mile-an-hour fastball."

"I didn't know boys in high school could pitch that fast," I exclaim.

"They can't."

We pause together. "But you've hit that speed before in the batting cage."

"A couple of times, yeah. I've never faced it in a game, 'cause nobody pitches that fast. Most guys would throw their arm out. I don't think I can hit it."

"You've put in the work. Your batting rocks and you know it."

He grins at me over the video chat. "I can't wait to see you, Lu. Only four more days until camp's over."

282

But he doesn't have to wait four days. He only has to wait two.

As a surprise, Ryan, Grace, and I road trip to North Carolina to see him play in the final game against DR. Our parents allow us to go alone since Coach Rice is driving up for the game too. He said Alex was one of the best players he'd ever coached, and he wouldn't miss such a big game, especially since he'd helped Alex get into the Duke camp.

When Grace, Ryan, and I arrive at the field, I jog down the bleachers to stand behind the first base dugout. The team is practicing on the nicest field I've ever seen. It looks like the pros.

Alex stands in his position at first base, chewing his gum and watching the batter, totally in the zone. The pitcher throws the ball and the batter swings and misses. The ball smacks into the catcher's mitt. Everyone on the field relaxes.

This is my chance.

"The first baseman's totally hot!"

The players jerk their heads my way. Alex sees me, gapes, and drops his glove. He sprints my way. He leaps over the wall and joins me behind the dugout, lifting me off my feet, spinning me around.

"You're here! I can't believe it. I missed you." He hugs and kisses me, tasting like cinnamon gum.

A Black man wearing a baseball uniform walks up, chewing gum too. "Rouvelis, what's going on here?"

"Coach, this is my girlfriend, Lulu. Lu, this is Coach Andrews."

The coach leans over the wall and warmly shakes my hand. "You came all the way from Tennessee?"

"Yes, sir, we drove. I wanted to see Alex play."

"Hold on to this one, Rouvelis," Coach Andrews says with

a wink. "Guys," he calls out to the team on the field. "Let's take a twenty-minute break." To Alex, he says, "Be back in twenty, Rouvelis."

Alex climbs through the stands to hug Grace and Ryan, who had hung back to give us a moment.

With wide eyes, Ryan stares out at the lush, green field. "I'm so proud of you, man."

Then Alex's teammates descend upon us, and he introduces me to boys from all over the country, guys who'll be playing in the major leagues one day.

Before Alex goes back to practice, he sits in the bleachers and pulls me onto his lap, seemingly not caring that his teammates are gawking at us.

"I'm so excited to see you," he says, tightly gripping my hand, glancing at my lips. "Can we hang out tonight? I'll take you to a pizza place I found that's pretty good, but it's no Niko's."

"Of course it's no Niko's, but yeah. I'd love to." I kiss his cheek. "I missed you so much."

"Me too. Never again, Lu. I never want to be apart from you so long again."

Never again.

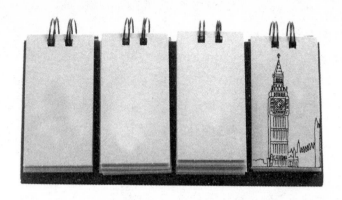

TODAY
SENIOR CLASS TRIP

We're staying at a hotel nearly thirty minutes outside of
London, because hotel prices here are astronomical. A field trip to
the moon would be cheaper.

The little hotel is gorgeous. Hydrangeas decorate the entrance-
way and British flags swing from light poles out front. Identical
black taxi cabs transported from 1940 idle along the curb. Inside,
the lobby is old-timey, like something from a century ago with white
tile floors and bellmen in actual bellboy caps and gold uniforms. The
complete opposite of a Holiday Inn back in the States.

Ryan sets his backpack down on the lobby floor. "Splendid,
chaps, it's simply splendid."

"If he keeps using that stupid accent, I am going to kill him,"
Grace says to me.

Coach Rice blows his whistle. "Okay, everybody, I'm gonna tell you your room assignments and pass out keys."

As Coach goes through the list of our names, it dawns on me that we're squeezing as many of us to a room as they can without breaking the fire code. Coach Rice says that Grace and I are rooming with Marcie, Dana, and Paige. Alex, Ryan, Max, Caleb, and Nick are staying together.

"One of you guys has to sleep on a cot," Coach Rice adds with a snort.

"Not it," Ryan announces.

"Not it," Alex jumps in.

"Not it," Caleb and Nick say simultaneously.

"Well, fuck," Max says.

The elevator is ancient and will only carry two people at a time. It creaks and groans, and no way am I climbing on that thing and plummeting to my death.

Instead, Alex carries my suitcase up four flights of carpeted stairs to my room and sets it inside. I wrap my arms around his neck and kiss him. "Thank you."

He presses his forehead to mine. "You're welcome. Let me go grab my suitcase, okay?"

"Okay."

Alex glances back as he leaves, his eyes lingering on me. Shit. He knows something's up.

Max starts to pass by, but I reach out and grab his elbow. "What gives? Why'd you whisper so loud on the bus? Alex heard you."

"C'mon, Lu. You have to tell him."

"I'm going to—maybe not until we get home, though."

Max runs a hand through his hair. "Look, y'all are finally good, and you're going to blow it by not telling him, and then I'll get all the fallout. You have to get your shit together."

I take a step back. "I didn't know being friends with me was so hard," I snap.

"Sorry," he mumbles. "That came out wrong. I just can't handle the idea of you being hurt again. I'm so worried about what's going to happen with you guys."

"Me too."

He sniffles, fighting back tears.

"Are you okay?"

Max shakes his head, shutting his eyes. "I'm going to miss you so much. I thought we were going to be close by in college, and we could see each other on weekends..."

I take his hand in mine. "I did too."

"And with Caleb being at a different school from me, I don't know what's going to happen with me and him. We haven't really talked about it, and I'm scared."

"Why do people always say that college is going to be the best time of our lives?" I ask. "It feels super terrifying."

Max nods slowly. "This really sucks. I don't want you to leave, but you have to do this."

He draws me into a tight hug, then pulls away, not looking back.

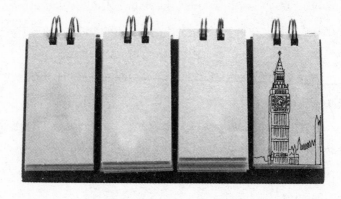

TODAY
SENIOR CLASS TRIP

My room is old fashioned and smells a bit musty like my great-grandfather's house in Florence, Alabama, but the beds seem clean, and it's not like we'll be here very much. I plan to spend as much time as I can in London itself.

I use the bathroom, feeling 100 percent better after I wash my hands and change my clothes. Travel always makes me feel dirty. As I'm leaving the restroom, Ryan arrives with Grace's suitcase, then tackles her to the bed.

"Ugh, at least wait until we're out of the room," Dana says, and she, Marcie, and Paige vamoose. I quickly make sure my passport is locked away in the safe, then go to find Alex's room, so I don't have to watch the Ryan and Grace show.

I knock on Alex's door and he lets me in. Caleb and Max are

stretched out on one of the beds already, Caleb with an arm tucked behind his head and Max resting his head on Caleb's chest. My best friend's eyes are red.

"What room are you guys in again?" Nick asks me.

"Four-oh-three, but Dana already went down to the lobby if you want to find her." He gives me a quick smile as a thank-you before leaving the room.

I raise my eyebrows at Alex.

He studies the look on my face. "Can you guys give us a minute?"

"Fine," Max says, taking Caleb's hand and climbing out of bed. "But you owe us later."

Once we're all alone, I flop down on Alex's bed. He lies next to me, intertwining our fingers together and kissing the back of my hand.

"Your dress is so cute," he says.

"Thanks," I say with pleasure. I love my long-sleeved navy mini dress covered with embroidered rocket ships. The hemline is scandalously short. I paired the dress with tights and my white sneakers.

"I love your new haircut," I tell him. Before our trip, he had it cropped short and sexy.

He is quiet for a minute before saying, "Can I ask you something?"

"Yeah."

With his other hand, he rubs the dark stubble covering his cheek. "We're okay, right? You'd tell me if something's wrong?"

I don't know if getting into RISD is technically wrong. It might not be right either. But I don't want to ruin his trip to London by telling him about it.

I never thought I'd get in. Now, it's like my single path has opened up to several different routes. How can I know which one is the best for Alex and me?

And which one is the best for *just me*?

"Yes, I'd tell you if something's wrong," I say, fudging the truth a little. I am going to tell him, just not right now.

"Last month. You know, when the condom broke—"

Oh my God, he's worried about that? "Alex, we're fine," I insist. "I promise."

"You're not, um, pregnant, right? Because if you are, we'll figure it out together. Whatever you want and need, I'm here."

I squeeze his hand, loving this guy so much. "We're good. You have nothing to worry about."

"Are you sure?" He holds his breath.

"I had my period last week."

His eyes narrow. "You did?"

Boys. "Don't you remember how moody I was?"

"I thought that was because the Phillies swept the Braves in the series."

I tickle his sides. "No, that's why *you* were moody."

He tickles me in retaliation, and I flip him onto his back, making eyes at him. "How much time do we have until we need to meet in the lobby?"

"Ten minutes."

I straddle his waist, fitting my body to his. Alex's strong hands grip my hips beneath my dress.

His Adam's apple shifts as he swallows, his face turning pink with heat as I reach for his belt buckle.

OCTOBER
SENIOR YEAR

"I have a surprise for you."

Alex had to work late tonight. Ever since he turned eighteen, his father has him close the restaurant and lock the doors after business is done for the evening. It's a big responsibility.

Alex asked me to meet him at Niko's at midnight for a surprise. Now that I'm a senior, Mom lets me stay out late so long as she knows where I'm going to be.

I pull her car into the dark parking lot. Hardly anything bad ever happens in our sleepy little town, but being alone at night makes me hyperaware, constantly looking over my shoulder for evil things, like a red balloon floating above a street gutter.

I sigh gratefully when Alex comes jogging out of the restaurant to meet me, rubbing his hands together in the cool air. The second

I'm out of the car, he's kissing me, grabbing both of my hands to stretch them high above my head. I sigh. His hips grind against me, a preview of what's to come later.

"What's this surprise?" I ask between kisses.

He twines his fingers with mine. "Come in."

He leads me inside Niko's. Only a few lights glow in the restaurant.

"It feels so lonely in here," I say.

"I know, right?" He kneads his hands. "To tell you the truth, it creeps me out being here alone."

I squeeze his biceps. "I'm sure you could beat the crap out of any robbers, Alex."

He takes my hand again. "It's not that... I don't like being in the dark. It makes me think about things. Like my grandfather. I miss him so much."

I bring his hand to my mouth and kiss it. "I know, me too."

Alex looks out over the restaurant. "And then I start thinking even darker thoughts. I start worrying about Yia Yia...and you."

"I'm fine."

"I know, I just worry."

"This is kind of a depressing surprise," I joke, trying to improve the mood.

After locking the front door, he leads me to a table at the very back of the restaurant. A tea light flickers on top of the red-and-white checkered tablecloth. "I nicked a bottle of red wine, and Demi made us that apple tart you like."

I do a dance for the apple tart. "Eeee!"

Ever since his older sister Demi started playing a larger role in management of the restaurant, she's been introducing new items to the menu—including the apple tart I've been having a love affair with.

I pull out a chair and sit at the table, ready to dig in. He pours us each a bit of wine. Not only do I like the fruity taste much more than beer or liquor, holding the glass makes me feel very grown-up.

"What's the occasion?"

"I wanted to tell you something about Papu."

"Okay," I say slowly. We didn't talk about his grandfather very often. Alex's feelings were still too raw.

"My grandfather left everything to my yia yia. The house, the restaurant." He takes a deep breath. "She had me over yesterday. Yia Yia wanted to talk about my future. She understands I want to play baseball, and if I don't make it, she knows I don't want to work here."

"What would you do if you didn't play baseball?"

Alex stares out the window. The bright moon shines over the fields beyond the restaurant.

"I dunno. Maybe engineering... What would you do if you weren't a writer?"

I sip my wine. "I'd be a political activist."

"Of course." He smiles. "Do you want some tart?" At my nod, he cuts us each a slice.

I pop a bite in my mouth. The mix of wine and tart zaps my head. Sugar overload.

"Anyhow, Yia Yia was talking about plans for the restaurant. Yia Yia said that I shouldn't worry about Niko's because Demi is really good at managing this place on the weeknights Dad stays home with Mom and the baby. I'm not so worried about leaving for college now."

"That's great," I exclaim.

"But I think Yia Yia felt guilty about it...you know, basically saying she was leaving the restaurant to my big sister instead of me."

I pump my fist. "Girl power."

Alex leans across the table. "Yia Yia asked if there's anything I wanted—anything that she might be able to help me with. I asked about the land out back. She and Papu were always talking about paving another parking lot."

I hold my breath.

"But I said we should do something to remember Papu. I said as long as the local nurseries are still willing to donate the seeds, we should give the land to the school in his name for a garden. You can start working on it whenever you want."

I squeal with laughter, clapping my hands. "Oh, Alex. I love you."

I clasp a hand over my mouth. Those words popped out. Those words I hadn't said since sophomore year. Shit. I pick up my wine and gulp.

When I finally meet Alex's face again, he's smiling over the rim of his glass. "I love you too, Lu."

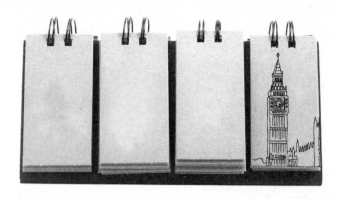

TODAY
SENIOR CLASS TRIP

Even though we were as quick as possible, Alex and I are still five minutes late to meet our tour group.

Being late is officially our thing.

I rushed to put my tights back on and now they feel bunched up around my thighs. I smooth the wrinkles out of my dress as we hurry to join our friends in the lobby.

"Alex, why's your hair all messed up?" Ryan asks loudly with a smirk.

Our entire class turns to look at us. Some smile knowingly. The Italian students give us curious looks.

"Thanks for gracing us with your presence, Rouvelis," Coach Rice says. "McDowell's right. Your hair's a mess."

Alex pats the top of his head. I grin sheepishly for pulling on his new, shorter hair so much.

Max comes over and whispers in my ear, "I'm sorry about before."

"Me too."

I check out his outfit. He's wearing jeans and a dinner jacket made up of multicolored, multi-design plaid squares, like a quilt. "I love this jacket."

He touches the sleeve of my dress. "And I love your rockets."

Lawrence the tour guide pointedly looks at his watch. "We need to leave if we want to stay on schedule." He pronounces it *shhedule*, which makes me groan because I know Ryan will start pronouncing it that way too.

The leader of the Italian group steps forward, her long chestnut hair bouncing. We learned on the bus that her name is Carina Abella, and she's the English teacher at their school. Is everyone from this particular area of Tuscany really, really attractive or what?

"Are we ready to go?" Ms. Abella says with an accent.

"Uh, yeah," Coach Rice replies, clearing his throat into a fist. His face is pink.

Ryan elbows Alex. "Oh shit, Coach has a thing for her."

"Good for him," Alex replies.

Marcie cranes her neck to look at Coach Rice. "He isn't married?"

"Oh, he's married," Alex says. "He's married to baseball."

"Coach is perpetually single," Ryan adds. "The most action he's gotten lately is when Alex pulled down his pants at first base a couple seasons ago."

Coach Rice hears this and gives Ryan a look.

To get to Central London, Lawrence leads us to a nearby Underground station called Greenford. Our tour group walks together down the sidewalk. Given Ms. Abella's excellent English, I am not surprised when I learn the Italian kids speak our language well and begin to weave in with kids from our school.

Alex and I are holding hands when Sexy McSexerson approaches us.

"Hello," he says, shaking our hands. "I am Elia."

"I'm Lulu and this is my boyfriend, Alex."

"Lulu? I have not heard that name."

"Short for Louise."

I make eyes at Marcie, urging her to walk beside us, but she's a deer in the headlights.

After a ten-minute walk, in which I learn how Elia's family is from Milan—where his dad is an executive for a beverage company—we arrive at the entrance to the London Underground. It's marked with a large red circle. The tube station reminds me a lot of New York's subway, only it's cleaner and more vivid, peppered with bright paint. Like in Manhattan, there are people from many different races and backgrounds.

We each buy an Oyster Card to ride the subway. To get to the train, we take an escalator up to an elevated, outdoor platform. Large black letters across the tile floor spell out MIND THE GAP. London is a very polite city.

Our group rides the tube to the Westminster station, which takes thirty minutes. It feels like forever, like driving from home to Nashville. A bunch of us take the opportunity to close our eyes because we're exhausted from the flight.

When we arrive in Westminster, we climb the stairs out of the Underground, passing T-shirt vendors. Some of the guys stop to buy tees that say *We Love London* and *God Save the Queen* and even *Mind the Gap.*

We exit the station, and Big Ben looms before us, the gorgeous clock set against a bright blue sky.

I gasp. This city is stunning, with lush trees interspersed between the buildings and around the square. The breeze is chilly; it's much cooler here than in Tennessee. I zip up my jacket over my dress.

I take my guidebook out of my crossbody purse and flick through it to the map of London to confirm the gorgeous building behind Big Ben is Westminster, where Parliament debates all things England.

My classmates and the Italians begin taking photos.

Tourists and people dressed up in suits and ties swarm in front of the massive building from another century. If not for all the honking horns and people wearing jeans, I'd swear I was in the 1800s.

Across the square is Westminster Abbey, where past kings and queens are buried. Oh, and Princess Kate and Prince William were married there.

"Look, Lu. There's the London Eye." Alex points across the bridge to the other side of the river Thames to the biggest Ferris wheel I've ever seen. By comparison, the Ferris wheel Alex and I rode together at Six Flags is a Lego.

As we come to stand under Big Ben, I remember how Dad flipped out about this trip. He didn't want me to come. A couple of months ago, a terrorist drove a van through here, right across Westminster Bridge, hitting a bunch of pedestrians. Three Americans died, including a man celebrating his twenty-fifth wedding anniversary.

"You'll be going to all sorts of tourist traps in London. It's dangerous," Dad had insisted.

"Bad things can happen anywhere," I'd replied.

Something similar had happened in New York a few years ago—a man drove a truck down a bike path, killing several people. But Dad didn't stop me from going to New York. Hell, an attack could happen back in Coffee County.

What would be the point of living if you cower at home all the time?

I want to live.

"Let's get a picture of all of us in front of Big Ben," Max says, recruiting Coach Rice to snap a photo of me, Grace, Max, Alex, Ryan, Caleb, Marcie, Nick, and Dana with our arms around one another. My smile wanes as I think about how we won't be together next year. If I'm not careful, I'll bawl my eyes out during graduation.

"Now, let's get one with me in it," Coach Rice says, passing Max's phone off to Lawrence to take a photo of him squatting in front of us, holding up the peace sign.

"Go home, Coach," Ryan says. "You're drunk."

"Coach, why're you hanging around us when that hottie Italian teacher is over there?" Alex asks.

Coach rubs the back of his neck. But instead of going to talk to her, he decides to check on another group of kids from our school.

"That's it," Alex says to Ryan. "We have to hook Coach up with Ms. Abella before the trip is over."

Ryan responds with a fist bump.

Only my silly boyfriend would come up with an idea like this. Can't adults figure out their own relationships?

But Coach Rice has been a great coach to them over the years, so I understand why Alex wants him to be happy.

Without him, Alex wouldn't have a scholarship to play ball for a top college team.

To get to the London Eye, we cross over the Westminster Bridge and then walk under an overpass and along the banks of the Thames.

I walk slowly beside the shoreline to see if anything interesting has washed up from the murky brown water. My guidebook says that people do this thing called mudlarking, where you wade out into the Thames at low tide and search for stuff people have thrown into the river over the past two thousand years. Everything from Viking belts to clay pipes, which used to be as common as cigarette butts under Queen Elizabeth I. One mudlarker even found a two-thousand-year-old Roman coin.

Being in the presence of all this history, from Westminster to Big Ben, makes me feel so tiny, my problems so insignificant. Is my story with Alex, even if I don't know how it ends yet, important?

"God, it smells like the 7-Eleven bathroom down here by the river," Ryan says, pulling me from my deep thoughts.

"Maybe it's just you, man," Alex replies.

"It's definitely Ryan," I say. "I love it here. It reminds me of New York."

"Me too," Alex says.

"Only it's more romantic," I whisper to him, and he wraps an arm around my waist.

Caleb and Max are walking in front of us, holding hands. They rarely, if ever, do this at home in Tennessee, where close-minded people like to make rude comments. Most kids at school have accepted them—and I know of at least a sophomore girl and a junior boy who came out after Caleb and Max got together—but adults in public aren't as welcoming. It makes me happy they feel comfortable here.

The place where you board the London Eye is full of school groups waiting to ride the giant Ferris wheel or one of the boat tours next door. After standing in line for what feels like forever, we finally prepare to climb aboard the London Eye.

"The wheel never stops moving," Lawrence says. "It's going very slowly, but you still have to climb aboard while it's rotating, so make sure you move quickly."

When the worker raises the barrier, we hurry across the plank into our compartment. Behind us, two workers wearing SECURITY shirts follow with mirrors attached to wooden poles, which they use to search under the seats, I guess looking for bombs or other threats. Once they finish their sweep, they jump off the car right at the last second as we swing upward toward the blue sky.

London stretches out beneath us. I can't imagine how romantic this would be at night. Maybe even the most romantic view ever.

The Ferris wheel is so big, it will take half an hour to fully rotate. Twenty of us fit comfortably into one car, including Elia and his group of friends. He hangs out with these two girls who are dating—Siena and Cat, and another guy, Leo.

Now that I've talked to Elia a little, I introduce him to Marcie. Elia says hello to her and smiles, but gets distracted when Leo says something in Italian to him, pointing through the glass at the London Spire.

"Maybe he's gay," Marcie whispers.

Caleb checks him out. "That boy is not gay. Trust me."

"How do you know?"

"He hasn't looked at me or Max once."

"Maybe you're not his type," I say.

Caleb gives me a pompous look. "Please."

Meanwhile, Alex and Ryan are whispering conspiratorially, sneaking glances at Coach Rice and Ms. Abella.

Alex claps once like he's in a huddle at a ball game. "It's go time."

Ryan walks over to Ms. Abella and points into the distance. "Do you know what that building is, Ms. Abella?"

At the same time, Alex calls out, "Coach, Coach, come take another picture of me and Lu."

"I'm not your personal photographer, Rouvelis," Coach Rice says. "I want to see the city too."

"Oh yeah, you're right," Alex replies. "Come stand here, it's a great view."

Right then, Ryan steps away from Ms. Abella and Alex guides Coach Rice into the place Ryan vacated. Coach Rice glances down at the Italian teacher and swallows nervously. Ms. Abella points at something and begins speaking to him. He smiles, and a few seconds later, he laughs. Then she chuckles too.

Alex pumps the air with his fist, celebrating.

Ryan dances in place like he's the absolute shit.

After the London Eye makes one complete rotation, we exit and join up with the rest of our class to begin a boat tour on the Thames. My group of friends chooses seats toward the back.

A very peppy British woman with a microphone stands at the bow of the boat. "Welcome aboard! Thank you for joining us here on City Cruises."

The boat begins to slice through the brownish water, which reminds me of the Cumberland back in Nashville.

"Off to your right, you'll see the replica of the Globe Theatre, where Shakespeare's plays were originally performed. The first Globe Theatre burned to the ground in 1613."

The boat glides beneath the London Bridge.

"Up ahead on your left is the Tower of London, built by William the Conqueror in 1078," says the tour guide. "Not only can you find the crown jewels here, but this is where King Henry VIII had Anne Boleyn beheaded."

"This boat trip is a little morbid," I say to Alex.

"A little? I would say it's a lot morbid."

The tour guide says, "It's actually Medieval Weekend at the Tower. Head on over there if you're interested in eating some venison or gruel, or shooting a crossbow."

Ryan sits up straight. "Oh shit. Coach, I want to go shoot a crossbow."

"You remember in the last game where you threw that ball a foot over Alex's head?" Coach replies. "Yeah, nobody's trusting you with a crossbow."

I settle into my seat and enjoy the views of historic buildings and the blue sky. "Remember the freshman year trip? Where we had our first kiss?" I say.

"You mean, where *you* attacked me with your lips?"

"Stop. You liked it."

"No, I loved it."

We kiss here on the boat, in front of all of London, and when we break apart, I sigh. "Nothing's changed."

"Nothing...and everything."

I weave my fingers between his and stare at his brown eyes. Most romantic view ever.

NOVEMBER
SENIOR YEAR

The doorbell rings.

I pull open the front door to find Alex wearing a gray suit, white shirt, and a shiny blue tie under his black puffy coat. For once, he isn't wearing his Braves cap. He holds a bouquet of purple, yellow, and orange wildflowers. I get up on tiptoes to kiss him, loving the way he smells of cinnamon gum.

"I love the flowers, thank you." I reach for them.

He pulls them away from my fingers. "Oh, these aren't for you. They're for your mother."

I pout. I want flowers. But seeing the look on Mom's face when Alex hands her the bouquet is worth not having my own.

She gives Alex a quick hug and examines the flowers. "Beautiful. Did you pick these?"

"Yes, ma'am, from my yia yia's garden. But don't tell her!"

While Mom putters around the kitchen, looking for a vase, Lila hugs him too. "You've grown like, a foot since I last saw you."

Since Lila started attending law school in Atlanta, she isn't home all that often. This past summer, she interned at our senator's office in Chattanooga, so she wasn't around to see Alex and I falling in love all over again.

"Alex? Is that you?" Dad calls from his study.

"Yes, sir."

"Come watch the game with me."

Dad loves Lila and me, but I think he secretly wishes for a son to watch football with.

Alex came to my house for dinner because he's never experienced a traditional Thanksgiving. His family always works at Niko's on holidays. I guess some weirdos want Greek pizza instead of sweet potatoes and cranberry sauce.

Grace, Uncle James, and Aunt Lilibeth arrive next. Aunt Lilibeth sets her green bean casserole on the counter and hugs everyone. Uncle James beelines out of the kitchen to watch football with Dad and Alex.

Lila brings down a bag of clothes she doesn't want anymore, and Grace and I rummage through the hand-me-downs and end up fighting over an itty-bitty red skirt.

"If it's that hot, maybe I should keep it," Lila says.

Grace and I look at each other. "We'll share it. Promise."

My parents made turkey for everyone else, while I have my own personal tofurkey. Alex tries a little, but he sticks his tongue out and goes straight back to the real thing. I love the green beans and mashed potatoes, and our parents even let Alex, Grace, and I have a small glass of wine.

In addition to my mother's flowers, Alex brought us pumpkin pie he made using the vegan crust from his restaurant. "This is so good," I groan as I shovel forkful after forkful into my mouth, making Alex smile.

Mom speaks to Alex quietly. "How is Ryan doing?"

Grace sits up straight like a meerkat.

Alex slowly chews his pie, then wipes his mouth with a napkin. "He's better since he moved in with his grandparents."

"I hope he knows we're here if he needs anything," Mom says.

"He does," Alex replies. "He's glad he could stay here to finish out high school."

After his mom moved to Florida, his dad decided to sell the house and move to Nashville. Something about being closer to work and having access to better golf courses. Good riddance, I say.

Later, I help Lila wash the dishes. She scrubs at caked-on mashed potatoes in a pot. "You seem really happy, Lu."

"I am."

"When you broke up with him the first time, it gutted you. None of us were sure about you dating him again."

"I wasn't either at first, to be honest, but everything's going great. It's just so easy with him."

"You've both relaxed a lot since I saw him a couple of years ago." She lowers her voice. "Are you being careful?"

I glance over my shoulder to make sure nobody else is around. "We haven't done it yet."

"Gawd," she exclaims. "Y'all were all over each other sopho-more year. I figured you were doing it like monkeys."

"Not for his lack of trying," I say with a laugh. "I want to...it just hasn't happened yet."

"I get that. I didn't do it until sophomore year of college."

"Really?" I exclaim. She had a serious boyfriend the last two years of high school.

"You'll know when the time is right."

Throughout the past summer, we fooled around outside by the Little Duck River, but now that it's getting colder outside we've been forced to relocate to his cramped pickup truck. Neither of us wants our first time to happen there, and his house is full of nosy sisters and a baby brother. Plus, my father would torture Alex in the dentist chair if he caught us in my room. Since retiring from the Air Force, Uncle James had been the town sheriff, but my Dad liked to say: "James may fight criminals, but I fight the real war against cavities."

Eye roll.

I don't tell Lila this, but Alex and I went shopping for condoms together last week, which was even more torturous than listening to my dad's joke about fighting the war against cavities. But being in an adult relationship means you do awkward adult things like buy protection at the drug store from the guy who's always asking everybody to join his Bible study group.

Alex comes into the kitchen, hugs me from behind, and kisses my cheek. Then he picks up a towel to dry dishes.

Lila leans over to whisper to me, "I'd do any guy who's willing to help with the dishes without being asked."

I elbow her, laughing. "Shut up."

Alex gives us a funny look as he dries a plate.

Later that afternoon, we sit on the love seat, my legs draped across his lap as we share another helping of pumpkin pie.

Alex gently touches my knee as he whispers in my ear, "My house is empty tonight."

"What? Really?"

"Everyone's at Niko's."

My heart begins to race. I press my forehead to his. "What are we doing here, then?"

He kisses my cheek.

We lie to my parents and say we're going to help out at Niko's with the rest of his family, when really we drive back to his empty house. His dog greets us at the door, begging for pets.

With Princess Peach on our tails, we climb the stairs to his room. On the wall behind his bed hangs my latest sketch of us kissing, along with every other drawing I've ever given him. I love that he takes such good care of them, even the ones from sophomore year.

"Did you make your bed?" I ask.

"And cleaned up my dirty clothes."

"Wow, somebody give this boy an Oscar."

I flop on his bouncy bed and curl up between his flannel sheets while Alex takes off his suit and exchanges it for jeans and a long-sleeved T-shirt. I pretend to close my eyes as he changes clothes, but I totally peek.

"I'm so tired," I whine. "I ate too much."

"If I'd known you were this into pumpkin pie, I would've bribed you with it years ago."

"Bribed me for what?"

"A kiss."

He climbs under the covers with me and gently pecks my lips. I snuggle against his shoulder and trickle my fingertips over his strong chest, draping my leg across him. He wraps an arm around me, settling his hand on my waist.

I'm feeling kind of full and need a nap, so I close my eyes. I doze off, and when I wake up, it's dark outside, and Alex is hugging me. We're wrapped around each other like starfish. He opens his brown eyes and gives me a drowsy smile.

"Hey, Lu," he says, lifting my braid to kiss it.

The house is still and we're alone—the perfect moment. The perfect moment to show how much I love him. Without words, I slip his shirt off over his head and unbutton his jeans, revealing black boxer briefs, and he helps me out of my dress and the fuzzy pink leg warmers I like to wear once the temperature drops below fifty degrees. When our clothes are gone, his arms pull me closer, cradling my body against his. My nerves have me trembling, but I'm also incredibly turned on as his hand roams up my thighs.

My voice wobbles as I ask, "Do you have the condoms?"

He nods at his nightstand. "In my drawer."

Desire is written all over his face, but his arms are shaking as he holds himself above me. He breathes heavily, almost as if labored.

"What's wrong? Are you okay?" I ask.

"A little nervous," he admits.

I lift myself up onto my elbows. "We can wait if you need to."

"No, no. I'm *mad* for you. I'm in love with you. I've been ready to do this with you for years."

I touch his cheek. "Then why are you nervous?"

A lock of his hair falls across his face. "I want to make sure it's good for you."

I laugh. "Alex, I love you. It's going to be good. The only problem so far is all this talking. Kiss me already."

Smiling broadly, he begins to kiss my hands, my fingertips, my neck, my *everywhere*.

Neither of us has any idea what we're doing—with the condom or the angle, and we figure it out together. It hurts at first, a sharp pinch. He moans, burying his face in my neck, and it feels so personal, it's almost overwhelming. It's like I suddenly know everything about him, and him about me.

"I'm scared," I whisper.

His big brown eyes find mine. "Do you want to stop?"

I shake my head.

"I've got you," he says as I hug him tighter. "And you've got me."

As he moves faster, it grows warm and full, and I never want it to end. The night progresses so naturally, it's hard to know where my body ends and his begins.

I always heard you shouldn't expect your first time to be perfect, and it isn't.

But after years of waiting and growing up, we are perfect for each other.

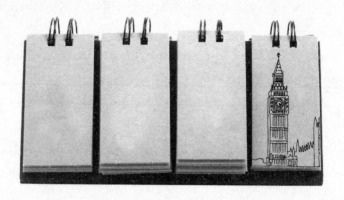

TODAY
SENIOR CLASS TRIP

When the boat tour is over, we walk back across Westminster Bridge.

Lawrence the tour guide and the teachers say we have two hours to explore the area around Buckingham Palace and Westminster Abbey, then meet back up at the Underground to go to Covent Garden for dinner.

I cannot believe they are letting us go off by ourselves in London. We have so much more freedom now that we're older. Not to mention, legal adults.

"Okay," Ryan says. "Here's the plan. We go to a pub."

"No," I whine. "We have to at least see Buckingham Palace. I mean, what if some hot lord's son is there looking for a royal bride? I have to at least throw my hat in the ring."

Alex frowns, while Ryan points at me. "You're right. And I could meet a lord's hot daughter."

Grace looks doubtful.

Max is nodding. "There's gotta be at least, like, one gay earl out there. Onward to the palace!" he says as if he's a knight brandishing a sword.

"We're going to Buckingham Palace and then to get a drink," I say to the Italians. "Do you want to join us?"

Elia glances around at my circle of friends. "Yes, thank you." He turns to the guys next to him and speaks in rapid Italian. They nod.

Buckingham Palace is only a short walk from Westminster. On our way we pass by 10 Downing Street where the prime minister lives. It's nothing like the White House in America, which is surrounded by fences and barriers and police with guns. I could walk right up to the front door of 10 Downing Street and knock. Not that I'm going to do that.

We continue past Churchill's War Rooms, where Winston Churchill ran the British response to World War II underground, and find ourselves in a park.

"Where are we?" Alex asks, holding out his hand to take my guidebook.

I pull it back and open it to the map. "St. James Park. I've seen this place before on that TV show about Queen Victoria."

A pair of joggers dart by our group, running alongside ducks waddling among a rainbow of flowers.

"This is amazing," Grace says as we're walking through the park. "This is where like, half the romance novels I read take place."

"We should reenact one," Ryan says, sweeping her in his arms from behind. "Hello, my lady," his voice booms in that ridiculous British accent.

"Can I see the map?" Alex asks me.

"I'm using it."

"I only need it for a second."

"It's my map. Why didn't you bring one?"

"Because I figured I'd use yours."

I shake my head at him. We bicker like this the entire way to Buckingham Palace, me aggravated that he keeps trying to use my map every two minutes.

"Just use your phone map," I say.

"Nah, the GPS will drain my battery."

"They're an old married couple," Ryan says to the Italians. A confused look crosses Elia's face. Maybe he doesn't know that phrase?

Then the enormous white palace comes into view. People stand in front of the gates, staring and taking photos and selfies. A flag is waving above the palace, which means the queen is home. According to my guidebook, her great-great-grandmother Victoria was the first royal to live here. A golden statue of Victoria looms above the traffic circle out front. Queen Elizabeth's direct line goes back a thousand years. Were any of my ancestors here in England? I need to try one of those ancestry websites ASAP.

Alex and I take a selfie in front of the gates, then I peer through the bars. A smattering of cars are parked in front of the castle. Are important people here, or is that where servants park?

After visiting the outside of Buckingham Palace, which is kind of a bust because tourists are only allowed inside in August when the queen is vacationing in Scotland, we walk past the palace walls behind the royal mews in search of a pub. I peer down a side street, where a bunch of British flags hang across the intersection. What a gorgeous city.

A few blocks away from the palace near the Victoria Underground stop, we find what we're looking for.

We enter the pub to find it mostly empty. It's midday on a weekday, and people are probably at work. The air feels musty and damp, and nearly every surface seems to be made of wood or stained glass. It's quintessential England. I love this place already.

The seven of us sit smushed together in a long wooden booth. Elia's friends take the table next to ours. Marcie sits at the end of our booth, where it's easier to stare at Elia. She's barely spoken to him, though, which is unlike her.

There are no strawberry daiquiris on the menu, so Max and I settle for Blueberry Basil Margaritas.

"I want the biggest ale you can give me," Ryan says to the server.

Alex studies the menu. "Is the imperial size the biggest? The twenty ounce?"

"I'll have two of those," Ryan says.

The waitress writes on her notepad. "Are you going to drink them quickly? Otherwise, the beer will get warm. You may want to stick to one at a time." She smirks at Ryan, clearly flirting with him.

"He said he'll take two," Grace snaps.

The waitress takes the hint and moves on to take everyone else's orders.

Once she leaves, Ryan says, "Are you jealous, Gracey?"

"Of course not." She crosses her arms. "I want good service is all."

"Aw, you're jealous," Ryan says, trying to kiss her cheek, and Grace pushes him away. They are so cute together, it hurts. It took forever for them to make it official, but now I can't imagine them not together. Just like I can't imagine being apart from Alex.

I sigh. Where is that waitress with my drink?

"This is so nice having drinks without worrying about the cops busting our party," Ryan says.

"Does that happen often?" Elia asks.

"Only every weekend at Goose Pond," Marcie says.

"You have an interesting accent," Elia says. "Is it Southern?"

"Yes," Marcie replies, "But I don't hear it."

"Neither do I," I say, even though I know we have them. Even Cady James Morrison commented on my Southern accent.

When the server returns and passes out drinks, Max slurps down his Blueberry Basil Margarita in what seems like a few sips. He proclaims it the most glorious drink he's ever had. "Can I get another?" he calls out to the waitress, who smiles and gives him a thumbs-up.

I tentatively take a sip of my margarita. The tequila zaps me. "Damn."

"Good?" Alex asks, taking a drink of beer.

"I'm going to marry this drink."

Alex elbows my side. "But what about me?"

"You'll have to marry both of us."

"You guys are kinky," Ryan says sarcastically. "Hey, let's play

316

a game. We'll ask each other questions, and if you don't want to answer, you have to take a drink."

"Okay," Max replies. "I'll go first. Ryan...where's the wildest place you've ever had sex?"

Ryan glances to his right at Grace, who gives him a look of a death. He picks up his beer and chugs.

When Ryan asks me, "Who do you like more? Grace or Max?" I take a gulp of my margarita. No way am I ruining friendships when I could take another sip of a delicious drink.

The game gets absolutely ridiculous. My head begins to cloud up. I can't even believe the questions my friends come up with—some of them so bad—there is definitely more drinking than answering going on. Questions like: *Have you ever stolen anything? Have you peed in the pool since you were a little kid? Have you ever walked in on your parents doing it?*

"Max," Ryan asks. "Where's the wildest place you've had sex?"

Grinning widely, Max begins to open his mouth to speak, when Caleb elbows him. "I'm saving myself for marriage," Max lies, which prompts Ryan to throw a peanut at his forehead.

When Max raises his arm to signal the waitress for a third margarita, I push his hand down. "Nuh-uh. You've had enough, bud."

He leans against me. "But whhhy? They taste so good."

"Because I worry about you. It's not like you drink tequila all the time."

"You always take care of me."

I press my forehead to his. "I love you, bud."

"Lu, I'm gonna miss you so much. I wish you weren't leaving," my best friend cries.

Alex leans around me to see Max. "What are you talking about?"

Max hiccups. "Oops."

Alex jerks his head my way. "Lu, what's going on?"

Grace furrows her eyebrows and Ryan sits up, his back ramrod straight.

"I'm soooo sorry," Max says, dropping his face into his hands. "I didn't mean to say anything."

I look at each one of my friends and begin to shred the paper napkin in my lap. "I applied on a whim...I couldn't believe it when I got the email. I was so surprised," I ramble.

Alex's eyes go wide...and frightened. "What are you talking about?" he says slowly.

"I applied to the Rhode Island School of Design. I sent *Here Comes the Sun* in as my application."

"It's one of the best art schools there is," Max adds, swaying into me.

My boyfriend looks like he's going to be sick. He takes a long chug of his beer. "Why didn't you tell me?"

"I never thought I'd get in. Why would they accept me?"

"You got in because you're incredible." Alex sucks in a deep breath. "Lu, I love you. But how the hell could you keep this from me?"

"I'm sorry," I whisper. "I've been trying to figure out how to tell you."

Alex gulps the rest of his beer, and with watery eyes, he stands and walks out of the pub.

Ryan glares at me, then abandons his almost-full beer to follow his best friend out the front door.

"Hey," Grace calls. "Y'all can't leave us with the bill."

I laugh softly at my cousin's joke, but she doesn't look happy with me either. "I thought we told each other everything."

"We do... I was trying to decide what to do, and when to tell everyone. I didn't want to spoil our trip."

"Well, you did anyway," she says, sounding choked up, and then my cousin's gone out the door too.

Max lurches over, holding his stomach. "Oh God, I drank too many basil thingies. I'm gonna be sick."

I quickly stand so he can get out of the booth.

"C'mon," Caleb replies in a sweet voice, helping his boyfriend up to go to the bathroom.

Marcie slides out of her side of the booth and circles around to sit next to me, putting an arm around me. "Are you okay?" she asks, as I'm wiping the tears away from my eyes.

"No, not really," I say quietly. "This isn't how I wanted everyone to find out."

"Everybody loves you and wants what's best for you. We just need to give them a bit of time to process the news. I'm sad too."

Marcie is going to Middle Tennessee State, the school I'd been planning to attend. We were talking about being roommates.

That's when I realize Elia has been watching all of this.

He picks up his beer and moves to sit across from us, watching Marcie comfort me. He gives her a small smile.

"May I speak?" he asks very formally, and I nod. "My girlfriend left for college last year. She is older."

"Oh, so you have a girlfriend?" I ask.

"We broke up when she left. She moved to Rome."

"Where are you going to college?"

He wraps his hand around his beer glass "I am not going to college next year. Perhaps the year after. I am moving to Switzerland for a job."

"A job?"

"An apprenticeship at a bank."

That sounds fancy. "I'm sorry about your girlfriend," I say. "Were you close?"

He shakes his head. "We were not like you and Alex. Not so serious...or right for each other."

"You can tell after knowing us for a few hours that Alex and I are right for each other?"

Elia raises a shoulder. "Yes."

"The queen could walk by and Alex wouldn't even notice, because he's too busy watching you all the time," Marcie says with a laugh, and Elia joins in.

I close my eyes. They're right. Alex and I are right for each other. It's going to hurt him so much when I go to Rhode Island.

If I go. Maybe I shouldn't.

The sad expression on his face when he learned I won't be living a short drive away... I never want to see that look again. If I go to Rhode Island, I'll see it every time I climb on a plane to leave him behind in Tennessee. I want to stay with him more than anything, but can our relationship survive a nineteen-hour car ride? A three-hour plane flight that neither of us can afford on a regular basis?

When my literary agent suggested I seriously consider RISD, one of the first things I did was look up the Vanderbilt baseball schedule to see if Alex will be playing in New England at all. They won't be. I knew when he agreed to play for Vanderbilt, he'd be traveling a lot for games, so it's not like I'd see him all the time.

But he'd always come home. To me. And now I'm leaving him.

"Lu, where did you go?" Marcie asks, pulling me from my thoughts.

"I wish I could've told Alex about RISD myself."

Marcie glares toward the men's restroom. "I can't believe Max."

"He didn't mean to spill," I say. "It was that damned margarita talking."

"You have good friends," Elia says. He smiles at Marcie again, and she smiles back, and I giggle a little to myself, that my heartbreak might lead to Marcie—as she put it—getting a piece of the Italian hottie.

Once I've paid the bill—using a big chunk of my spending money, and we collect Max and Caleb from the bathroom, we leave the dark pub and emerge into blue skies again. Alex, Ryan, and Grace are sitting across the street on a bench. I let out the deep breath I was holding, relieved they didn't leave us behind.

Marcie glances to her left, then begins to step onto the road.

"Wait, wait," Elia says, putting out a hand to stop Marcie, pulling her against his chest. He points down at the street, where white paint spells out LOOK RIGHT. She must've forgotten they drive on the other side of the road here and was about to step into oncoming traffic.

She gazes up at him. "Thank you."

He holds her hand to cross the street, and I do a little celebratory dance for my friend.

I'm about to follow them to meet up with Alex when my phone chirps. I swipe the screen on to discover a notification with Peter's name. I quickly calculate the time difference. It's about ten in the morning in New York.

I inhale deeply, step back from the sidewalk to lean against a building, and open the email.

Dear Lulu:

I have some news. An editor loves your book and is interested in working with you! Her name is Val Martinez and she's a junior editor at a science fiction imprint called Apollo. Unfortunately, however, the editorial board at Apollo wants you to revise and resubmit the book before Val can make an official offer. Speaking frankly, you may choose to revise and resubmit to Val based on her feedback, and still not receive an offer. It's a risk.

Your book is still out with ten other editors right now, and any one of them might be interested in making an offer, but they might have a different vision from Val and Apollo. I'm going to reach out to the other editors to let them know we have interest from another house, which may spur them to work more quickly to review your material. Apollo is a leading sci-fi publisher, after all.

I know you're out of the country at the moment, but

Val would like to set up a phone call as soon as possible to get to know you and talk about Here Comes the Sun. Like me, Val is particularly impressed with your grasp of science and the rich detail of your book.

I wish I was giving you news of an offer. Getting on the phone with Val is a good opportunity, and I think you should take it, so you can at least hear about her ideas for the book and see if it's in line with your vision.

Let me know.

Congratulations!

Peter

Holy crap. A New York City editor who works for a real live publisher read my book! An editor wants to put my book on shelves in bookstores. Holy shit. I quickly forward the email to my parents and Lila with a note that says: !!!!!!!!!!!!!!!!!!!!!!!

I grin to myself, but it starts to fade. Another revise and resubmit? I already did this once with Peter. My writing still isn't good enough?

After I revised for Peter, he agreed to become my agent, but what happens if I do this for an editor and the editorial board still says no? Peter said that could happen.

This seems like all the more reason I need to attend RISD. What am I going to do?

I store my phone in my purse and begin walking again, to catch up with my friends.

323

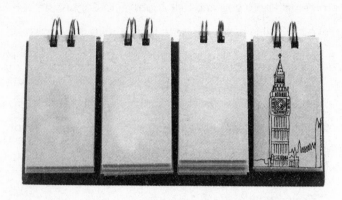

TODAY
SENIOR CLASS TRIP

When no traffic is coming, I look both ways and cross the street.

Everybody is lounging on benches waiting for me. Some of my friends are smiling and having a good time, but others are not.

Max is saying to Alex, "I'm sooo sorry, man. I didn't mean to upset you."

"It's all right," Alex says, helping Max to remain sitting up.

For the record, margaritas and Max do not mix well. He looks like a rag doll.

"Can you give us a minute, Max?" I ask, helping Alex to pass him off into the care of Caleb, who can't stop grinning at his drunk boyfriend.

"I am totally documenting this for the future," Caleb says.

"Nooooo," Max says again, as if in slow motion. "At least tell people I was drinking whiskey shots."

Alex leads me to a bench in the little square park where they've been hanging out. The Victoria Underground station is across the street, and a bus stop is behind us. Two of the London red busses are picking up riders. People won't be able to hear us here.

We sit together, not touching, which scares me to death.

Alex nervously flips his phone over in his hands. "I'm sorry I ran off like that. I got scared and freaked."

"I'm so sorry I hadn't told you yet. I was going to... I wanted to get my thoughts in order first, and I didn't want to upset you in London."

He pulls me into his arms. "I know, Lu. I'm so proud of you for applying and getting in. I should've said that first."

I snuggle against him. "Thank you."

"We do need to talk about it, though. And what it means for us." He pulls back from me.

"I love you, no matter what," I say.

"I love you too," he replies, but he's not meeting my eyes. A car driving by lays on its horn. "It's so hard being away from you, Lu. I don't feel like myself. It's like part of me is missing."

"Like last summer, when you were at Duke."

"Right. Or when you visited your sister in Atlanta over Christmas and New Year's. I missed you so much."

"I know. It hurts me too."

He takes a sharp breath. "I already committed to Vanderbilt. If I'd known you were considering Rhode Island, maybe I could've looked at teams up there."

"Vanderbilt is your dream, Alex. They have the best team. You have to go there."

His eyes are glassy. "What are we going to do, Lu? I don't want to be apart from you."

Marcie walks up next to me, clasping and unclasping her hands. "Guys," she says quietly. "I hate to interrupt, but we need to walk if we're going to make it back to the group on time. Coach Rice probably won't let us out of his sight if we're late. And none of us want to have a teacher as a buddy for the rest of this trip."

Alex and I stand to begin the short walk back to Westminster Abbey, where I'm going to say a gazillion prayers to God asking for us to be okay.

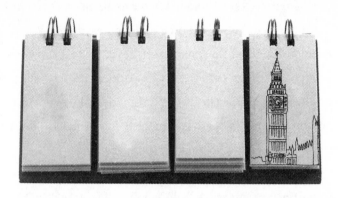

TODAY
SENIOR CLASS TRIP

It's about five o'clock when we arrive to meet our group for an early dinner and a nighttime bus tour of London, but my body doesn't believe it. It has no idea what time it is. I want a nap.

Lawrence the tour guide announces we're taking one of the big red city busses from Westminster to Covent Garden. I've never ridden a city bus, even in the States, so this is all new for me. I stare out the window, liking how we're so high above the other traffic.

Coach Rice and Ms. Abella sit together at the front, which is making Ryan absolutely bonkers.

"If they're not sharing a bed tonight, I'll eat my hat," Ryan says.

"What kind of hat? Like a sombrero?" Caleb asks.

"Yeah, I'll eat a sombrero."

These guys are never going to grow up.

I take out my tablet to quickly write down what the inside of the bus looks like. I also jot down a few notes about Westminster, the London Eye, and the Thames. If I ever write a story here, I'll need to remember the details. As I'm working, my eyes start to feel heavy. I rest my head against Alex's shoulder. My eyes close.

Before I know it, the bus screeches to a halt. "Lu, hurry, it's time to go," Alex says, helping me to my feet.

Sleepily I make my way off the bus and down the stairs to the sidewalk. I pat my purse, to make sure it's safe. It feels lighter than usual—oh shit.

"I left my sketchpad on the bus!" I point at it as it pulls away from the curb.

Alex gasps, drops his backpack, and sprints after the bus. Traffic is heavy, so the bus is not going too fast, but it's still too fast for Alex to get the driver's attention.

I chase after him, running as fast as I can. He runs for two city blocks, waving his arms and screaming at the driver. He dangerously crosses diagonally across an intersection to the far side of the street. The bus finally stops, its doors open, and Alex runs aboard to get the tablet. Seconds later, he appears at the bus door and lifts the sketchpad, showing me he found it.

I wave at him from across the street. He waves back with my sketchpad.

I bounce up and down on my tiptoes, grinning. "Thank you," I mouth at him as cars rush by in the street.

He smiles back.

He looks to his left, then begins to step out into the street. A bus screeches its brakes. Oh shit, he didn't look right. Cars here drive on the other side of the road. He should have looked right.

Alex didn't look right.

———————

The bus careens to a stop.

Alex stumbles backward onto the sidewalk. My sketchpad goes flying onto the concrete. His heel catches on the curb and he crumbles, breaking his fall with his hands. Another second and that bus would've killed him.

"Alex!" I scream.

I rush to him. He's breathing heavily, eyes clenched shut, one hand carefully holding his other wrist.

"Oh no, oh no," I cry. "Your arm. Are you okay?"

He pulls me down to the ground next to him, holding me tight. "I'm fine, we're fine. I love you."

"I love you too."

"Is your sketchpad okay?" he asks.

I glance down at my tablet on the sidewalk. The screen looks like a spider cast a web against the black starless sky.

It's shattered.

"Who cares?" I say with tears falling down my face. "Your arm! You have to play baseball. You have to!"

He's cradling it against his chest. That's the arm he catches with. He needs it to play first base. Without it, can he still play for Vanderbilt? I cry harder.

Coach Rice skids to a stop next to us. He kneels and places a gentle hand on Alex's shoulder. "What's wrong?"

"My arm," Alex replies, out of breath. "Hurts like hell."

"Can you move your fingers for me, Rouvelis?"

Alex gingerly lifts his arm and moves his fingers.

Coach Rice sighs, taking off his baseball cap to run a hand through his hair. "It's not broken. We should still find an urgent care facility or hospital to make sure it's okay."

"I'm fine," Alex says, stretching his fingers and wrist. "Get me an ice pack and some Ibuprofen...and let me sit here. I need to catch my breath for a minute."

He leans against me, breathing heavily, kissing the top of my head. I gently run fingertips over his sore wrist.

Carrying Alex's backpack, Ryan runs up and falls to his knees. "You okay, man?"

Alex nods at his best friend. Ryan squeezes his shoulder.

Alex uses his good arm to reach back for my broken sketch-pad. "Oh shit," he mumbles as he examines the screen. "Did you back up all your work, Lu?"

I shake my head. "Not the new stuff, but it doesn't matter."

"We really should go to the doctor," Coach Rice says. "Your wrist is your future. We have to take care of you."

But Alex shakes his head. "I don't want to miss tonight."

"Okay," Coach Rice says, not sounding okay at all. "We'll ice it and give you an anti-inflammatory, but if it swells at all this evening, I'm taking you in."

While the rest of our class continues into Covent Garden, Alex, Coach Rice, and I stop at a drug store called Boots.

Coach Rice stays outside. "I'm going to call your mother, Alex, and I need to call the principal too."

Alex comes out of his daze long enough to say, "No matter what they say, I'm not going home early."

Alex moves slowly beside me through the aisles. I've never seen him like this before. He stares at the shelves for at least a minute, like he can't figure anything out, like he's reading a foreign language he doesn't know.

"Do you want me to pick everything out?" I say.

He nods, rubbing his eyes with his good hand.

I shove an ace bandage into a basket, then slam some Ibuprofen down next to it. My hands shake as I pull a box of ice packs off the shelf. Dried tears streak my cheeks as I pay for everything.

I almost lost him. Fresh tears fall from my eyes.

Outside on a bench, Coach Rice is waiting for us. "I talked to your mom. Give her a call when you have a minute, okay?"

Coach Rice rips open the ace bandage and quickly wraps it around Alex's sprained wrist. "Your arm doesn't look too bad. I'm sure it'll heal up in time to start weight lifting at Vanderbilt. We'll need to stretch it and take good care of it." The ice pack goes on next.

Alex breathes in relief. "That feels good."

"I'm so sorry," I whisper. "It's all my fault."

"It was an accident," he mumbles. "God, this day sucks. First you tell me you're leaving, and now this."

Coach Rice gives me an alarmed glance. "Why don't we head on to Covent Garden. You can find a place to sit and grab something to eat."

Lawrence the tour guide meets us outside the entrance. He rushes up, a worried expression on his face. "How are you doing?"

"Fine," Alex says, but his voice is anything but. I wrap my arm around his waist, feeling him stiffen beneath my fingers.

Ms. Abella hurries toward us as well. "Is everything all right now?"

A big smile appears on my boyfriend's face. "It is now, Ms. Abella, and it's all thanks to Coach Rice. He's the best."

Alex elbows his coach, who rolls his eyes at Alex's matchmaking.

"Seems like you're okay for now," Coach Rice says.

"Yeah, we can meet up with Ryan and everybody," Alex replies.

"Let me know if you need anything, or if you change your mind about the doctor, okay?" Coach Rice says.

"Okay. You should take Ms. Abella to get some wine," Alex says, which makes the Italian teacher smile and shake her head, totally on to him.

"Let's go," Ms. Abella says to Coach Rice, and he follows her like a puppy.

Lawrence tells us about Covent Garden on the walk inside the plaza. "It's been around for over four hundred years, and I promise you'll enjoy it. It has great shopping and plenty of options for food."

Covent Garden is a large enclosed glass structure held up by gorgeous stone buildings. I immediately fall in love.

I wrap my hands around Alex's elbow on his good arm and walk in with him. Twinkling lights fill the trees. The smell of bread wafts over from a bakery. We pass an Apple store that's completely mobbed with people. But beyond that is a square where a band is playing.

"Can we sit over there and listen to some music?" Alex asks. His eyes are tired with pain and worry. We find a bench facing the stage to sit on together. For two songs we lean against each other in silence, just listening, just being together. The band is an acoustic eighties tribute band.

"Mom and Dad would be going apeshit if they were here," I say. "They live for eighties music."

"Mine too," Alex says with a small smile.

I caress the back of his neck with my hand, and lean closer. The weather is getting even chillier outside. "How does your arm feel?"

He wiggles his fingers for me. "It's definitely not broken, but it's bothering me a little. It hurts."

"Maybe we should go to the hospital."

Alex pulls a deep breath in through his nose. "I don't think I can handle that tonight, Lu...all this stress is too much... Maybe I'm more scared than actually hurt, you know?"

"I was terrified. For a second I thought that bus was going to hit you."

"I can't believe it didn't," he exclaims, letting out a deep, shaky breath.

"I can't believe you ran back for my sketchpad."

"I know how much it means to you."

"And it shattered anyway." I let out a sob, hating that my boyfriend almost died for it. I run a fingertip along his arm. "I know how much baseball means to you. I could never forgive myself if I messed up your future."

He leans down to kiss me. "Lu, you're my future, not baseball."

A tear spills down my face. "You're my future too. I'm going to stay with you. I'm going to decline RISD."

"You're my future," he says again. "But you have to go to Rhode Island. I'd never forgive myself if you stayed for me."

"I'd never forgive myself if you gave up Vanderbilt for me…"

Alex stretches his hand again. "What if I don't make it in baseball?"

I squeeze his knee. "Don't talk like that."

"Today showed me that anything can happen. One injury could screw everything up."

"Coach says your arm will be fine."

"Forget my arm for a minute." His eyes glisten. "I can't lose you, Lu."

"I can't lose you either. What are we going to do, though? A long-distance thing?"

"We don't have to figure everything out tonight, Lu, but I'm up for it for you are." More tears fall out of my eyes. "There's always fall break and spring break and the holidays. We can figure out ways to visit each other… Maybe we could even try Skype sex."

"Oh my God, have you been talking to Grace?" I playfully smack his thigh, and he kisses my cheek. "But what if you meet someone else? I wouldn't want to worry about you with other girls."

"I don't want anybody but you," he says. "I haven't since you got us locked in that escape room together."

"That was your fault, not mine!" I smile at him, and he grins back. "You never would've made it out of there without me."

"I was about to say the same thing to you." He sits up a little straighter, looking around. "What do you want to grab for dinner?"

I stand, extend a hand, and say, "Let's go find our friends."

Of course we find our friends at the pub.

Ryan and Grace are standing at a high-top table, laughing with Caleb and Max. Marcie is smiling up at Elia as they sit cozily next to each other on barstools. Everybody has a drink in front of them except for Max.

"Caleb cut me off before I even got a drink," he grumbles.

"We could get Shirley Temples," I say, making my best friend's eyes light up.

Alex's teammates crowd around him and examine his wrist as if it's a precious jewel.

"Are you all right?" Grace asks Alex, biting her lip.

"I hope so," he says quietly. His face droops, and Grace gives him a hug.

Marcie leaves her spot beside Elia and comes close to me. "Is everything okay?" she asks me quietly.

"We're all good," I say.

Ryan, who apparently was eavesdropping, raises his ale glass. "To Alex and Lulu being all good!"

Not only do my friends toast, but so do a bunch of other random people in the bar. Alex drapes his healthy arm around me.

Grace nudges Ryan. "Go get Alex and Lulu some drinks."

"And some ice for my wrist," Alex calls out.

I leave my boyfriend for a moment and walk over to my cousin. She hasn't met my eyes once since this afternoon. "I'm so sorry, Grace. I should've told you first."

"Yes, you should've. I'm pissed, but I'm so excited for you."

I hug my cousin, and she squeezes me back. "I'm going to miss you so much."

"We'll text all the time, right?"

"Always."

Suddenly another set of arms comes around us. I glance up to find Max hugging us both. "I think what you meant to say is that we'll group text."

Once Ryan comes back from the bar with the drinks, Alex lifts his glass.

"To friends who buy me things," Alex says with a laugh.

"To Alex's arm being okay," Grace says.

Caleb lifts his glass. "To the best boyfriend ever...who somehow is getting tipsy off a Shirley Temple."

"Just for that, you're sleeping on the shitty cot tonight," Max replies.

"To our class president, who pushed the principal and school board hard for this trip to London, even though it was beyond the endowment annual budget," Alex says, toasting me, and everyone cheers my name.

"To getting my picture taken at Platform 9 ¾ tomorrow," Max says, hugging me.

After I won the election, Alex told me I had fought dirty to beat him. Of course I ran again on a campaign of convincing the school to get solar panels, but I also made *Harry Potter*-themed posters. Over the years, I spent time listening to my classmates, and that's how I knew I needed to frame my speech around pushing for a senior trip to England so we could go to *Harry Potter* movie sets.

Marcie lifts her glass. "To Lulu getting a book deal and becoming famouser than Stephen King!"

"Oh," I say. "I totally forgot to tell y'all. I got an email from my agent earlier today. An editor is interested in working with me. It's not a book deal yet, but it could be."

My friends erupt, yelling at me.

"How could you not tell us?"

"You've been sitting on this all day?"

"Lu! You should've mentioned it."

Alex loops his good arm around my waist, pulling me against him. He rests his chin on my shoulder. "What does the email say?"

I take my phone out of my purse. With everything that's happened in the past couple of hours with Alex's arm, and enjoying being in Covent Garden with my friends, I haven't checked my phone.

First I notice new emails from my parents and Lila, excited about my earlier email regarding Apollo's revise and resubmit request. Mom is already planning a book release party. Dad says he told every patient who came in this afternoon. Lila demands to read any contractual material I might receive.

As I continue scrolling through my notifications, I'm surprised to see several missed calls from a 212 number. On top of that, there's another email from Peter with the subject line NEWS!!

With shaking hands I open Peter's email.

Dear Lulu:

After I let the other editors know we had interest,

there was some scrambling on their part. We received an offer from Mina Tung at Libris. Congratulations!

Mina Tung is an executive editor, has been in the business a long time, and doesn't need to wait for the editorial board to make an offer. Like Apollo, she particularly loves your science and world-building, but she's also a big fan of the love story between Nera and Ander.

I told Mina how old you are, and she couldn't believe you wrote such a compelling romance at your age. She said it's clear you understand true love. Although, she's still reeling from your ending.

The offer memo is attached. You don't have to accept this right away. Let me go back to Libris and try to negotiate for more money. Also, I'll let the other editors—including Val Martinez at Apollo—know we have an official offer. This may spur Apollo to change their minds about the revise and resubmit. If they don't make an offer ASAP, they're going to lose you to Libris or another house.

I will let Mina and Val know you're traveling for the rest of the week, but that we'd like to set up conference calls for Monday.

Enjoy the rest of your trip. Congratulations again!

Peter

"Oh holy shit," I yell. Libris is one of the biggest publishers on the planet.

Alex reads the email over my shoulder. "Oh my God, babe. Open the offer memo."

He kisses my cheek as I click on the PDF.

I lose my breath. My first thought is that it's enough to pay for plane tickets to see Alex's games.

That's when Ryan shoves his head between us and reads the number. "Drinks on Lulu! She's rich."

I'll never forget this moment. Not because of the book deal. Not because of the money. But because of the looks on my friends' faces as they toast and congratulate me for years of hard work.

And I toast them for sticking with me through it all.

We climb aboard a London tour bus and choose seats on the roof.

I zip my jacket all the way up to my neck to keep out the chill, but it's not helping. "I'm so cold," I whine.

Alex snuggles me close.

The bus makes its way slowly through Piccadilly Circus. With its bright billboards, it's sort of like London's version of Times Square. Considering how much I didn't like Times Square, I'm surprised I love Piccadilly. The loneliness I felt in Times Square is nonexistent here. Here, laughing alongside my friends, I feel like I'm a part of something bigger.

Maybe it doesn't matter where you are—maybe it's who you're with.

"Let's make a pact we'll all meet up on May seventh next year," Alex says.

"But what if we have finals?" Grace asks.

"Or we're on different schedules?" Marcie adds.

"What if you have a ball game?" Max asks.

"Then we'll figure out what's the first day we're all home, and we'll get together," Ryan says.

When I was younger, I wondered if happily-ever-afters were realistic. Were they a myth? I still don't know the truth. Someone could get hurt anytime, anywhere. A friend could choose a different path. A lover could leave. Family can change their minds.

There's only one thing I know for sure.

I gaze around at my laughing friends, smiling under the bright lights of London.

No matter what, we'll find our way back.

ACKNOWLEDGMENTS

One of my most vivid memories from growing up is when I went with my junior high French class to France. We traveled to Paris, the Loire Valley, Mont Saint Michel, and Saint Malo. I was only fourteen, and I'd never been so far away from home before on my own. I couldn't wait to visit all the castles I'd been reading about for months, but other kids on the trip were more interested in drinking and making out than seeing artwork and practicing their French. Like Lulu, I decided to focus on the travel to get as much as I could out of the trip. Not only did I fall in love with traveling, I also grew up. As much as I wanted to, I couldn't ignore the drama around me. Those feelings and memories have stuck with me all this time and became the inspiration for this book. To me, traveling has an almost fantasy aspect to it, and I wanted to explore how it can inspire us to take chances in our personal lives, and ultimately, grow. Dear reader, if you ever have the opportunity to travel, I hope you take it! Go everywhere, talk to everyone, and eat everything.

This story took me longer to write than most of my other books. I'd first like to thank my readers for sticking with me! I have so much gratitude for my agent, Jim McCarthy, for his creativity, advocacy, and endless cheerleading. Uniquely, this book had a wonderful team of editors who helped me shape Lulu and Alex's story from beginning to end: Molly Cusick, Annette Pollert-Morgan, Kate Prosswimmer, and Cassie Gutman. Thank you to everyone at Sourcebooks for ten great years of publishing.

To my early readers, you were critical to me figuring out what worked, and I can't thank you enough: Andrea Soule, Trish Doller, Mary Hinson, Tiffany Schmidt, Tiffany Smith, Brett Werst, Tiffanie Ing, and Gail Yates. Thank you to Eythan Schiller for your travel anecdotes and all that time we spent brainstorming; Robin Talley, for assisting with my synopsis and several critical scenes; and Jessica Spotswood, for helping to fine-tune my opening pages. Joe Helein, Lizeth Cruz, and all my friends at the gym, for working with me to stay healthy and happy. I'm very grateful to Cristin Bishara, for helping me plot out this story's ending during a long walk on the beach! Finally, thank you to Don, for always supporting my writing and for reading all my terrible first drafts. I love you.

ABOUT THE AUTHOR

Miranda Kenneally grew up in Manchester, Tennessee, a quaint little town where nothing cool ever happened until after she left. Now, Manchester is the home of Bonnaroo. Growing up, Miranda wanted to become an author, a major league baseball player, a country music singer, or an interpreter for the United Nations. Instead, she became an author who also works for the U.S. Department of State in Washington, DC, and once acted as George W. Bush's armrest during a meeting. She enjoys reading and writing young adult literature and loves *Star Trek*, music, sports, Mexican food, Twitter, and coffee. She lives in Arlington, Virginia, with her husband, Don, and cats, Brady and Ryan, and dog, Jack. Visit mirandakenneally.com.

FIREreads

§ #getbooklit

Your hub for the hottest young adult books!

Visit us online and sign up for our
newsletter at FIREreads.com

 @sourcebooksfire

 sourcebooksfire

 firereads.tumblr.com